MIDNIGHT
MOVIE

THREE RIVERS PRESS • NEW YORK

MIDNIGHT MOVIE

A NOVEL

TOBE

HOOPER

with ALAN

GOLDSH

Hooper

Copyright © 2011 by Tobe Hooper

Published in the United States by Three Rivers Press, an imprint of the Crown
Publishing Group, a division of Random House, Inc., New York.
www.crownpublishing.com

Three Rivers Press and the Tugboat design are registered trademarks of
Random House, Inc.

Library of Congress Cataloging-in-Publication Data
Hooper, Tobe, 1943–
Midnight movie : a novel / Tobe Hooper with Alan Goldsher. — 1st ed.
1. Motion picture producers and directors—Fiction. 2. Supernaturals—Fiction.
I. Goldsher, Alan, 1966– II. Title.
PS3608.O5955M53 2011
813'.6—dc22
2010040358

ISBN 978-0-307-71701-6
eISBN 978-0-307-71702-3

Printed in the United States of America

Book design by Maria Elias
Cover design by Kyle Kolker
Cover photographs: © Julian Andrew Holtom/Flickr/Getty Images (zombie);
© Roger Charity/Getty Images (brunette screaming);
© Peter Dazeley/Getty Images (blonde screaming); © Ting Hoo (back)

10 9 8 7 6 5 4 3 2 1

First Edition

AUTHOR'S NOTE: *Some wise guy dubbed it the Game Changer, which, as you undoubtedly know, was shortened to the Game. It was a flip, dismissive way of referring to an ugly, unexplainable situation, but I suppose that's the way America rolls; the cavalier way our public dealt with it was the only way they could deal with it. If you turn something awful into a joke, you can trivialize it, and if you trivialize it, you can convince yourself it isn't real.*

Many researchers still contend the Game was not an actual virus, but rather an event. An event? Seriously? The Super Bowl is an event. The Game was . . . fucked-up. To me, tagging it as an event was another way of making the horrible palatable.

In some areas—most notably Texas, Southern California, and the northeastern seaboard—it oozed through the populace like lava, whereas the northwestern and midwestern sections of the United States (save for Chicago) went all but unscathed. The international ramifications have yet to be fully determined, but aside from the outbreak that practically wiped a tiny town in Italy called Montciano San Galgano off the map, it appears that the rest of the world got off easy. Fortunately, as of this writing, there have been no signs of a second outbreak either in the States or abroad, and experts are confident that the Game will remain dormant. Nobody, however, is saying that the Game is definitely over. How could they? They barely know how it started.

I guess the media didn't want to really, truly face it. The mainstream outlets reported on the effects—of course they did; laying down the facts at hand is easy—but nobody went after the cause. There were plenty of websites that spewed out theory after theory, but, as is often the case, the overwhelming majority of Netheads were dismissed as hysterics, or conspiracy nuts, or crazies looking for attention. Listen, it's

2011, people; yeah, the blogosphere and the social networks have their fair share of oddballs, but there're also hundreds of thousands of people who're plugged into reality, who know what they're writing about. You have to pay attention. I did, and it was a damn good thing, because if this book didn't exist, I honestly believe the Game would be forgotten, and that would be really, really bad, because those who don't remember the past are condemned to blah blah blah, et cetera, et cetera, et cetera, and next thing you know, welcome to Outbreak City, population: you, your family, your friends, and your lover.

The fact is, if the media and/or the scientific community had looked even just a little bit harder, they'd have figured it out. In this day and age, anybody can figure anything out . . . if they want to. If a pissant journalist like me could find answers, imagine what a real reporter could've done. Shit, I tracked down a journal by a guy who was practically a real-life Jack Bauer with three phone calls and a discount plane ticket to Chicago. You mean to tell me there wasn't a G-man or a New York Times scribe out there who could've done what I did? Give me a goddamn break.

Yes, it was a scary situation, scary as all hell. But, as my new friend Tobe Hooper might say, "Nut up, you pussies, and do your fucking job."

—Alan Goldsher, March 2011

PART
ONE

March 15, 2009

SOUTH BY SOUTHWEST FESTIVAL SCHEDULE

FRIDAY, MARCH 31 @ MIDNIGHT
TOBE HOOPER'S *DESTINY EXPRESS*
Screening and Q & A
The Cove
121 Third Street
(512) 343-COVE

We're not going to lie here, folks: This is one weird-ass booking, probably the weirdest-ass booking of this year's extravaganza. We loves ourselves some Leatherface, no doubt, but do we really need to see a film that the auteur behind *The Texas Chainsaw Massacre* slapped together when he was still using training wheels? Apparently the SXSW brain trust is also concerned about the turnout, because they stuck the sixtysomething-year-old director off in a club just north of the boondocks, *way* far away from Sixth Street, at a bar that is arguably the diviest dive in Texas. Not just Austin. *Texas.* And that's saying something.

No idea what the flick is about. All the press release said was, "Who knows what lurks in the young heart of Tobe Hooper? Find out Friday blabbitty blah blah, bullshitty bull bullshit." There's a chance that *Destiny Express* is good—Hooper is Mr. Chainsaw, after all, and it's possible that he had chops even as an adolescent—but the guy *was* sixteen when he made it, and it *was* 1959, so we're skeptical. Sure, he could've been Herschell Gordon Lewis before there was a Herschell Gordon Lewis . . . but he also might've been Richie Cunningham dicking around with daddy's neat-o video camera.

The Decemberists are playing at the exact same time. So we'll wait for the DVD.

TOBE HOOPER WITH ALAN GOLDSHER

TOBE HOOPER *(film director)*:

I wasn't anywhere close to awake when the guy called. It was first thing in the morning, like eight o'clock, and I'd been at the studio editing that remake of *Carrie* for Fox until well after midnight, and I didn't hit the sack until after four, and I was in deep REM sleep, and having some fucked-up dream about bowling, and then there's the *ring, ring, ring,* and I'm awake. Sort of.

Nobody *ever* called me on my landline, so I'd never bothered to get my answering machine fixed, so that fucking phone just kept ringing, and ringing, and ringing. My first instinct was to kill it, to shoot it dead, to send it back from whence it came. But my gun was in the safe in my office in the coach house, and the thought of getting out of bed, then going downstairs, then going outside, then jimmying open the door—no way I'd find the damn key before the phone stopped—then trying to remember the combination of the safe, then opening the safe, then grabbing the Colt, then putting bullets in the chamber, then going back upstairs, and then shooting the phone seemed like a lot of effort. So I picked up the receiver.

I coughed and cleared my throat right into the mouthpiece, then said, "What." That's all. Nothing good could come of an eight-in-the-morning phone call, so I figured the quicker we got down to business, the better. Screw pleasantries.

The dude said, "Mr. Hoopler? Toeb Hoopler?" He said "Toeb" rather than "Toe-bee." An eight o'clock phone call with a mispronounced first name and a butchered last name. Fuck, man.

I said, "Can I help you with something?" I kind of disguised my voice, deemphasizing the Texas accent. I don't know why, really. It's not like he would've recognized me or anything—if he didn't know how to say my damn name, it's doubtful he would've known my damn voice—but you never know. If he didn't know I was me, maybe I could tell him he had the wrong number.

The dude said, "Toeb, my name is Dude McGee, and I'm calling from the South by Southwest festival in Austin, Texas."

I was a fan of South by Southwest, so I decided to not curse him out and hang up. I said, "Hold on," then I put the phone down, went to the bathroom, took a leak, flushed, washed, squirted some Purell on my hands, then picked up the receiver again. I asked the guy, "Your name is Dude?"

He laughed a little bit, then said, "Nickname. I'm a big *Big Lebowski* fanatic. Big, big, big."

Eight o'clock in the morning. Mispronounced name. And a Coen brothers obsessive. I again considered getting the gun, and again decided it was too damn much work. I said, "How can I help you, Mr. McGee?"

He said, "Call me Dude."

I said, "I'll call you Mr. McGee."

He was quiet for a sec, then said, "Okay, Toeb"—still mispronounced, mind you—"here's the deal: A guy who knows a guy who knows a guy came across a print of *Destiny Express*." He gave a weird laugh, then said, "Remember that one?"

It took me a second. Or two. Or three. Or a hundred. And then, *lightbulb*. I said, "Mr. McGee, where the hell did you get a print of *Destiny Express*?"

He said, "*I* didn't get it. It was a guy who knows a guy who knows a guy."

I said, "A guy who knows a guy who knows a guy."

He said, "Yeah. A guy who knows a guy who knows a guy."

I said, "So you're telling me that the guy who knows the guy who knows the guy broke into my mother's house? Because as far as I know, the only print was in my mom's basement." It actually wasn't my mom's house anymore. It was mine. I'd been renting it out on and off since I moved out to Los Angeles ten years back. Free money for those dark days. See, when you make the kind of films I make, and when you write the kind of screenplays I write, and when you hate dealing with major studios as much as I do, you have a lot of dark days.

Dude said, "Toeb—"

I said, "It's To-*bee*."

Dude said, "Sorry, To-*beeeeee*," all sarcastic-like. Prick. He went on: "I can assure you that nobody broke into your mother's house. The fact is, I don't know where the guy who knew the guy who knew the guy got it. But it doesn't really matter, because everybody at South by Southwest is excited about it, very excited. We'd like you to come down to the fest and screen the film."

My initial reaction was, *No way.* Yeah, it would've been nice to go back to Austin and check out the fest, but I didn't even recall what the hell *Destiny Express* was about—I was pretty sure there was some zombie sex involved—and I didn't want to get up in front of a room full of horror geeks (geeks such as myself, mind you) and sound like a dumbass. But I *was* curious, so I decided to let the conversation play itself out.

I said, "Where would we be doing this dog-and-pony show? The Performing Arts Center?" The PAC, which was smack in the middle of the University of Texas campus, was just about the coolest auditorium in Austin. They staged musicals, and big concerts, and film festivals, and the like. Sometimes the goddamn Wiggles performed there, but I couldn't hold that against the PAC bookers. You got to pay your employees, because everybody's got to feed their family, and a Luis Buñuel retrospective wasn't going to rake in the dough like goddamn Greg, goddamn Jeff, goddamn Murray, and goddamn Anthony. And don't ask me why I know all the goddamn Wiggles' names. I'd rather not discuss it. Suffice it to say that if those Aussie freaks ever show up at my doorstep, I'm getting my Colt.

Anyhow, Dude said, "Nope. Not the PAC. We wanted it to be more intimate. We were thinking about the Cove."

I said, "The Cove? Man, I guess you guys don't think much

of me." You don't go to the Cove to watch a movie. You go to the Cove to shoot pool on what is undoubtedly the shittiest pool table in Texas, and get into a fight, and find a girl who'll let you put it where your girlfriend won't let you, or buy some shitty skunk weed, or get royally fucked-up on warm beer and watered-down whiskey. If you're keeping score, I've done all of the above.

Dude said, "Yeah, sorry about that, Toeb—"

I said, "Toe-bee."

Dude said, "Right. To-*beeeeee*. I know it's a shithole, but it was the only venue that wasn't booked. But it doesn't matter where we do it. We could do it on a bedsheet tied between two phone poles, and it'd still be great. You'll lead a discussion. You'll sign autographs. You'll shake hands. You'll hang out. You'll have a few Black Straps. We'll fly you down, and put you up, and feed you, and get you onto every guest list on Sixth Street. And we can pay you, I don't know, ten grand?"

If I'd have been drinking something, you'd have seen the biggest spit-take you can imagine. I said, "Ten grand? You're shitting me."

Dude said, "What, ten's not enough? How's fifteen sound? Or twenty?"

I said, "Insane. Twenty sounds insane. Hell, even *two* grand is insane."

He said, "Insane good, or insane bad?"

I said, "*Insane* insane. Listen, Dude, I know for a fact that you can only fit about sixty people in the Cove—"

He interrupted. "Actually, they did some remodeling. It's *way* bigger now."

I said, "How much bigger is *way* bigger?"

Dude said, "Like, the capacity is ninety. They've expanded by a third. Pretty awesome, right?"

I said, "Okay, let's you and me do some simple math here,

Mr. McGee. If you were going to break even on this, you'd need to sell the place out for about one-fifty a ticket. Nobody's paying a buck fifty to see a movie that some smart-ass kid did. Maybe they'd pay one and a half bills to see, I don't know, Leatherface fuck up Dick Cheney live onstage. But not this. Not some teenage vanity film. Seriously, Dude, why in God's name would you fork over five figures for this?"

Dude said, "Prestige. You're Toeb Hooper—"

I said, "I'm not *Toeb* Hooper, man, I'm Toe-*bee* Hooper."

Dude was quiet for a second. I heard some papers ruffling, then he said, "You sure about that? I'm pretty certain it's Toeb."

I almost hung up on him then and there, but—and I'm not proud of this—I wanted to hear him out, because I needed the bread. My last two movies had tanked, and I was still paying out the nose for that goddamn divorce—which I'm sure you read about in the papers, and I'm not going to get into it right now—so my bank account wasn't in any shape to finance a film. Plus, the last payment for *Carrie* hadn't come in yet, and the Fox accounting department wasn't known for its speed, so who knew when the hell that would show up. Twenty grand could get me to Greece, where I was hoping to shoot my new flick, which I was going to finance myself—it was a splatterfest straight out of 1975, and even with the *Saw* flicks doing their thing and putting asses in seats, there wasn't a studio in town that'd touch *this* one—and I could scout locations and start putting together a crew. That way, when the *Carrie* money showed—and when I got another investor or three on board—I could get started immediately.

So I told Dude, "First off, I can promise you that it's Toe-bee, not Toeb. And second off, have you actually watched *Destiny Express?*"

He said, "Yes. It's brilliant."

I said, "Thanks, man. Now, what the hell's it about?"

ERICK LAUGHLIN (*weekend film critic for the* Austin Chronicle, *lead singer and guitarist for Massacre This*): The *Destiny Express* press release showed up on February 27. I immediately thought about doing a long profile on Hooper, but that moron Dude McGee couldn't, or wouldn't, schedule an interview quickly enough for me to hit my deadline. He did, however, invite me down to his office to watch the movie, with the proviso that if I wrote about it, I wouldn't give away too much of the plot. I told him that professional reviewers and spoilers don't mix, so he said I could drop by whenever I wanted to. I told him I'd be there in an hour. Or less.

We critic types are supposed to be unbiased, but I have a major affinity for old-school horror—give me some Hitchcock, some Hammer flicks, and some George Romero, and I'm a happy boy. But I've always had a special place in my heart for Tobe Hooper, thus the moniker of my lame little punk trio. All of which was why the second I hung up with Dude McGee, I MapQuested directions to that moron's office, hopped onto my bicycle, and sped across town.

Turned out his office wasn't an office. It was a basement. In his parents' house. Where he was living.

Dude looked like a low-budget Harry Knowles—big and bearded, but without Knowles's charming sense of self-deprecation. He was of indeterminate age—maybe twenty-five, maybe thirty-five—strident, and obnoxious, and the close confines amplified both his loudness and his loutishness. He asked me if I had any trouble finding the place, then he belched. It smelled like salami. Actually, the whole place smelled like salami. I told him no, I found the place just fine, then I asked him if we could get started, because I wanted to turn this article in by the end of the day. That was a lie. I just wanted to see the movie, then get out of there, because the scent of luncheon meat was seeping into my pores.

But he insisted on giving me the grand tour. To the right, there were his five wide-screen monitors that enabled him to simultaneously play five different video games or watch five different DVDs. To the left, his, quote, *astoundingly valuable comic collection*, unquote. Now, I know very little about comics and even less about collecting, but one thing I am aware of is that you're supposed to put each book in a plastic cover, then store them in a condition-proof container of some sort, like a file cabinet or a safe. Dude had his books in bales of one hundred, tied together with twine, sitting inside of moldy, battered, uncovered cardboard boxes piled up to the ceiling. My younger brother Arthur collects comics, and I knew he'd be appalled if he saw Dude's casual, uncaring method of storage.

And the farther we went into the basement, the worse the salami smell became.

Dude led me through the maze of ratty boxes, high-end computer equipment, and a very tiny but very fancy-looking chemistry lab to a big utility room. In between a furnace and a rusty washer/dryer, he'd set up a movie screen, the kind of pull-down, marked-up screen that I used to watch filmstrips on in second grade. At the other end of the room, there was a single folding chair and bridge table, on top of which sat an unstable-looking movie projector. Dude told me to take a seat, then asked me if I wanted a beer. I said no, thanks, I should watch the movie so I can get back home and write the article. I pulled out my notebook— not my laptop, but actual, honest-to-goodness paper—and Dude slapped it out of my hand.

I said, "What the hell, man? What's the problem?"

Dude said, "You can't take notes, and if you insist on doing so, I'll throw you out on your ass." He was smiling while he said it. Not sure why. Maybe to soften the blow.

Now, if this wasn't a Tobe Hooper movie, I'd have told Dude to fuck off and then left. But it *was* a Tobe Hooper movie, so

I sucked it up and told him to roll film. He said, "Excellent. Forgive me if I won't be joining you. The first ten minutes were enough for me."

I thought, *Thank God*, then told Dude, "I'll be fine." Frankly, I was ecstatic he was leaving. He was one of those people whose innate wrongness made every interaction uncomfortable and distracting, and since I couldn't take notes, I needed to be completely focused on the movie.

So. *Destiny Express.*

The credits were pretty funny, although I don't think they were meant to be. It was a sexy little high school girl wearing a Catholic schoolgirl uniform, flipping through cue cards, kind of like Bob Dylan eventually did in the "Subterranean Homesick Blues" video several years later. I doubt D. A. Pennebaker got the idea from Tobe Hooper, but it was oddly similar. The first card said, "A TOBE HOOPER FILM." The second: "DESTINY EXPRESS." The third: "STARRING GARY CHURCH." The fourth: "CO-STARRING HELEN LEARY." The fifth: "AND CLAIRE CRAFT." The sixth: "CAMERA AND SOUND BY DARREN ALLEN." The seventh: "MAKEUP AND SPECIAL EFFECTS BY WILLIAM MARRON." The eighth: "WRITTEN, DIRECTED, CONCEIVED, AND BRIEFLY NARRATED BY TOBE HOOPER." Only six people. Talk about a skeleton crew.

Then there was a jump cut to a suburban cul-de-sac that was filled with birds, and trees, and perfectly coiffed lawns. The camera panned around in a half circle before stopping on a young man—a boy, really—sitting on a porch, staring off to his left. He coolly turned forward, gazed into the camera, then nodded and said, "Good afternoon, dear viewers. My name is Tobe Hooper. You don't know me. I could be a nice guy. I could be a liar and a thief. I could even be a killer. You can believe everything I tell you. Or you can ignore every word that I say. Or you can burn this film into a pile of ashes." He paused, ran his hand through his crew cut, then said, "But if I were you, I'd listen carefully. Because I have the camera. And I know the truth."

He stood up and began pacing back and forth, no longer looking into the camera. "I'm speaking to you from Austin, Texas. It's a quiet little town, Austin is. Nobody pays much attention to us. That's a bad idea. Like I said, you should listen carefully. You might want to get your friends and family to join you in front of the screen. They need to see this."

And then there was another jump cut to a man—or possibly a boy made up to look like a man—curled in a fetal position, wearing a filthy, tattered shirt and no pants. He was covered with some sort of dark glop, probably mud, but since the movie was in black and white, it was hard to tell exactly what it was. The thing—I guess you could call it a man-boy—stayed on the screen for a total of only two seconds, enough time to make one hell of an impression, then it cut back to Tobe, who said, "Did you see that? I know it was only there for a second, but I couldn't let you see it for too long. Because you'd go mad. And then you'd die. And then you'd become undead. And then you'd kill your loved ones." Another cut to the man-boy, who was now limping across the screen, with some kind of clear slime oozing out of his ass.

And then back to Tobe. "Some people think the word 'zombie' derives from the word 'jumbie,' which is how people in the West Indies refer to ghosts."

Another quick shot of the man-boy. The clear slime was now leaking from both his ass and his ears.

Back to Tobe. "Some people think it comes from 'nzambi,' which is African for 'spirit of a dead man.'"

Back to the man-boy, whose eyes were now leaking a thick, dark goo. Pretty good special effects for a sixteen-year-old. I made a mental note to ask Tobe about it at the screening.

Back to Tobe. "But we here in the South, here in the stinking bowels of Texas, we believe that it comes from the Creole word 'zonbi,' the translation of which is, *A dead man brought back to life without free will or the ability to speak.*"

And then the man-boy limped slowly into the frame and hacked off Tobe's arm with a machete.

As I watched the blood gush out of Tobe's shoulder, I actually gagged. I don't know how blood looks when it's coming out of a freshly amputated limb, and I don't know if young Tobe Hooper did either, but this looked pretty damn real. The oozing ass and the leaking eyes were excellent special effects, but the arm-chop was astounding.

After a few seconds of staring blankly at the camera, Tobe collapsed into a heap, his scream mixing with the zombie's mournful moan. The zombie licked the blood off the machete for about a minute—which is a long time, when you think about it—then sat down on his haunches and began to slurp up the fresh puddle of blood still dribbling from Tobe's shoulder socket. Then he turned to the camera and stuck out his tongue, which was coated with a combination of Tobe's blood and that weird zombie goo. He stood up and limped toward the camera, raised his machete, swung it forward, and then the screen went black, like he'd killed the cameraman.

It was a brilliant start, and had Tobe been able to sustain the momentum, he could've turned pro right then and there. Unfortunately, the moment the "story" kicked in, *Destiny Express* went straight into the crapper.

Ed Wood's *Plan 9 from Outer Space* wasn't even out yet so there's no way that Tobe could've stolen anything from Ed, but there were numerous similarities. The acting in both was horrible, for instance, but Tobe's situation was more forgivable, because his performers were probably all in their teens, while Wood's were adults. Both plots were incomprehensible, but quality-wise, Tobe's flick wins a head-to-head competition, because visually speaking, it was a lot more stylish, and the gore factor was off the meter.

Destiny Express featured two more human amputations; one zombie castration; an alligator attack; a sex scene between the man-boy and the female lead that, I'm embarrassed to say, got me a bit excited; and finally, a machete-versus-hammer battle between the zombie and girl lead that ends up with the two of them making out while covered in blood and slime. No clue what any of that has to do with either *destiny* or *express*.

It was a humorless piece of work, but, like the opening credits, the closing credits were funny in a weird way. The cue card girl reappeared, and, when she flipped to her third card, the zombie materialized behind her and bit off her ear, then sucked the ear hole until they both collapsed onto the sidewalk, the zombie clearly in ecstasy, the girl clearly dead. The end.

It was only an hour long, and I had the afternoon free, and since Dude McGee had disappeared, I rewound the film and gave it another watch. It was just as confusing the second time around. Try as I might, I still couldn't figure out how he made the amputations look so convincing. And that castration . . . horrifying, man, just horrifying.

I stumbled my way out of the utility room, past the weird little laboratory, past the boxes, past the comic books, and back into Dude's basement apartment. He reluctantly tore himself away from his computer bank—it looked to me like he was playing three different splattercore games at once, but it could've been one game spread out on three screens—then said, "So how'd you like it, Mr. Erick McLaughlin, Mr. Massacre This, Mr. Film Critic, Mr. *Austin Chronicle,* Mr. Austin Powers?" He spit onto the floor, farted, then gave me a weird giggle. I chose to ignore all three.

I told him the movie was interesting.

He then asked, "Are you coming to the screening? It'll be a

ton of fun. More fun than a barrel of zombies who have clear goo leaking from their orifices."

I said, "I doubt it. Twice was enough."

He said, "Twice, eh? And you survived." He did that weird laugh again, then said, "If I'm you, I wouldn't even consider missing it, because maybe you could slip Tobe a Massacre This CD, and he could use it in his next movie."

I thought that was actually a pretty good idea, but I didn't want Dude to believe I had any respect for him. Yeah, I'd been around him for only five minutes, but he's the kind of guy who you can safely label a douchebag after only two. I told him to put me on the list, and I'd try to make it.

He said, "I'll give you a plus-ten. Bring your friends."

I told him thanks, then made a quick exit. He belched again, and I almost sprinted up the stairs. That salami smell was making me nauseous.

TOBE HOOPER:

The flight from Hell-Lay to Texas was uneventful. Thank you, Ambien.

There was supposed to be a car waiting for me at the airport to take me straight to the club. Didn't happen. Wasn't surprised. South by Southwest wasn't known for its attention to detail. So I flagged a taxi. I didn't want to be *that guy*, the Hollywood type who rolls into town and bitches about a ten-dollar cab ride.

I hadn't been to the Cove in who knows how long. The last time I was there—or at least I *think* it was the last time I was there; I might've gone another night after that and had such a crappy time that I forced it out of my brainpan—I got into a fight with three drunk dudes that ended with me getting a pool cue broken over my head. And I can't fight for shit, so no surprise that I got the bad end of it.

Anyhow, when I got there, I saw that Dude McGee either lied or didn't know what the fuck he was talking about. They hadn't expanded the Cove by a third; they just took out the pool table and the jukebox, which meant you could fit maybe fifteen more people in there. The Cove wasn't a place to hang out anymore. It was a place to get fucked-up: no pool, no music, just crappy booze. There was nothing else to do there but drink, and maybe get a blow job in the bathroom. And, of course, fight.

On the plus side, the girl selling the tickets at the door was a fucking knockout. Not that I'd do anything about it—I was old enough to be either her older father or possibly her younger grandpa—but she made the outside of that dump look a hell of a lot prettier.

JANINE DALTREY (*University of Texas senior*):
Dave Cranford, my old boyfriend, called the day before the *Destiny Express* thing and asked if I'd like to take a shift at the Cove. I said, "Are you serious? I already told you I'm never setting foot in that place again." The last time I went, I was there for only five minutes before some guy—who, it turned out, was a regular customer—stuck his hand on my ass. And he didn't just smack it or pinch it; he ran his finger up and down the crack, like, twice. I screamed at him to back the hell off, but he didn't, so I pulled out a trick I learned at the self-defense class I took my sophomore year and stomped his foot with one of my heels, then elbowed him in the sternum, then got right on out of there. Dave told me later that I broke his fifth and sixth metatarsals. Good.

So, you know, screw the Cove.

Dave said, "All you'll have to do is collect the cover charge. You can sit outside the door. You don't even need to set foot in the place. I know you need the bread."

He was right. I did need the money. Six months before, I'd

taken a leave of absence from my bartending gig at the Iron Cactus to cram for midterms. My manager wouldn't give me the job back after I was all done with my tests, because he threw all my shifts to one of the servers who had really big tits and was in the habit of leaving her top four buttons unbuttoned. The manager actually told me that my B-cups weren't cutting the muster. I told him to fuck off, and that he was going to hear from my lawyer, and that it was cutting the *mustard,* not *muster.*

He said, "If I give you severance pay, will you keep the lawyers out of it?"

Like I could afford a lawyer anyhow. But he didn't know that, so I told him, "What kind of severance are we talking about here?"

He said, "Five hundred bucks?"

I shot for the moon and asked, "How about a thousand?" We agreed on seven-fifty. I was a month behind on rent, and two months behind on gas and electric, so the money was gone before I even touched it. By the time I got the call from Dave, I was at rock bottom. I could've called my parents for help, but it was too damn embarrassing.

So I asked Dave on the phone, "How much can you get me?" I told myself the minimum for a night at the Cove was one bill.

Dave said, "How does five hundred sound? Plus free drinks. Plus I can get your sister on the guest list."

My little sister Andrea didn't have any money either, so I thought she'd enjoy a free evening on the town, even if that particular piece of town was disgusting. "Okay. So what's the deal? I'm guessing it's a South by Southwest thing."

He said, "Yeah, it's a movie. You know *The Texas Chainsaw Massacre?*"

I said, "Never saw it. But I suppose it makes sense to show it at the Cove."

He said, "Nah, they're not showing *Chainsaw.* It's a movie by the guy who directed it. He made it when he was a kid, like back in the 1940s or something."

I said, "Sounds like a blast. Andrea will *love* it." I was being sarcastic. The only movies Andrea watched were romantic comedies and indie films about people who fall in and out and in and out of love. She was sappy like that. She was super-cute—if I'm being honest, I'd say she was cuter than me, and I've been told that I'm pretty cute—but she'd never had a real boyfriend at that point, and I was always afraid that her dream version of dating was clean and pretty, and she'd be disappointed when she learned that there were going to be plenty of arguments, and that sex is usually wet and messy, and you usually have to clean up the wet stuff before you cuddle, and even when you're in love with somebody, you'll still get butterflies when a random cute guy tells you how nice you look. I could've told her all that, but I thought it would be better for her to find out about it herself. I mean, I had on-the-job love training, and I turned out okay.

Anyhow, Dave said, "Great, we really appreciate it. The screening's at midnight, and the doors open at nine, so get there at eight. Cool?"

I showed up right on time, because I'm a Virgo, and Virgos *always* show up on time. Virgos also do a lot of waiting around, because nobody else in the world ever shows up on time, Dave Cranford included. The Cove was locked when I got there, naturally, so I went back to my car and sat down on the hood. It was still light out, but I wasn't concerned about getting harassed by anybody. The Cove itself is gross, but the neighborhood is okay. It's almost like somebody plucked the bar out of a shitty area in Houston, airlifted it over to Austin, then dropped it, like, *boom!*

So I'm there in the parking lot, chilling out on my hood, and this older guy comes over and asks if I work there. He had a scraggly gray beard and nerdy John Lennon glasses, and he looked relatively harmless, so I actually answered him. I said, "Not really. Just for tonight. One time only. This place is disgusting. I'm collecting the cover charge, and my plan is to stay outside all night."

The guy nodded, then said, "What if you need to use the bathroom?"

I said, "I'll hold it."

Then he said, "What if you hear people screaming and laughing at the movie? Wouldn't you maybe step in for a minute or two?"

I said, "Doubt it."

He said, "That's too bad. I bet you'd enjoy it."

I said, "You've seen it?"

He said, "I made it."

I said, "Oh, you're the *Chainsaw* guy."

He kind of laughed, then said, "Yeah, I'm the *Chainsaw* guy."

I said, "Cool. What's the movie about?"

He said, "I don't fucking know."

TOBE HOOPER:

I don't remember much that happened to me from age zero to age fifteen. From fifteen on, I'm pretty good, although there're big chunks of my late teens that sometimes get *real* hazy, which I blame partly on the weed and partly on the fact that all I did was think about movies. But before that, it's virtually nothing. I lost most of my memory on the street in front of my mother's house. Literally.

I was playing concrete hockey with my buddy Scott Frost. I do recall that Scott was a helluva hockey player, man, both on the street and on the ice. There weren't too many ice rinks near where we grew up—back then, hockey and Texas didn't really mix, and if you take the Dallas Stars into consideration, that's really still the case—but if Scott'd had regular access to a rink and somebody around to teach him the finer points of the sport, who knows what would've happened? Anyway, even though I don't recall the specifics, I'm sure that whenever I played with Scott, I always tried to make certain that I was on the same team as him, because if you played against him, you were royally fucked.

Taking into account my massive memory-suck, whatever I know about Scott, I learned from somebody else. Everybody I've spoken to said Scott was a good egg, popular, a fellow who always did the right thing. Apparently he was a precocious bastard, too; he was dating a college freshman when he was a high school sophomore. Some say he knocked her up. He must've really had something on the ball, because in that day and age, it was a rarity for boys in their mid-teens to be getting laid, especially by a college coed. Today, kids are screwing in elementary school. Man, I wish it'd been like that back in my day.

From what I was told, it was only the two of us that afternoon, just me and Scott. Apparently our hockey game consisted of me whacking the puck at his net, then him taking a whack at mine. I'd bet that every once in a while, I stopped that hard orange plastic round thing with my gut or my chest, but most of the time, the damn thing probably went right in between my legs or over my shoulder. I'd also bet that I didn't get a single goal off old Scotty.

Our street wasn't ever busy during the day. The neighborhood was all stay-at-home moms and their little rug rats, and there weren't too many two-car families, so while the daddies were at work, the road was free and clear. And even when cars did come by, they'd just honk their horns, and we'd get our asses onto the sidewalk. Except for that red fucker.

I found out later that the Corvette wasn't actually *red* red: it was *Roman* Red. Those Corvette dickheads can call it whatever they want to, but I've been to Rome, and I didn't see anything that shade of red.

I remember seeing the red Corvette plow around the corner, and I remember waking up in the hospital with a fucking turban around my head.

I remember the doctors poking and prodding the shit out of me, and I remember it hurting like hell, the worst physical pain I've felt. *Ever.*

I remember my mother telling me that I flew fifteen feet in the air, and landed face-first on the pavement, and cracked my skull. Some of my brain fluid apparently leaked onto the street. The next time it rained, my memory was washed into the sewer.

And I remember my mother saying that Scotty flew about twenty-five feet. He went headfirst into a streetlamp. He was dead before he hit the ground.

Fuzzy memory, man. So when that beautiful girl in the Cove's parking lot asked me what the deal was with *Destiny Express,* I told her the truth: "I don't fucking know."

JANINE DALTREY:
He introduced himself as Tobe Hooper, then we shook hands. His hand was kind of clammy, which I chalked up to it being unseasonably warm, like a zillion degrees. He seemed like a nice old fart, so I asked him, "Can you take a guess what it's about?"

He said, "I'd rather let the movie speak for itself. All I'll say is that it's probably a combination of funny and bloody. That's me in a nutshell: funny and bloody."

I said, "If there's a lot of blood, there probably won't be much laughing. Plenty of screaming, I'd bet."

He scratched his beard, then said, "Yeah, but here's the thing: It's scarier if there's some humor involved, because life, although it is generally fucked-up beyond recognition, is oftentimes pretty damn funny. If something's funny, it becomes more real, and if it's more real, it becomes more scary."

I said, "I suppose I see your point. But, if I can be honest . . ."

He said, "I'd hope for nothing less."

I said, "Look at those *Scream* movies. Or look at the Freddy Krueger movies. They were pretty funny, but they were less scary than *The Ring*. That wasn't funny at all."

He smiled, then patted me on the shoulder and said, "Honey, if I wasn't old enough to be either your older father or your younger grandpa, I'd ask you to dinner and a movie."

I said, "And I'd accept."

He said, "Ah. That's nice. It appears that we're having a moment here."

And before he could go on, this beat-up car flew into the parking lot, then screeched to a stop right behind my car. The door opened, and this fat guy practically fell out of the car, looking as drunk as your typical Cove patron. He walked over, and the first thing I noticed was the orange stain on his white T-shirt; it looked like he'd gotten into a fight with a bowl of buffalo wings. The second thing I noticed was that he smelled like salami. Gross. He looked me up and down and said, "Nice tits. I don't know why you got fired. Me, I think B-cups are *awesome*." Then he turned to Tobe and said, "What do you think, Toeb? What're your favorite-size breast-a-sauruses? Are you a double-D man? Do you like sticking your face in the cleavage and doing a bronski? Or do you like flat, perky ones like this chick here?"

Tobe coughed loudly and spit a loogie at the guy's feet, then said, "Dude McGee, I presume."

TOBE HOOPER:

I was this close to punching him in the face, but I was out of shape, and he had about three thousand pounds on me, so I hawked a couple of yellow ones by his shoes. He just laughed, then cut a huge fart that you could smell even though we were hanging out in the great outdoors. I did, however, say, "If you mispronounce my name again, I'll hit you. And if you speak to this girl like that again, I'll cut you."

Dude belched, then, with what was some impressive aim, spit a goober right on top of one of my goobers and said, "You don't have a knife on you, Tobe." He pronounced it right. Hallelujah, praise Jesus. "And even if you did, it'd probably be in your safe, and even if it was in your safe, you'd probably be too lazy to get it. Don't write a check with your ass that your cock can't cash. Or something like that." Then he wiped his hand on his pant leg and offered it up for a shake. "Pleasure to meet you."

I'm from the South, and southerners are gentlemen, so I've never refused a handshake in my life . . . but there's a first time for everything. I said, "Sorry, Mr. McGee, but I have a terrible cold, and I left my Purell back at the hotel. I'll have to owe you that shake."

He said, "And I'm holding you to that. Wait here." Then he went into his car trunk, pulled out a film canister, and said, "Here it is, the moment you've been waiting for. Ladies and gentlemen, may I introduce to you the one, the only, *Destiny Express*!" He held it out to me, then said, "Would you like to check it out? Or are you afraid that you'll give it your terrible cold?"

Over the years, I've developed a pretty good bullshit-o-meter, and this dude was pinging in the red. I took a deep breath, counted to five, then said, "I'd love to check it out, Mr. McGee." I reached for it, then he yanked it away.

He said, "Say 'please.'"

Then the pretty blond girl said, "Jesus Christ, just give him the movie!"

McGee leered at her chest and said, "Only because you asked me so nicely." And then he handed it over.

The canister—which certainly looked to be the original one—was clean and dust free, but it still smelled musty, kind of like wet newspapers. On the label, I'd written in some sort of marker, "TOBE HOOPER'S 'DESTINY EXPRESS.' DO NOT VIEW WITHOUT THE PERMISSION OF THE DIRECTOR/ SCREENWRITER!!!" I don't remember doing that, obviously, but it sure sounded like something that the teenage version of yours truly would come up with: pretentious and snotty.

I opened it up, and there it was, the only existing print of my teenage dabbling into the great world of moviemaking. I took out the reel and unspooled a few frames, but it was too dark to really see anything. I asked Dude, "Have you watched this?"

He said, "Have I? *Have* I?!"

The pretty girl said, "Yeah. Have you?"

He said, "I have . . ."

I said, "What did you think?"

He said, "You didn't let me finish. *Not.* I have *not* watched it. Wait, that's a lie. I watched ten minutes of it. That's all I could stomach." Then he patted his fat gut and said, "And that's saying something."

I said, "Does that mean it was too gross for you?"

He belched again, then said, "Something like that." Then he pointed to the club and said, "Shall we?"

I gave him back the film and said, "You go ahead. I'll meet you."

As we watched him go, the pretty girl said, "If that's your audience, remind me never to make a horror movie."

I said, "Shit, girl, remind *me* never to make a horror movie."

FROM: GaryChurch@gmail.com
TO: Church_Warren@LTDLaw.com
SUBJECT: Blast from the past
DATE: March 15, 2009

Greetings, O Brother of Mine—

You're not going to believe this one. Guess what arrived
in the mail today . . . and not an e-mail, mind you, but
an honest-to-goodness letter. A note from our ol' pal Tobe
Hooper. Long time no hear from that sumbitch, right? Doesn't
he still owe you a few bucks? But seriously, folks . . .

So yeah, he sent me a handwritten note! No e-mail for the
Hooperman. No shocker there, though. I bet he's a total
technophobe. I wouldn't be surprised if he still edits his
movies by hand. Anyhow, the note was short and sweet.
He invited me to some music convention in Austin that's
showing that movie of his I was in when I was, what, 16?
17? 14? Who can remember? Clearly not me, because I didn't
even remember its existence until that very moment. And he
must've wanted me there badly, because included in the
envelope was a first-class ticket to Dallas and a voucher for
a limo to Austin.

Good timing. I just wrapped that Shawn Levy thing—my first
foray into comedy, after decades of horror, so you can finally
get off my ass about spreading my acting wings—and I have a
spare couple of weeks.

No clue how he got my address. But I don't really care. It'll be great to see the guy. He is, as they say, a good egg. I'll send you a report.

Love,
Gary

AUTHOR'S NOTE: *As far as I know, no other member of the* Destiny Express *team was summoned to the screening. Hooper professes no knowledge of who sent Church his invitation. One can assume it was McGee, but that can be neither confirmed nor denied.*

TOBE HOOPER:

And then, right as I was falling half in love with the girl who was named Janine Daltrey, a limo rolled up, and I started laughing. How could I not? I mean, a limousine pulling into the parking lot of the Cove is like a giant ruby levitating out of a huge pile of human excrement. The limo door opened, and out came a blast from the past: Gary Church. Gary goddamn Church. Man, I almost shit a ruby on the spot.

Like I said, I don't remember much about my early childhood, but my teen years are a little clearer, and I sure as hell remember Gary. Because in my neck of the woods, which was populated mostly with hammerheads and dullards, Gary stood out.

The best thing about Gary was, he was a stand-up dude. Like if you made plans to meet at a restaurant at 6:00, he'd be there at 5:58. Unfortunately, I'd usually show up at 6:58, but he was such a good guy that he'd hang out until I got there and only complain a tiny bit. If *I* was waiting for *me* at a restaurant, and *I* showed up an hour late, I'd have complained my ass off, then I probably would've kneed myself in the balls for good measure.

Gary brought a helluva lot to the table. In high school, he was a brainiac who always got straight A's, but unlike the other brainiacs in our school—all four of them—he wasn't the least bit uncool. He managed to balance work with play better than anybody I've ever met, before or since. It helped that he had an innate intelligence that allowed him to finish a two-thousand-word paper on Chaucer, or Homer, or astro-fucking-physics in two hours. That all left him with plenty of time to wreak havoc. With me. Which we did. All the damn time.

I remember once we got ahold of a full bottle of blackberry brandy, which, at the time, I thought was the elixir of the gods, but I now realize is the foulest shit you can drink. We slammed that thing down in a couple of hours, then, for the hour before we puked up our collective guts and passed out, we took a baseball bat to every mailbox in a five-block radius. Juvenile shit, man, but it was fun.

Our hijinks weren't always of the innocent variety. We stole probably a hundred books and magazines from good ol' Mr. Ralph's newsstand, which we didn't need to do, because our respective parents gave us plenty of spending money, plus the local library had everything we could ever want. Why did we do it, then? Because there was something outlaw about reading a stolen piece of merchandise. Knowing they were hot made those pulp mysteries and horror tales come across as creepier. And cooler.

We dug reading. During the summer, the two of us would sit in one of our backyards, on the lawn, and spend the entire afternoon poring over whatever book we'd ripped off that day. I gravitated toward guys like Jim Thompson, and Spillane, and Chandler, whereas Gary was into nonfiction crap like . . . well, truth be told, I don't remember exactly what kind of nonfiction crap. Once in a while, just for the fuck of it, one of us would bring along something heavy, like *Atlas Shrugged,* or *Critique of Pure Reason,* or maybe some Genet thing. Our other friends thought we were odd, and our enemies thought we were complete fucking morons. Me and Gary, we didn't grow up in the most intellectual of areas, which is why we clung on to each other for dear life.

Girl-wise, Gary was way ahead of the game, just like Scott Frost was. I mean, the dude was balling a twenty-four-year-old when he was fifteen. Seemed like everybody in town was getting older ladies into the sack but me. Gary told me all about it, but in a respectful way, like he wouldn't say shit like, "I blew my load all over her huge tits." That wasn't the way he was wired. No, good ol' Gary liked to talk about how sweet her hair smelled, and how smooth her skin was, and how her entire body tasted like caramel. Sometimes I wish I could've taken that kind of approach with the ladies—especially with a certain Oscar-nominated brunette who shall remain nameless. Anyhow.

Gary was into everything: history, sports, music, philosophy, and, of course, movies. He wanted to be an actor practically from day one. He'd drag my ass to the Ernest Lord Theater at least twice a week, and we'd see a Hitchcock flick, or some John Ford, or some John Wayne, or something—cross your fingers, please, please, dear Lord—with Kim Novak. I initially watched all these flicks just to watch, to be entertained, but not Gary. He was all about camera angles, and the finer points of acting, and story development, and all the kind of shit that even today I need to brush up on. I suppose if you break it down, if there's no Gary Church, there's no Leatherface.

After we finished up high school, he went out to California to make it as an actor. Now, he wasn't particularly good-looking—we're talking five foot eight and a buck forty soaking wet, with a too-early-in-life receding hairline—but he had a charisma that charmed casting directors and looked great on the big screen. Unfortunately, since he was so short and average looking, nobody gave him a shot at carrying a movie. They didn't even give him a chance at *helping* carry a movie. He became, for my money, the greatest horror third banana in Hollywood. If you needed a sympathetic best friend to kill off in the second act, Gary was your man. And the dude knew how to die a good death.

I moved out to Hell-Lay after *Chainsaw* hit, and for a while, it was like old times for me and Gary, except without the broken mailboxes and cherry bombs. When I was hard up for cash, he'd take me out for a meal, and when I was lonely, he'd set me up on a blind date, and when I wanted to show a studio exec a script, he'd do his damnedest to get me an appointment. Gary was a mensch, man, a true mensch.

When I started getting busy directing, and he started getting busier acting, we lost touch, and I have to foot a larger part of the blame for that one. I'd get so wrapped up in a movie—"obsessed" is a better word, I suppose—that I wouldn't meet him for lunch, or grab a drink, or even return a damn phone call. When we managed to connect, I told him he shouldn't take any of it personally, because I didn't return *anybody's* phone calls or meet *anybody* for lunch. But after a while, how can you *not* take it personally? I couldn't blame Gary when he stopped reaching out. After all, I'd stopped years before.

We'd run into each other around town—if you've been in the industry for a while, you eventually run into *everybody* at some point or another—and it was always pleasant. He'd talk about his many acting gigs, and I'd talk about my too-few directing gigs, and we'd make promises to get together, and, of course, it never happened. I felt so guilty about the whole thing that I started avoiding him at parties and premieres, so when he stepped out of that limo at the Cove, well, that was the first time I'd seen him in almost a decade. My initial reaction was, *Man, I'm a dick for blowing this guy off.* But when I got a gander at his smiling face, all the regret, all the guilt, and all the self-flagellation fell by the wayside, and I ran over and gave him a big-ass bear hug.

JANINE DALTREY:
Tobe and his friend yipped and jumped around like little kids, and it was the sweetest thing. If you talked to Tobe for a minute or two, you might think he was kind of a crusty fellow and blow him off. But if you saw him hugging his pal like that, you'd give him a second chance.

Tobe held Gary by his shoulders at arm's length and said, "As I live and breathe, it's Gary Church. My God, brother, you look amazing." And I have to admit, Gary did look pretty good . . . and pretty familiar. I guessed that since he rolled up in a limo, and since he was buddies with a fancy director like Tobe Hooper, that he was a *somebody*. I made a mental note to look up Gary Church on IMDb when I got home.

Gary took a playful swipe at Tobe's scraggly old beard and said, "I wish I could say the same for you. Manscape much?"

Tobe smacked Gary's hand away, then laughed and said, "Nobody gives a rat's ass about how we working stiffs behind the camera look. You pretty boys, you're the ones who have to do the . . . what did you call it?"

Gary said, "Manscaping."

Tobe laughed. "Right. Yeah. Manscaping. Maybe that's what I'll call my next flick. The pitch: Yuppie dude gets attacked by a haunted lawn mower. You can play the lawn mower."

Gary said, "It would be my honor. And it'd be nice to work together again."

Tobe said, "Yeah, right. Again. Say, do you remember what the fuck this movie was about?"

He shrugged and said, "Meh."

FROM: GaryChurch@gmail.com
TO: Church_Warren@LTDLaw.com
SUBJECT: My film debut
DATE: March 18, 2009

Good morning, Mr. Busy Lawyer Man—

Thanks for not writing back. As usual. You bastard.

Since I last e-mailed you—an e-mail that, I should re-remind you, you didn't answer—I've been thinking about Tobe. Do you recall when I shot that movie with him when we were, what, 15? 16?

I remember that script wasn't much to write home about—there was a whole lot of "I'm going to kill you, you terrible man" and "How could you do that to my girlfriend?" and "Let's cut him off at the pass"—but he was a kid, and how many kids back then knew how to write dialogue? (For that matter, how many adults right now know how to write dialogue?) He told me that if I didn't like what was on the page, I should feel free to change it up so it sounded more natural, like it was something that I'd actually say. The problem was, I was about as good an improviser as he was a screenwriter, so what was originally "How could you do that to my girlfriend?" became "How dare you do that to my girlfriend?" It dawned on me that we wouldn't be winning any Oscars.

But I will say that, amateurish as it was, the screenplay made sense: Hapless man (played by me) meets zombie . . . hapless man becomes zombie . . . hapless man tries to turn loving girlfriend into zombie . . . hapless man's innate goodness sublimates zombie-ian tendencies . . . hapless man turns girlfriend into zombie, and they live happily ever after. Or, I suppose, they're undead happily ever after.

We shot it as written, and even though Tobe kept telling me to mess with the words, I did my part mostly verbatim. I might've tried to stretch if I hadn't been covered in this god-awful zombie slime for the entire shoot. He never told me what that shit was made of. All I know is it stunk like, well, like shit, and when it got above 85 degrees, it congealed. I know you remember that part of it, because you used to rag on me about A) how bad I smelled, and B) how much time I spent in the shower. Does this ring a bell?—"HEY, ASSHOLE, YOU'VE BEEN IN THE CRAPPER FOR AN HOUR, AND I CAN STILL SMELL YOU OUT HERE! ARE YOU WASHING UP OR JERKING OFF?!" Brotherly love at its finest . . . you dick.

I remember getting hurt a couple of times. Not badly, just some bumps, bruises, and cuts. The worst was when we were shooting this scene at a makeshift swamp he'd created in his backyard. I was attacking my girlfriend, who was played by Helen Leary (remember her? That cheerleader girl? My God, she was hot), and she was fighting back with a scimitar that Tobe fashioned out of two yardsticks, aluminum foil, and Elmer's glue. She gouged me in my neck, and some of Tobe's shit-slime rubbed up on it, and it stung like crazy. I went into Tobe's house, washed it on up, splashed some whiskey on it, and went back to work. We were already behind schedule and over budget (LOL), and we did what we had to do.

So yeah, that was my first film experience. What with the slime, and the heat, and the long hours, and the badly choreographed alligator attack (Jesus, I haven't thought about that stinking alligator in years), and the nonexistent salary, it prepared me for Hollywood better than any acting class ever would've.

The funny thing is, I never saw the damn movie. It should be a trip.

Love,
Gary

ERICK LAUGHLIN:

I've met who-knows-how-many celebrity types, and aside from the time when I interviewed Jessica Alba at a photo shoot that she spent most of wearing only a thong and what could best be described as pasties, I've never once gotten tongue-tied. Stick me in a room with George Clooney or Meryl Streep, and I'm fine. Stick me in a room—or a parking lot—with Tobe Hooper, and that's another story.

I pulled my bike into the Cove lot, and there he was, the man himself, a big, fat smile on his mug, chatting with a short, balding guy. I didn't want to bother them, so when I saw Janine Daltrey sitting on the trunk of her car a few feet away from Tobe, I wandered on over.

Janine, who, as usual, was looking beautiful, gave me a kiss on the cheek, then patted the trunk and said, "Pull up a chair. How's it going? How's the band?" I knew her only a little bit—she was more friendly with my drummer, Theo—but I always liked her, partly because when she asked you a question, she actually listened to the answer, which is something that isn't always common in my circle of friends. Another reason I liked her: She was fucking *hot*.

I told her, "Okay, I guess. Actually, not really okay. Our last gig was pretty sucky. Our bassist, Jamal, canceled at the last minute, so Theo and I had to do a White Stripes guitar/drums duo thing. It didn't suck as badly as it could've, I guess, but it still did suck." Then I went on and on about a couple movies I'd recently screened, but I'm certain I didn't say anything noteworthy, because by that point, I was trying to listen to Tobe's conversation.

Janine saw right through me. She said, "Erick, go talk to the guy. He's perfectly nice. He won't bite you." I didn't say anything. I didn't move. Finally, she jumped off the car, grabbed me by my elbow, pulled me up from the trunk, hauled me over, and said, "Tobe Hooper, Erick Laughlin. Erick Laughlin, Tobe Hooper.

Tobe, Erick here is a film reviewer and a musician. You two should have plenty to talk about."

Tobe stuck out his hand and said, "Music and flicks. A man right after my own heart. Pleasure to meet you. Listen, I don't mean to be rude, but could we jaw after the movie? I'm catching up with my old pal Gary here."

I shook his hand and said, "Are we talking Gary as in Gary Church?"

Gary said, "My man, if you know my name, you must really be a *serious* film nerd."

I said, "Well, I am. But that's not it. I saw *Destiny Express* yesterday. You were *the guy*."

Gary nodded and said, "I was *the guy*." Then he laughed, looked at Tobe, and said, "Thing is, I don't know what guy that was, exactly."

Tobe laughed. "Me neither. How about that, Erick: You know more about this piece-of-shit movie than either the star or the director." He paused, then asked, "*Is* it a piece of shit?"

Talk about a loaded question. If I said, *No, it's not a piece of shit, it's an interesting little film,* they'd think I was a moron after they saw it, because, for the most part, it *was* a piece of shit. But if I said, *Yes, it is a piece of shit,* I'd totally offend one of my favorite directors.

Tobe said, "Well, I guess I have my answer."

I said, "I didn't say anything."

Tobe said, "The answer lies in your silence, my new friend. After the flick, I'll buy you a beer, and you can tell me what you thought the smelliest part of that turd was." Then he clapped me on the shoulder and went back to chatting with Gary.

Just then, Dave Cranford, the meathead who manages the Cove—who, for some unexplainable reason, Janine dated for several months—called out to Janine, "Hey, blondie, get your ass in here! It's time!"

She called back, "There's nobody here, David! Relax!"

He said, "Just get in here!"

She whispered to me, "Diiiiick," then yelled to him, "On my way, muffin!" She took my hand and dragged me along with her. "I'm not facing this shit by myself. I'm hiring you to be my escort for the night."

I said, "Yeah? What am I getting paid?"

She said, "My undying gratitude. And that's priceless."

Andi-Licious

The Useless Musings of Sophomoric Sophomore Andrea Daltrey

FRIDAY, MARCH 31

I *HATE* THE COVE, BUT I'LL SEE YOU THERE!

My sister invited me to a SXSW movie screening at the Cove tonight and I'm going even though the Cove is the crappiest place in the known universe. But I have nothing else to do, so what the heck. Maybe I'll meet somebody. But then the question becomes, who will I meet at the crappiest place in the known universe that'll be worth meeting? Another question is, what kind of movie will they be showing there? Like, what kind of movies do they show at the crappiest place in the known universe? Whatever it is, I'm sure it'll be lame but I'm going anyhow, because it's better than sitting in my room watching the Discovery Channel and waiting for the phone to ring.

Hmmm, what should I wear? Maybe that low-cut thing Janine got me, because she's always going on about how I should quit hiding my bod because it's smokin'. (She's the one with the smokin' bod.) I don't know, whatever, it's boiling outside, and I'm sure the Cove doesn't have the air conditioner on, so maybe I'm better off dressing lightly anyhow.

Details to follow tomorrow . . .

MIDNIGHT MOVIE

JANINE DALTREY:

So Erick and I are on our way into the club, and, shock of shocks, my little sister Andrea rolls up, rocking a low-cut top and some low-hanging jean shorts. I gave her a wolf whistle and said, "Somebody's on the prowl tonight."

She gave me a hug and said, "This is the crappiest place in the known universe. I'm not prowling."

Now, Andrea was a girl who needed to prowl. If you saw her walking down the street, you'd totally think, *Sexpot.* She had a Barbie doll figure, you know, huge boobs, and a tiny waist, and a big butt . . . and that butt swayed like a pendulum. Andi got gawked at all the time, but she was so oblivious about that kind of thing that she didn't even realize it. Me, I can tell in a heartbeat when some guy is checking me out.

Here's the thing: Andi was a virgin. She'd had boyfriends, and I know for a fact that she'd been to second base, and I have a hunch that she went to third, even though she'd never confirmed it. She gave her high school squeeze a hand job, but apparently that traumatized her so badly that she hadn't touched a cock since. Most every other girl in Texas who wasn't a Catholic was fucking by the age of fourteen—myself included—but Andi was different. She was either saving herself, or she wasn't into sex. She just *looked* like she was into sex.

Ever since we were kids, like from when I was sixteen and she was fourteen, I told her that she could talk to me about *anything,* and if she had any questions, she should ask, no matter how stupid or embarrassing she thought it might be. She took me up on it exactly once, and it was her first day at college. We were in her crappy little dorm room, and I was helping her unpack all her clothes, then, out of nowhere, she asked me, "How do I know if I've had an orgasm?"

I told her, "If you have to ask, sweetie, you probably haven't had one."

TOBE HOOPER WITH ALAN GOLDSHER

She said, "I *definitely* haven't. But if it happens, how'll I know?"

I asked her, "Do you know where your clitoris is?"

She said, "Yeah."

I said, "Have you, um, *experimented* with it?"

She said, "Not really."

I said, "Okay, here's your assignment. Each night for the next week, diddle around down there for a few minutes and get back to me. You might figure it out for yourself."

And that was the last time I discussed sex with little Andrea Daltrey.

She asked me if she could sit with me by the door while I sold tickets, and I told her, "Why? Don't you want to mingle with everybody?"

By then, there were probably a couple dozen guys on the scene, none of whom looked like Andi's type. Actually, I didn't know what Andi's type was, but I *did* know that these guys weren't it. I had a hunch she wasn't into the men of Comic-Con.

There were only two girls there, and they were clinging on to their boyfriends for dear life; they both looked miserable, like they'd been dragged there against their will. The single guys seemed to be jazzed up about the movie, so even if there were some prospects there for Andi, they probably wouldn't be able to tear themselves away from the screen.

Andi's clueless when it comes to dealing with the opposite sex, but she's a sharp cookie in every other venue of her life. She looked at the crowd and said, "Seriously, sis, this is nerd central." She pointed to a guy wearing a *Texas Chainsaw Massacre* T-shirt, carrying a plastic chainsaw, and said, "Like I'm going to let that guy ruin me for my future husband."

I said, "You have a point. But you *could* stand some ruining." I flicked the top of her left boob, then said, "And with those, you can find somebody to ruin you *easily*."

She smacked my hand away and said, "Just for that, you're buying me a beer."

I told her, "It's Black Strap or nothing."

She blew out a big puff of air, then said, "My God, I hate the Cove."

TOBE HOOPER:

I don't get out much. Being *in* is crazy enough, so who needs *out*?

Before all that Game shit went down, my typical day probably would have sounded like a snooze to the regular nine-to-fiver. Actually, it probably would have sounded like a snooze to a ten-to-sixer, or an eleven-to-sevener, or a midnight-to-nooner: wake up; shit; eat; smoke my one butt for the day; watch two movies; eat; watch another movie; maybe write, maybe not; eat; sleep; repeat. For a dude like me, that's a lot of day.

The only times I got sociable, truly sociable, were when I was making a movie or doing a signing at a horror convention. On a film set, behind the camera, communication is king, and if you can't get your vision across to your DP, or your lighting guy, or your second-unit director, you're fucked. As for in front of the camera, that's another story. Sometimes actors don't *want* to communicate. I'll take a malleable amateur who's eager to learn something, who takes a big-picture view of the project, and who doesn't bitch about the size of their trailer over a megastar any day of the week. You might not end up with a perfect performance, but at least it'll be *real*, and if something's real, then the horror is more horrifying.

As for those movie and comic conventions, suffice it to say that when I want to, I can work a room with the best of them.

Since I'm not out in the real world all that often, I have very little sense of how the real world feels about me. Even when I do get out, it's not like I'm recognizable—the only directors that the general public recognizes are the bigmouths like Marty Scorsese, or Woody Allen, or Spike Lee—and that's fine with me. I offer the world what I offer the world: scary flicks. I'm not trying to make a grand statement or anything. I want to entertain, and I do that best from behind the camera, not in front.

So when I was out in front of the Cove jawing with Gary, and all these folks started wandering over, and introducing themselves, and asking me to sign their *Chainsaw* DVDs, and quizzing me about what I'm working on, and wondering what the hell *Destiny Express* was about, I was pretty shocked, and—I'm not going to lie here—flattered. I don't seek one-on-one acceptance, but when I get it—especially if it's unsolicited—it feels pretty good.

FROM: 3105151842@verizon.net
TO: Church_Warren@LTDLaw.com

So I'm standing in the parking lot of this dive bar in Austin,
bored as all get-out, waiting for the fancy-schmancy *Destiny
Express* screening, and my man Tobe is getting mobbed—
that is, if you can call 30 people a mob. Obviously he has
a following, but I've never had visual confirmation of said
following. It's needless to say the crowd is as geeked out as
your typical paranormal crowd, and it's also needless to say
that it's 99.9999 percent male. If you see Emma, tell her she
doesn't have to worry about me getting a taste of strange.

Despite their obvious Tobe worship, these people look
relatively sane . . . LOL. I'm looking at one young gentleman
who, way back in the day, we'd have called a preppy. He
has the perfectly coiffed coif, and a pink Izod shirt, and
Top-Siders, which I didn't even know they made anymore.
And there're a couple of white kids who evidently wish like
hell that they were black, what with their shirts that hang
down to here, and their shorts that hang down to there,
and their strategically placed tattoos and piercings. Then
there're a couple of old fogies . . . like us! Well, more an
old fogy like you: They look like boring, slightly overweight
lawyers. Again, LOL.

These people aren't letting Tobe go, so I'm going into this
dump of a bar and getting myself a brew. Apparently all they
have is Black Strap. Gross. Anyhoo, I'll text you a report
after the flick.

SENT FROM MY VERIZON BLACKBERRY

ERICK LAUGHLIN:

I was leaning against the wall, staring at the stars, enjoying the breeze, and trying to not stare at Andrea Daltrey's breasts when I felt a tap on my shoulder and smelled a waft of luncheon meat. That's right, you guessed it, it was my old pal Dude McGee.

He giggled this weird, high-pitched giggle and said, "Glad to see you made it, Erick, Earache, Erick the Half a Bee, Erich von Stroheim."

I grunted a nonanswer.

He said, "I'm kind of surprised you're here. Wasn't twice through the movie enough?"

I leaned away from him. He made me feel dirty. I said, "I'm here for the Q and A."

McGee nodded. "Ah. The Q and A. I'm here for that, too. Lots of Q's, I have."

I said, "Like what?"

He belched—surprise, surprise—then said, "Like how did he make such a masterpiece at such a tender age?"

I asked him, "You think it's a masterpiece?"

He said, "Of sorts."

I said, "What's your favorite scene?"

He said, "Oh, I don't have one. They're all good."

I said, "Okay, what's the scariest moment?"

He said, "They're *alllll* scary."

I said, "I was pretty impressed that he was able to get such a nice color scheme."

He said, "I couldn't agree more."

I said, "The movie is black and white. You didn't watch it at all, did you, you dipshit? Not even the ten minutes you claim." It was unbelievably rude for me to call a guy I was meeting for only the second time a dipshit to his face, but he brought out that side of me.

He shrugged and said, "So what? I'm not the critic. You are."

He made a shooing motion at me, then said, "So get in there and go criticize." And then he wandered toward Tobe.

TOBE HOOPER:
My throng of fans—such as it was—gradually made their way into the bar. I was about to follow when somebody grabbed me roughly by the wrist. I turned around quick, ready to swing. You don't grab a man by his wrist from behind.

It was Dude McGee. He turned the grab into a sweaty handshake and said, "There's that shake, Mr. Homer. We're even. So I never asked if your flight was satisfactory."

I said, "It was perfectly satisfactory." I didn't mention that nobody came to pick me up. Why bother? "And it's Hooper."

He said, "Of course it is," then he put his hand on my back, nudged me toward the club, and said, "Shall we?"

I gently pushed his hand away and said, "No offense, Mr. McGee, but you're awfully touchy-feely. I'm not a fan of touchy-feely. No offense."

He ran his index finger up my spine, then pulled his hand away and said, "No offense taken." Then, as if out of nowhere, the film canister appeared in his hand. "Are you excited? Because I am. I've watched it countless times all by my lonesome, but this is my first chance to see it with a crowd. Exciting, very exciting, very, *very* exciting."

I said, "Sure, exciting. Listen, can you give me a rundown? I don't remember a damn thing about it."

Erick, the kid with that Massacre This band, called over, "He hasn't watched it, Tobe!"

I asked McGee if that was true. He said, "I *feel* like I watched it. Isn't that good enough?"

I said, "No. It's not good enough. So why'd you set this up? What if it's a piece of shit?"

McGee said, "You're Toeb Hoopster—"

I said, "Tobe Hooper."

McGee said, "And you did *My Texas Chainsaw Attack*—"

I said, "*The Texas Chainsaw Massacre*."

McGee said, "So I know deep in my gut that it's not a piece of shit."

I almost said something about how deep his gut was, but that wouldn't have been polite. Say what you will about southerners, but we're usually nice to strangers, even when they smell like delicatessens and have a habit of touching you in what has to be considered a strange manner.

He said, "Mr. Laughlin, Mr. Laughing Boy, Mr. Laugh-a-Minute will tell you. It's not a piece of shit, right? Right?"

Erick took a deep breath and said, "It's kind of a piece of shit."

ERICK LAUGHLIN:

I tried to suck the sentence back into my lungs. I mean, I'd just told Tobe Hooper that something he made was a piece of shit. I was a dick, right? Right.

If I may put on my objective critic's hat for a second, I'd have to say that, like with every filmmaker in the world, some of Tobe's flicks are better than others. But none of them could be considered a piece of shit.

Except this one.

Fortunately, Tobe laughed. "Okay, lay it on me, brother. What's shitty about it?"

I said, "I don't know if I'm qualified . . ."

Then Janine, who I hadn't even realized was listening, piped up. "Erick, Jesus Christ, you're a goddamn film critic. Give him your goddamn review."

Tobe said, "Yeah, Erick. Give me your goddamn review."

I took a deep breath—it was more of a sigh, really—and said,

MIDNIGHT MOVIE

47

"Okay, the script is a mess, and the story is barely existent, and aside from your pal Gary, the acting is atrocious."

Tobe clapped me on the back and said, "Sounds awesome to me. Let's go watch this."

I said, "I watched it twice yesterday—"

He interrupted, "And twice was enough. Don't worry, brother. I'm glad you didn't blow smoke up my ass." He gestured at the front door and said, "I'm sure there'll be plenty of smoke blowing from that lot. I'm going in. Catch you after."

As Tobe walked away, I called after him, "The effects are good!"

He laughed and said, "You're full of shit, pal, but your heart's in the right place."

March 31, 2009—This was my seventh SXSW in seven years,
and I decided it was to be my last. I never thought of
myself as age conscious, but I realized after my fifth
show in two nights that I was, I was. The people in the
clubs were young enough to be my children, and the people
in the bands were young enough to be my grandchildren.
The music was fine, sometimes even spectacular, but was
it worth getting slam-danced into? Was it worth being a
magnet for spilt beer? Was it worth paying for the flight
from Chicago to Texas, the hotel, the cover charges, the
drink minimums, and the flight back to Chicago? By 2009,
the answer was a resounding no.

After three consecutive nights of music, music, music,
I was in the mood for a change. I considered attending
one of the literary panels, but the only one that was not
sold out was a panel discussing a new movement called
"mash-ups." I did not know what a mash-up was, nor did I
care to learn.

There were several film screenings and discussions,
some of which had potential but not that much potential.
The only non-music event I was truly compelled to go
to was a movie by the gentleman who made *The Texas
Chainsaw Massacre*. It was either that or back to my hotel
room.

MIDNIGHT MOVIE

twitter.com

 ScaryBarry off to see DESTINY EXPRESS!!! mad psyched!!!
6:31 PM March 31 **via** web

 FarceCycle @ScaryBarry Don't gloat. It's unbecoming.
6:33 PM March 31 **via** web

 ScaryBarry the lights went off. DESTINY EXPRESS, ALL ABOARD!!!
9:42 PM March 31 **via** web

 FarceCycle @ScaryBarry Repeating: Don't gloat. It's unbecoming. Dick.
9:51 PM March 31 **via** web

Andi-Licious

The Useless Musings of Sophomoric Sophomore Andrea Daltrey

THE DATE: TODAY

THE TIME: MY TIME

THE TITLE: THE TITLE

I don't remember the lights going off, but I do remember drinking some gross beer, and I remember the movie starting, and I remember being scared, and I remember being grossed out.

I remember some guy touching me, and I remember where he touched me, and I remember thinking he shouldn't touch me there without my approval.

I remember I wanted to ask him to stop, and I remember not being able to open my mouth.

I remember this funny feeling in my stomach, and I remember my knees shook, and I remember my tummy did a squiggle.

I remember my nipples getting hard, and I remember looking for him.

I remember him being gone and I remember being sad.

MIDNIGHT MOVIE

JANINE DALTREY:

It was a gorgeous night, and I was having fun chatting with Erick—who I'd always gotten a kick out of—so I decided to skip the movie. As for Andi, I figured she could fend for herself. She was a friendly girl, and I was sure she'd strike up a conversation with one of those horror nerds and be A-okay.

So Erick and I blabbed for a while. Like way too many guys in their early twenties, Erick didn't ask a damn thing about me, but at least he was interesting to listen to. As was almost always the case, he talked mostly about his band, and how frustrated he was with the whole thing, and how fucked-up the record industry was, and how he wanted out, but he *had* to play music, and if he didn't, he'd die. I appreciated the passion, but having grown up poor, I didn't get the appeal of being an impoverished artist. I'd have been happy getting an advertising degree, and moving to, say, Phoenix, and getting a gig at some boutique agency that offered health insurance and three weeks' vacation.

Erick also told me a story about his whole band getting some bad shrooms at a show in Denton, then spending the whole ride back to Austin vomiting inside, and outside, and even on top of, their van. Gross, but funny. It was nice that he wasn't trying to charm me into the sack. I mean, you don't seduce a girl by telling her puke stories.

ERICK LAUGHLIN:

I was *totally* trying to charm her into the sack.

JANINE DALTREY:

Finally, about a half an hour after the movie started, I told him he should go in. He said only if I joined him. So in we went.

TOBE HOOPER:

Erick was wrong. It wasn't a piece of shit. It was a big, heaping piece of shit under a big, heaping pile of vomit, under a big, heaping pile of diarrhea, under a big, heaping pile of horse guts, under a big, heaping pile of maggots. I almost hoped a critic from a major newspaper was there, just so I could see what the fuck he'd write. A. O. Scott would've had a field day with good ol' *Destiny Express*.

Gary was sitting off to the far side, so I made my way over to find out what he thought about the whole thing. Right as his character was eating the arm off our female lead, Helen Leary, I tapped him on the shoulder and said, "Now that, Gary my man, is emoting."

He punched me in the stomach and said, "Shut the fuck up, man. You say another fucking word, and I'll fucking equalize you."

I wanted to say *What the fuck, Gary?* but the punch knocked the wind out of me, and I couldn't get out a single word. All I wanted to do was sit down, but there wasn't a chair in the general vicinity, so I wobbled over to the bar, plopped onto a stool, and tried to catch my breath and figure out why Gary gut-shot me. I assumed he thought I was somebody else, and I'd startled him. But that was still weird, because the Gary Church I knew wasn't a hitter.

The vibe in the Cove was weird, man. Just fucking weird.

FROM: 3105151842@verizon.net
TO: Church_Warren@LTDLaw.com

This movie is fucking awesome. I'm getting a print. You're
watching it. It's a revelation.

SENT FROM MY VERIZON BLACKBERRY

twitter.com

 ScaryBarry snorted 1 line off of the bar and im
wrecked. teeth hurt. awesome flick.
March 31 11:31 PM **via** web

 FarceCycle @ScaryBarry Jealous. Call me tomorrow.
March 31 11:33 PM **via** web

March 31, 2009—I watched maybe two minutes of the
movie and was appalled. It was a litany of violent acts
under the guise of a zombie story. It had no redeeming
qualities. I headed to the door but was tripped, possibly
on purpose, by a slovenly young man. He put me in
a headlock and said, "Aren't you enjoying this?" He
breathed his fetid breath into my face, and I felt a wave
of nausea that almost doubled me over.

I said, "No, I am not enjoying this," doing everything
within my power not to vomit.

He said, "I think you are." And then he tightened his
hold on my neck. The next thing I remember, I was lying in
my hotel bed with a plastic mask covering my face.

TOBE HOOPER:

I can't tell you how many times I've stood in the back of a theater during a *Chainsaw* screening, listening to the screams of the audience . . . and nothing else makes me happier. Knowing that I've given a willing crowd some nightmares is a beautiful feeling, man, simply beautiful.

The screaming that started halfway through *Destiny Express* wasn't as gratifying. Actually, it scared a little bit of the shit out of me.

This knockout girl next to me at the bar hopped off her stool, sat down on the floor—that disgusting Cove floor—and started pulling on her hair, like she was trying to yank it out of her goddamn head. I knelt down and said, "Honey, stand up."

She grabbed me by the back of my neck and gave me a kiss. A bolt shot from my stomach, to the top of my spine, right down to the tip of my dick. I was about to tear her clothes off when she pulled away from me and went back to work on her hair. The bolt went away, but my dick stayed hard. I adjusted my shirt to cover the evidence, stood up, and asked the bartender for another beer. He picked up a shot glass, turned around, and pitched it against the back mirror, shattering the entire thing into a collection of glass knives, then he said, "What the fuck did you say, old man?"

I looked around to see if anybody was going to come and settle the dude down. Nothing. They were staring at the screen, transfixed by my piece-of-shit movie. I turned back to the bartender and said, "What do you think of the flick?" I don't know if he knew who I was. I hoped he didn't, so I could get an honest answer.

He picked up a beer mug and threw it on the floor as hard as he could, then yelled, "*It's fucking awesome, maaaaaaan! Fucking awwwwwwwwesome!*"

Nobody even blinked. A small part of me wanted to knock over the projector, stand up in front of the room, and ask, "What the fuck is wrong with you people!" Another small part of me wanted to get the hell out of Austin and never come back. But most of me was paralyzed, so I just stood there.

Andi-Licious

The Useless Musings of Sophomoric Sophomore Andrea Daltrey

THE DATE: TODAY

THE TIME: MY TIME

I had the weirdest dream about the cock.

The cock. The cock. The cock. Let us examine the cock and what it can do.

One thing it can do is be sucked and spit into a lucky girl's mouth. It sometimes tastes like a lollipop, but other times, it tastes like a sweat sock.

It can get hard, and it can get soft, then, after a while, it can get hard again.

It can be fun, and it can be scary, and it can be a weapon.

Also, it can be a divining rod to the heart. At least that's what I'm told.

JANINE DALTREY:

Erick and I tried to go into the club, but one of the horror nerds was standing in front of the door, and he wouldn't budge. After I asked him politely to move, he put his hand in between my boobs and pushed. Hard. If Erick hadn't been standing directly behind me, I'd have fallen ass-first onto the concrete.

He caught me and said, "Are you okay?" Legitimate concern.

I said, "I'm fine."

He said, "Good." Then he stepped around me and threw the flat of his palm at the guy's nose. I took that self-defense class, and I was well aware that if done right, that move could actually force a bone chip toward your attacker's brain. Erick was an underfed indie rocker, and I didn't think he had enough strength in him to break anything other than his own hand.

It didn't matter. The guy caught Erick's hand well before it made contact, then he twisted his arm behind his back and yelled right into his ear, "You got a problem, *motherfucker?* You want to *go?* You want to *bring it?* You think you can handle *this?* Go ahead, *bitch.* I'd *love* it."

Just then, Dude McGee practically fell out of the door, and, just like that, the guy let Erick go . . . but not before giving him a backhand across the cheek. It looked less painful than humiliating. The guy shoved Dude against the door and roared, then head-butted the wall and walked into the club.

Dude kind of laughed and told Erick, "You know, this is one of those flicks that works better on the big screen. Maybe before it gets released wide, Mr. Toeb Hoopster can do it up in 3-D."

TOBE HOOPER:

Finally, finally, finally that abortion ended, and thank God. I wanted to be gone. People were breathing heavily, and the place was a veritable bad breath factory. And that weird vibe was still here, there, and every-fucking-where.

It was the kind of vibe that you feel when you walk into an underground boxing match. There was a sense of anything-can-happen, and if something happens that isn't good, nobody's going to stop it, because nobody's in charge. You can smell the boxers' athletic sweat, and the crowd's booze sweat, and you want to get the fuck out of there, but you're afraid that if you make any quick moves, somebody'll bash a folding chair over your head before you even get to the door, and then somebody'll steal your wallet while you're lying unconscious in the middle of the aisle.

If it wasn't my movie, I'd have bailed out of that club in a heartbeat.

When the lights went up, things reverted to some sense of normality. The crowd went nuts . . . but in a good way. Nobody yelled. Nobody screamed. Nobody threw a beer mug. Nobody punched me in the stomach. It was all applause. Warm, appreciative applause.

I looked over to Gary's table. He gave me a big smile and a double thumbs-up, then mouthed, "We rock!" I polished off my beer, then, hoping I could get drunker before the Q & A, asked the bartender for a shot of whatever brown liquid was closest. He picked a couple pieces of mirror out of his hand as if it was nothing and said, "You got it, Mr. Hooper. That was a brilliant piece of work. I'm going to order the DVD of *Chainsaw* the second I get home."

After he gave me my drink, I asked him, "Are you okay?"

He said, "What do you mean?"

I pointed at the floor behind the bar and said, "Brother, you're standing in a damn mountain of glass."

He looked around, then shrugged and said, "Just another day at the Cove, man. Just another day at the Cove."

I almost said, *Another day at the Cove? Broken shit all over the floor is another day at the Cove?* But I held my tongue. It didn't seem like the time for a philosophical discussion about the true meaning of fucked-up-ed-ness. All I did was throw down the shot, then, as I headed toward the other side of the club, the girl who'd kissed me gave me a chaste peck on the cheek and said, "I don't like scary movies, but that was wonderful." I felt nothing. It was like being kissed by my cousin.

I gave her elbow a squeeze and said, "Thank you, darlin'. Sorry about the . . . confusion during the flick."

She gave me a smile that you could actually describe as virginal and said, "What confusion?"

I pointed at her beer and asked, "How many drinks have you had?"

She shrugged and said, "Three, I think. But that's nothing for me." She puffed up her big ol' chest and said, all blustery, "Despite my tininess, I'm far from a lightweight."

I couldn't help but laugh. "I believe you. Now I got to go to work."

Many of the filmgoers touched me as I wound my way through the club. Nothing lascivious, mind you. Just pats on the back, and handshakes, and in a couple of instances, I got my hair tousled. I yelled across the club, "Gary, you'd best get your ass up here! I'm not doing this alone."

Everybody laughed; then, when it quieted down, he yelled back, "Yeah, you are! It's your night, Tobe!"

twitter.com

 ScaryBarry took a scary shit in the scary cove bathroom. i think i pooped out some of my guts.
April 1 12:48 AM via web

 FarceCycle @ScaryBarry You're all class. Wish I could be there with you.
April 1 12:55 AM via web

 ScaryBarry @FarceCycle too late. gonna try and score some more blow before I split. j/k.
April 1 12:59 AM via web

ERICK LAUGHLIN:

I'd survived *way* worse beatings. The unofficial count: once in junior high, five times in high school, once in college, and four times after Massacre This shows. None of them were totally my fault—I'll take some responsibility, because sometimes there's a bit of a disconnect between my brain and my mouth—but I've never been randomly attacked. And it fucked me up physically *and* mentally . . . but I wasn't fucked up badly enough that I didn't stagger into the club for Tobe's Q & A.

The guy who'd hit me was sitting at a table right by the door. He raised his beer at me, gave me one of those chin-nods, and said, "Sorry, man. 'Roid rage. It happens. Let me buy you a drink."

I said, "Fuck off, asswipe."

He laughed. "I hear you, man. Too bad you missed the flick." He pointed at Tobe and said, "Can't wait to hear what this dude has to say."

I must've looked royally pissed, because Janine draped her arm over my shoulders, guided me to the other side of the room, and said, "What say we sit down and listen to your hero regale the masses?"

I said, "That sounds good." And then I thought, *It'll be even better if you keep your arm around me.*

TOBE HOOPER:

In general, Q & A's are either awesome or terrible, and what with most of my viewers off in Never Never Land, this one wasn't looking good. I didn't know what was going through those folks' heads, but I was pretty sure it wasn't a question about how I lit that alligator scene. There were other factors, too, factors that I personally will foot the blame for. How can it be a good Q & A if the dude who's being Q'ed doesn't know any of the goddamn A's?

They pelted me with questions about how I got the dismemberments to look so realistic, and what kind of cameras I used, and how long the shoot was, and where I did my editing. After each question, I yelled over to Gary, "Do you know?" Everybody laughed. They thought I was kidding. I wasn't.

Finally, after about fifteen minutes of this utter nonsense, I said, "Anybody want to ask me something about *Chainsaw*?"

Some wag yelled out, "Screw *Chainsaw*. What happened on *Poltergeist*?"

Ah, *Poltergeist*. Lot of rumors about my involvement with that one, and you'll hear only rumors because nobody'll talk about it, myself included. I said, "No comment. Next question."

Silence.

I said, "All right, y'all, I'm outta here. Thanks for coming. And I'm glad you enjoyed your ride on the *Destiny Express* . . . because I sure as hell didn't." Then I ran to the back of the room and gave Gary a quick good-bye hug, told him I'd call him when I got back to town—and I meant it, this time—then told the bartender to get me a cab and get me a cab fast.

The taxi showed up ten minutes later. There was a hotel room booked for me across town, and my flight was scheduled to leave three days later, but I had a case of the willies like nobody's business, so I went right to the airport and traded my ticket in for the next flight out, which turned out to be six o'clock, so I had to sit in the terminal for three hours, but I didn't care, because I wanted out.

Hell-Lay had never, *never* sounded so good.

PART TWO

AUTHOR'S NOTE: *Today, if you do a Google search of "The Game" and "virus," or maybe "The Game" and "symptoms," you won't find much of interest. Why? Nobody's really sure. See, a goodly amount of the Net coverage of the Game evaporated into cyberspace. Much of that, I suspect, was due to personal choice; a lot of the writing about the disease—especially from those who were suffering one of the harsher symptoms—is at once appalling and embarrassing, and if it were me who posted it practically against my will, I'd want it erased, too.*

When the Game was at its worst, a shocking number of websites fell off the map, and this was one area where I was unable to track down any concrete information. Nobody in the government would speak with me, no reputable tech reporters would talk, no nothing. It was the one time during the whole process that I wished I had some honest-to-goodness press credentials.

But I was able to track down a wonderful hacker who was able to resurrect a number of blogs and chat boards that were thought to have been gone forever, and even though he was unable to offer any answers as to why this stuff disappeared in the first place, we should all be grateful that there's something.

Andi-Licious

The Useless Musings of Sophomoric Sophomore Andrea Daltrey

APRIL 1, 2009

THE EMPRESSES' NEW CLOTHES

I don't have any money, and neither does Janine, but my sister knows how to shop. She's always trying to buy me new stuff, but I feel guilty accepting her offers because I know how broke she is, plus my feeling has always been, how many outfits does one girl need?

The morning after I spent all that time at the creepy, creepy Cove, I felt so dirty that even after a two-hour bath with multiple refills, I needed something to make me feel pretty again, so I called up sis and said, "Let's go thrifting!" She squealed like I told her I'd won the lottery or something, and if she's happy, then I'm happy.

Once we were at the store, I went kind of nuts . . . but to my credit, I only went nuts at the super sale rack. I ended up walking out of there with four blouses, two skirts, and a pair of what sis called "fuck-me pumps." I loved it all so much that on the way to the parking lot, I gave her a huge hug and a wet, juicy, silly kiss on the lips. She shoved me away, then wiped off her mouth and got all flushed. It was awkward, but whatever. We'd had a superfun day, so it was all good.

MIDNIGHT MOVIE

69

FROM: GaryChurch@gmail.com
TO: Church_Warren@LTDLaw.com
SUBJECT: Ouch, babe
DATE: April 3, 2009

Hey, Warren—

You know how I always get those headaches? No? You don't?
THAT'S BECAUSE I NEVER GET HEADACHES. And I have a bitch
of one now. And four Advils every three hours (which, according to my GP/quack/Dr. Feelgood, is a therapeutic dose) ain't
cuttin' it. But I'll survive.

Out of nowhere, I landed what could be an interesting gig.
Wes Craven, he of *Scream* and *A Nightmare on Elm Street* fame,
is doing a parody filled with horror third and fourth bananas,
er, I mean horror character actors. Ironically, I'm playing the
fourth banana, making me the lowest banana in the bunch.
But when you've got bills to pay, it's always banana time.
Details from the set to come.

Hey, how come I haven't heard anything about your latest
whatzhername? Details, please, Counselor.

Love,
Gary

twitter.com

 ScaryBarry craving fast food and coca cola and coca caine
April 3 12:04 AM via web

 ScaryBarry scarfed down taco hell, drank a liter bottle, and snorted a line. feeling way better. more, more, more!!!
April 3 1:01 AM via web

 Freekydeeky Anybody know how to make meth? Have the equipment, need the ingredients and ratios.
April 3 1:13 AM via web

 ScaryBarry @Freekydeeky badass methmaker right here baby
April 3 2:04 AM via web

 FarceCycle @ScaryBarry Seriously, Barry? Meth making? Did you finish your Brit Lit essay yet, dickhead?
April 3 2:25 AM via web

 Freekydeeky @ScaryBarry Barry, hit me up via e-mail
April 3 2:31 AM via web

 ScaryBarry @Freekydeeky lost your addy
April 3 2:51 AM via web

Freekydeeky @ScaryBarry Freekydeeky420 (at) Yahoo.
April 3 2:54 AM via web

FarceCycle @ScaryBarry @Freekydeeky Please tell
me you dumbasses aren't discussing meth recipes on
Twitter. If anybody asks, I don't know either of you.
April 3 3:11 AM via web

ScaryBarry @FarceCycle @Freekydeeky what can i
say? if somebody needs help, i'm there for them. j/k.
April 3 3:29 AM via web

FROM: BarryKlein1998@gmail.com
TO: Freekydeeky420@yahoo.com
SUBJECT: recipe
DATE: April 3, 2009

steve—

i kind of wrote this myself. haven't done a test run, but
somehow i know it'll work.

barry

*****

2 boxes of Contact 12-hour Time Release Tablets
½ bottle of Heet
1 gallon of Muriatic Acid
1 quart of Coleman's Fuel
1 pound of IAMS Cat Food
2 cans of frozen orange juice
½ gallon of Acetone
2 bottles of iodine tincture, 2%
8 oz. of dried "oregano"
½ pound of mulch
1 lb. of Scott's Rose and Bloom food
2 bottles of hydrogen peroxide
½ can of Red Devil's Lye
2 gallons of distilled water
1 gallon of tap water
1 gallon of "used" toilet water
2 oz. of rat blood

April 3, 2009—And then I died. At least I felt as if I did.

I cannot stop thinking about the plane trip back to O'Hare. The moment I arrived at the airport, the second I set foot in a terminal, a terminal that was not particularly crowded, I felt claustrophobic. That was not a surprise, as I have many phobias, claustro being likely the most enervating. Nonetheless, it has been years since the last attack, an attack that I still believe was brought on by a stressful discussion between MariAnne and me, but that is not germane to this particular event. That attack was in private, whereas this was very public. I had never had an attack in such a wide-open area, and I certainly would never have guessed that it could even happen like that. Think about it. Claustrophobia and giant airports, in theory, do not mix. Then again, what do I know? I am not a doctor. At least not that kind of doctor.

I did not know if I was assigned a window seat, an aisle seat, or a center seat, but none of them sounded appealing, so I bit the bullet, so to speak, and upgraded to first class. Nine hundred dollars. From Texas to Illinois. Astounding, simply astounding.

I had flown first class only once previously, and enjoyed it immensely, but that was for a Department event, thus they footed the bill. Since this one came from my pocket, I was far more critical. But considering my mood, and my flop sweat, and my shaky stomach, and my trembling knees, and my hollowed-out joints, I believe I would not have been happy or comfortable anywhere.

We'd been in the air for about an hour when the

compulsion started. But "compulsion" might not be the right word. "Craving," maybe? "Unquenchable desire"? "Fixation"? Call it what you will, but it was impossible to ignore.

The skies had become turbulent, and the "Fasten Seat Belts" sign was crystal-clearly on, but I stood up nonetheless, took a step toward the cockpit, and knocked on the door. The attendant was right behind me and said, "Dr. Gillespie, please return to your seat." I would normally find it a nice touch that the flight crew remembered my name and title, but at that moment, it was unnerving.

I told her that I needed to speak with the pilot immediately. She put a hand on my elbow, trying to placate me as if I were a child or a crazy person. (It could be argued that right at that moment, I was both.) I have no clue what I said next. All I recall is the stewardess guiding me back to my seat, after which I again strode to the cockpit and pounded on the door. A large male crew member dashed through the curtain that separated first class from coach, then shoved me down into my chair and said, "Sir, if you do not calm down, we are going to have a couple of air marshals meet you in Chicago, and nobody wants that."

I do not know whether it was the threat of arrest or the threat of physical violence that brought me down to earth, but whatever it was, just like that, I snapped back into myself. That compulsion to meet the pilot was gone. The irony is, on the way out of the airplane, when the pilot offered his hand, my first instinct was to punch him in the jaw. Fortunately, I was able to sublimate it.

When I returned home, I poured myself a stiff drink, gave my schedule a once-over, and cursed. Two days from now, it is off to New York, for a meeting with some midlevel brass. I didn't even bother unpacking my suitcase. I asked myself the same question I always ask myself when prepping for these meetings: How, after years of research and mountains of intel, can these people not know how to infiltrate a cell?

April 4, 2009

Jesus H. T. Fucking Christ, did Janine look good the other night, or what? Why she's my ex-girlfriend instead of my current-girlfriend-giving-me-a-blow-job is beyond me. Jerked off while thinking about her this morning in the shower. Jerked off while thinking about her in my car before work. Jerked off while thinking about her right before I sat down and started writing this very entry.

But before I jerked off just now, I called her cell. It rang once, then went to voice mail, which means she screened me. I hate that. If she doesn't want to talk to me, answer and tell me. I'm a big boy. I can handle it. I survived after she dumped my ass for that guy in her yoga class, so I'll survive getting blown off on the phone.

I think I'm going to quit the Cove. I'm getting paid shit, nobody tips, the clientele is pathetic, and the chances of meeting a woman who's not a total ho are slim at best.

I miss Janine. Maybe I'll pop in on her. Maybe not. Maybe I'll jerk off again. I don't know.

FROM: GaryChurch@gmail.com
TO: Church_Warren@LTDLaw.com
SUBJECT: Doctors do little
DATE: April 6, 2009

Warren—

Doctors in L.A. are a joke. Good luck getting a same-day
appointment, or quality one-on-one care, or a useful
diagnosis. It's not like the doctors back home are anything
to shout about, but man, these California physicians suck.

Last night, my head was throbbing so badly that I went to
the emergency room. (If I knew somebody who sold Vicodin,
I would've gone that route, but sadly, the only illegal drug I
know how to procure is Mary Jane Wanna.) I insisted they run
every test imaginable—fuck it, the Screen Actors Guild has
a good health plan, so why not take full advantage of it?—
which meant an MRI, a CT scan, a ton of blood work, and,
worst of all, a spinal tap. You ever had a spinal tap? Don't.
They hurt like a bastard.

Anyhoo, I got my wish: a two-week supply of Big V. And we're
not talking Viagra, although I wouldn't mind some of that
right about now. At least it would be a distraction from the
orb of pain that is my head.

Gary

Andi-Licious

The Useless Musings of Sophomoric Sophomore Andrea Daltrey

APRIL 9, 2009

I HAD ONE!

So I was laying in bed last night thinking about nothing in particular, and then all of a sudden, I had I guess what you could call a vision. But it was so real that it might've even been a hallucination. I couldn't say for sure, because I've never hallucinated before. Anyhow, it was a man. Not a man I'd ever seen before. Just a man.

He was in my room, and he kneeled down by the side of my bed and told me that I shouldn't be scared, that he'd take care of everything. Naturally, I was freaking the hell out . . . that is, until he started rubbing right where I'd gotten waxed last weekend with the tips of his fingers.

It made me shiver. It felt so real, like he was there in the room with me. He traced his fingertips up my tummy, right to the bottom of my breasts, and then back down again. He went back and forth and back and forth, and finally he went all the way down there and he did a little flick, and this tingle started from my ankles, and shot up my legs, then through my thighs, then it went right past down there and all the way to my head.

MIDNIGHT MOVIE

7 9

Then he was gone.

My eyes were shut, and I think I was asleep and dreaming, but it's possible I was fantasizing about this ghost guy, or maybe the shaved-head guy in my women's studies class, or my trig teacher, the very hot Mr. Lawrence Ellison (oh my God he's hot!). Whatever I was thinking about, I woke up with my hand in between my legs, and it was soaked, and I was rubbing, and rubbing, and rubbing on this one spot, and it was perfect. It dawned on me that I had a real, honest-to-goodness orgasm. It was like I won the lottery or something.

I hope Janine doesn't read this. I shouldn't even be blogging this. But I can't help it. I want to SHARE! No, I HAVE to share! It's really really really weird. My brain is telling me to tell you, and if I don't tell you, I should poke myself in the eye with a fork.

EXPLOSION IN ROUND ROCK KILLS THREE, INJURES 12

FIVE-ALARM FIRE CONTINUES TO RAGE

APRIL 11, 2009

BY LEANN MORGAN

Round Rock, TX—An explosion in an apartment building located in Round Rock that housed what police are calling a "crystal methamphetamine laboratory" killed a University of Texas student and two local teenagers, as well as injuring 12 bystanders. Of the 12 injured, eight are in critical condition at the St. David's Round Rock Medical Center.

The three deceased are Steven Lackey, 21, the primary occupant of the apartment; Karen Czarnecki, 19, and Angela Gallo, 19.

The explosion sparked a five-alarm fire that raged for 15 hours across three city blocks. The property damage is estimated to be $1.5 million.

An eyewitness said, "It looked like a bottle rocket shot out of Steve's window. When the spark landed on the street, it made kind of a mushroom cloud, then it looked like the street went up in flames. It reeked something awful. You can still feel the stink."

Detective Pedro Rodriguez commented, "Crystal meth has been a major problem in our area for the past decade. There have been countless explosions in countless so-called labs across the city, most of them contained. Obviously this one is, by far, the worst. We are putting together a special task force that we hope will go a long way toward putting an end to the epidemic."

Funeral plans for the three deceased have yet to be disclosed.

twitter.com

ScaryBarry r.i.p. freeky.
April 11 9:18 PM via web

FarceCycle @ScaryBarry WTF, dude?!? Was that you?
April 11 9:28 PM via web

ScaryBarry @FarceCycle i don't know. i doubt it. what i fed him was mostly bullshit. thought it wouldn't do anything.
April 11 9:31 PM via web

FarceCycle @ScaryBarry The key word there being "mostly." You need to talk to somebody.
April 11 9:33 PM via web

ScaryBarry @FarceCycle not talking. moving on.
April 11 9:45 PM via web

FarceCycle @ScaryBarry I'm talking.
April 11 9:51 PM via web

ScaryBarry @FarceCycle don't.
April 11 9:59 PM via web

GTownRepresent @ScaryBarry You're the guy, aren't you? Send it to me via Direct Message.
April 11 10:06 PM via web

ScaryBarry @GTownRepresent send what?
April 11 10:17 PM via web

GTownRepresent @ScaryBarry Send IT! And don't
fuck with me. You know what IT is.
April 11 10:38 PM **via** web

ScaryBarry @GTownRepresent it?
April 11 10:51 PM **via** web

GTownRepresent @ScaryBarry Do not fuck with me.
Have ur addy and phone#.
April 11 11:02 PM **via** web

ScaryBarry @GTownRepresent whatever dude
April 11 11:09 PM **via** web

GTownRepresent @ScaryBarry Send it.
April 11 11:28 PM **via** web

ScaryBarry @GTownRepresent right
April 11 11:30 PM **via** web

GTownRepresent @ScaryBarry SEND IT SEND IT
SEND IT SEND IT SEND IT
April 11 11:40 PM **via** web

ScaryBarry @GTownRepresent jeez, relax, it's on the
way
April 11 11:48 PM **via** web

GTownRepresent @ScaryBarry If I don't get that
recipe by the morning, I'm on YOUR way, bitch.
April 11 11:58 PM **via** web

April 13, 2009

Splitting fucking headache. Blood on pillow. Of course there is. I hit myself on the head with a hammer. Maybe it was a chisel. I don't remember. Fingers hurt. The only thing that makes anything feel better is chewing on tinfoil. It's gross but it works.

Can't stop thinking about Janine. Can't stop. Can't stop. Love her so much. I want to be in her. I want her to be in me. Thinking about her sometimes makes me feel better. When I think about her and suck on the foil, things seem almost normal. There isn't that weird blue fog around everything. The world doesn't smell like salami. I don't feel like ramming my face into the mirror, then running one of the shards up and down my tongue.

I want to see Janine so bad so bad so bad, but she won't take my calls. Fuck it, I'm going over. And I'm not even going to shower. She used to like the way I smelled after a workout, she was a freak like that, so it shouldn't matter that right now I reek.

I'm gone. I'm out. Janine, here I come.

JANINE DALTREY:

Right after we established ourselves as a couple, Dave became this wishy-washy, indecisive guy. It was always, *I love you, I hate you, I love you, I hate you.* Our relationship was defined by blowout arguments and awesome makeup sex. But that's not a relationship, now, is it? For a while, I thought it was. But that was when I was a freshman, and I didn't know any better.

So naturally we broke up and got back together I-don't-know-how-many times. It was always casual, so the breakups went down when we met somebody else, and the reunions happened when we were lonely. When he started calling me, I wasn't lonely, and when his calls became more frequent and more desperate, I started screening them. I wasn't seeing anybody, but I wasn't lonely.

On the night of April 13, like around eleven thirty, I'm in my jammies, brushing my teeth, face covered in this blue exfoliating cream, ready to crash, and my doorbell rings. We have a security camera by the front door, so I checked out the monitor, and there's Dave, looking wasted. I said, "What're you doing here, David?"

He whined, "I miss you, Janine. Like soooooo much." He tended to get needy when he was really drunk.

I told him, "I'm about to get into bed."

He said, "Perfect timing!"

I said, "Not really. Why don't you go home and sleep it off? How did you get here?"

He said, "I walked." Still whiny.

I said, "I'll call you a cab."

He said, "That's really nice of you. Can you come down and wait with me?"

I said, "Dave, it's almost midnight. I've got my face shit on."

He said, "Wipe it off and keep me company. I don't feel good. My stomach hurts."

He sounded like a five-year-old crying for his mommy. I'm such a sap that I said, "I'll be down in a sec." I called him a taxi, rinsed off most of the exfoliating crap—I missed a bunch of it, because I was in a rush to get down there, then get back up again—and met him on the front doorstep.

Dave's a good-looking guy, but that night, not so much. He had that I'm-drunk-as-shit pink complexion—a regular thing for him when he gets his drink on; he's part-Irish—but it was way worse than usual. I could tell his eyes were bloodshot, even in the dark. His long black hair was all stringy and dirty, like he hadn't washed it in a while. I told him, "Sweetie, no offense, but you're a mess."

He gave me this weird smile, opened up his arms, and said, "You're so pretty, Janine. Gimme a hug."

A hug was not that big of a deal. I could handle that, no matter how sweaty or smelly he was—and he was really smelly, like he had booze and bologna sweat leaking from his pores. I put my arms around his waist, and he started squeezing me. *Hard.* Like so hard that I had trouble breathing and talking.

I kind of hit him on the back and managed to gasp out, "You're hurting me, David. Let go."

He said, "You hurt me, Janine." He pulled me into him even tighter.

I said, "How . . . did . . . I . . . hurt . . . you?" I was getting light-headed from the loss of air and nauseated from his stench.

He said, "That night at the movie." *Squeeze.* "That stupid zombie slasher movie." *Squeeze.* "You looked so good." *Squeeze.* "And you were talking with that writer guy." *Squeeze.* "And that hurt."

I started pounding him on his back and said, "Jesus . . . Christ . . . let . . . me . . . go . . ." It felt like I was going to black out. He gave me one last squeeze, then let me go, then reached out and pinched my nipples *hard*, something that, in the right context, I thoroughly enjoyed. This was as far from the right fucking context as you could get.

He said, "You looked so good. You had on that short black skirt that I like so much, and that cute little red T-shirt, and those sandal heels, and all I wanted to do was hug you, and kiss you, and you wouldn't even come inside the bar." Then—and this is something that I never imagined I'd ever see—David Cranford started crying.

Of course my stupid nurturing instinct kicked in, and despite his obnoxious late visit, and despite the hug that almost broke my ribs, and despite the fucked-up nipple pinch, I wanted to make him feel better. I put my hand on his arm and said, "David, I'm sorry. I never meant to—"

Before I could say "—hurt you," he took my hand and put it on his crotch. His dick was hard, but, like, *scary* hard. It had been a while, but I totally remembered how big he was. Still, this felt noticeably bigger. He ground my hand into his dick and said, "Squeeze it. Squeeze it *hard*. Squeeze it as hard as I was squeezing you."

I tried to take my hand back, but he held it even tighter and pushed it even closer. I kind of started crying and said, "Stop it, Dave. Let me go."

He softened, then loosened his grip, got down on his knees, and said, "Oh my God, I'm so sorry, baby. I didn't want you to cry. I just wanted a hug and a hand job." Then he grabbed me around the waist—gently, mind you—and buried his face in between my thighs.

I was so stunned that I couldn't move; for that matter, I couldn't even think. We stayed like that for probably a couple of minutes, both of us crying. A few people walked by, but none of them stopped; I'm sure that from the outside, it looked like we'd just had a fight and were in the process of making up. Finally, the cab showed up. I told Dave, "Listen, your ride's here. Go home and we'll talk about this tomorrow. We'll go to the park."

He looked up at me with these pathetic goo-goo eyes and said, "You promise?"

I said, "I promise."

He stood up, then said, "Okay. I'm holding you to that." And then he walked to the cab, opened the door, and got in. Before he slammed the door shut, he checked his watch and said, "You know what, Janine? It's twelve oh-three."

I said, "Right. Past both of our bedtimes."

He said, "But that means it's tomorrow."

I said, "David, go."

He said, "And you promised we could go to the park tomorrow."

I said, "Right. Tomorrow."

He said, "It *is* tomorrow." Then he told the driver to fuck off, hopped out of the taxi, and was immediately in my face. He yelled, "*It is tomorrow! We're going to the motherfucking park!*" And then he picked me up by my hair and kicked me against the front door to my building like I was a soccer ball.

The next thing I remember, I'm lying in a hospital, both of my arms in traction, a breathing tube down my throat, and my little sister is fucking a doctor at the foot of my bed.

POLICE REPORT

CASE TITLE: Daltrey Assault

DATE/TIME REPORTED: April 14, 2009/2:14 AM

INCIDENT TYPE/OFFENSE: 240 (a) (1) ASW/Assault with a Deadly Weapon

LOCATION: [REDACTED] **REPORTING OFFICER:** Crowley, Morris (141)

INTAKE OFFICER: Melvin, Neal (318) **APPROVING OFFICER:** Morton III, Joseph (010)

PERSON(S): Janine Anne Daltrey **SEX/RACE/AGE:** F/W/22

PHONE: [REDACTED] **ADDRESS:** [REDACTED]

OFFENDER(S): David Wilson Cranford **SEX/RACE/AGE:** M/W/27

PHONE: [REDACTED] **ADDRESS:** [REDACTED] **PROPERTY:** Public location

VEHICLE: On foot

NARRATIVE: On April 14, 2009, David Wilson Cranford of [REDACTED] in Austin, TX, was placed under arrest at [REDACTED] for a public attack on Janine Anne Daltrey of [REDACTED] in Austin, TX.

When I arrived on the scene at [REDACTED], Cranford was repeatedly kicking Daltrey's prone body. She was wearing a thin white T-shirt and pink shorts. The shirt was ripped and exposed her breasts. Both items of clothing were covered in blood, but I could not immediately determine specifically where the blood was originating from. She had multiple lacerations on her face and arms, but the cuts were not gushing.

Daltrey was emitting a high-pitched scream, thus I knew Daltrey was conscious. I yelled at Daltrey to get her attention, but she was not lucid enough to respond. Cranford turned around and demanded I leave, then lifted Daltrey parallel to the ground and dropped her face-first, dislodging three of her teeth. I unholstered my weapon and gave him a verbal warning to stand down. Cranford advanced, so I fired my weapon, hitting him in the knee. Cranford continued moving forward. I fired at Cranford's other knee, yet he continued to advance. When Cranford was arm's length away, I removed my TASER from my belt and discharged it on his left temple. Cranford collapsed onto the sidewalk, where I placed him in handcuffs and took him to the squad car. Once at the car, he began thrashing wildly and attempted to bite me. In order to contain him, I was forced to hit him on the head with the butt of the TASER.

Once Cranford was in the rear seat of the squad car, I radioed for both backup and an ambulance, then when Officers Rangold and Martinson arrived, I asked them to guard Cranford while I canvassed the area for eyewitnesses, of which there were several. Lucille Wharton of [REDACTED] in Austin, TX, said she witnessed Cranford dragging Daltrey along the concrete by her hair for approximately fifty yards. Michael D. McGee of [REDACTED] in Las Vegas, NV, added that Daltrey was facedown while being dragged and pointed out what appeared to be two teeth lodged in a crack on the sidewalk approximately twenty yards from the spot where I subdued Cranford. Dorian Stanger of [REDACTED] in Austin, TX, pointed out a trail of blood that led to Daltrey's apartment building approximately two hundred yards away.

I gained entry to Daltrey's apartment building, where I attempted to interview all the first-floor tenants. Marissa Robertson, whose unit is approximately ten yards from the front door, was the only tenant who was willing to speak. Robertson told me that at approximately 11:45, she heard Cranford and Daltrey conversing through the security system for several minutes, after which Daltrey came down to street level. An argument ensued, then Robertson heard a loud "crash," after which she looked out the window. She witnessed Cranford lifting Daltrey from the ground. Daltrey hit Cranford on the chest, after which Cranford slapped Daltrey with the back of his hand. Cranford then dropped Daltrey onto the ground and kicked her in the ribs, the stomach, and the knee. Cranford then lifted Daltrey from the ground, threw her into the air, and, as she came toward the ground, kneed her in the chest. Cranford then took Daltrey by her hair and dragged her to the sidewalk. Robertson did not follow.

I returned to the arrest scene. After bringing Officers Rangold and Martinson up to speed, I entered the front of my patrol car and read Cranford his Miranda rights. Cranford spit at me several times, then tried to break the rear window with his head. After five attempts, he gave up. (Note: He remained conscious the entire time.) I then drove Cranford to the Precinct, where Officer Melvin took Cranford's statement.

Andi-Licious

The Useless Musings of Sophomoric Sophomore Andrea Daltrey

APRIL 14, 2009

UM

I went to visit Janine at the hospital and it was awful. She was beaten up, bloodied, and in a coma. There were tubes sticking out of everywhere, and the young doctor said she was going to make it, but he didn't know when she'd get better.

He was so nice and cute that I wanted to thank him, so I stood up and gave him a hug and a little kiss on the cheek. Then, all of a sudden, I felt him get hard, and it was weird, because it wasn't like I did anything sexy. I just kissed him on the cheek. I wasn't wearing anything cute, just some sweat clothes, but he got really hard, he started breathing all heavy. It was nice.

He closed the door to the room, then asked me if he could kiss me on the mouth. I said okay, because I had to. I couldn't help myself. So we kissed, and he got so hard so hard so hard. I had to touch it, even though I wasn't good at touching, but I did anyhow, because I had to had to had to.

The second I touched him, he squirted all over the place. I'd never seen so much at once. He stayed hard, then asked if he could touch me, and I said okay. I pulled off my sweatpants and my panties, then I leaned against Janine's bed and spread my legs a bit. He rubbed me with his index finger, and the second he touched me, I got so wet, like I've never gotten wet before, and just like that, I had an orgasm. Now that I'd discovered orgasms, I wanted to keep having them.

I almost passed out, and he kept touching me, and I kept cumming and cumming and cumming. I grabbed him by his lapels and threw him against the closed door, then I wrapped my legs around him and put him inside me. I didn't care about protection or anything. All I wanted was him inside me.

When I kissed him, he came so hard and so fast. When I took him out of me, his cock was shooting out this blue gooey stuff, and he passed out, and I didn't care. All I wanted to do was fuck and fuck and fuck some more.

So I told Janine's unconscious body that I'd be back soon, and I came back here to write this, and now I'm going back out to fuck somebody, and I'll tell you all about it, I promise I promise I promise, because it gets me hot knowing that I'm getting you hot and now that I know what it's like to be hot I'm going to stay hot.

April 19, 2009—I have been studying sleeper cells since long before 9/11 and was recently told by a high-ranking White House official that I possess as much, if not more, knowledge of a cell's inner workings than anybody in the government. This is not a fact I am necessarily proud of, but the cell movement throughout history is fascinating, and its development in the Middle East even more so.

How can one not be fascinated? How can one not want to learn about specially trained secret agents who are sent to another country and assimilate into the culture, waiting for the moment when their handler contacts them to commit an act of terrorism that, while it is a means to an end, might lead to their death. But to them, to the believers, death is life.

For the sake of plausible deniability, many cell members do not even know the existence of their comrades. Cell Member #1 may live in the same city as Cell Member #2 and not know of his existence. Cell Member #3 may be friends with Cell Member #4 without ever realizing that they are coworkers of sorts. Gripping, simply gripping.

There are considerably more cells in the United States than one would expect. Al-Qaeda has offshoots in Tucson, Santa Clara, Houston, Orlando, Boston, and Portland. Hamas has been spotted in Los Angeles, Kansas City, Oklahoma City, and Dallas, as well as in my very own town of Chicago. There is the Muslim Brotherhood in Tulsa, and al-Gama'at al-Islamiyya in Detroit, and the

Algerian Armed Islamic Group in Seattle, and Abu Sayyat in San Francisco, and on, and on, and on.

I know how they work, and I know how to make them work better. I know the proper way to make a pipe bomb. I know how to create sarin gas out of common household items. I know American sleeper cells better than the cell members themselves. It is my job, and I am an expert.

Becoming a member of one of the above will not be a problem.

Welcome to the Truth About Zombies

April 19, 2009

Possibly interesting news from the world of the undead, kiddies. TTAZ member Gorgeous Gorge knows somebody who knows somebody who saw these four college kids in the Oakwood Cemetery in Nowheresville, Texas, digging up what was likely a grave. (WTF else could it be they were digging up? It's not like you're going to find anything else in a cemetery other than a grave.) Apparently there was moaning and a heinous stench. (Sounds pretty zombie-centric to me!) Gorge's friend's friend's friend sent us a cell picture: **Click here for photo**.

That, dear readers, is what we in the zombie industry refer to as "indisputable evidence." Granted, the zombie industry's definition of "indisputable evidence" is far different than that of the rest of the world. See, we take what we can get.

Keep your eyes peeled, and drop us a note if you see anything.

COMMENTS

Bullshit picture. Doesn't prove anything
Adam from Cleveland, OH
April 20, 1:10 AM

I know exactly where that is, and I've seen some weird shit going down back there for the last two weeks. First of all, I can attest to the stench. You can smell it from five blocks away, and even farther if you're downwind. Second of all, there're always people going in and out of the cemetery at night. I know for a fact that most of them are dipshit high school kids getting drunk and tipping headstones (stay classy, Texas), but some of them, not so much. I can't attest to any gravedigging, but, like I said, weird shit.
P.S.—Yo, Adam from Cleveland, enough with the negative vibes. No haters allowed.
Brenda from Austin, TX
April 20, 2:42 AM

There was a little piece in the *Dallas Observer* about it last week. I can't believe none of you saw this. Weirdly enough, the link for the article is dead, so I typed it up for y'all. Check it out:

"Word out of Austin is that the undead are walking the streets . . . or at least that's the word from our photo intern Paul Chase, who claims that three of his friends who live by the Oakwood Cemetery have disappeared off the face of the earth, and his feeling is that they were murdered by zombies who have risen from the grave, and they will be reanimated when the time is right. We can't prove it . . . but we can't disprove it, and Paul is a good man, so we'll run with it."

Full disclosure: I know Paul Chase. He wouldn't make this up. I've had a call in to him since I read the article but haven't heard back. I promise I'll post any news I can find.
Craig from Austin, TX
April 20, 7:02 AM

---

i died today and i was reborn and it was beautiful and you bitches are all missing out. it's easy. bash your head against a mirror and eat the glass. put your head under the tire of a city bus. put some gasoline up your ass and light a match. then wait. they'll come. and it'll be worth the wait.
Zombie Jim from You Don't Want to Know, TX
April 21, 12:04 AM

Interesting. Very, very interesting.
Morris Frost from Las Vegas, NV
April 21, 12:10 AM

Zombie Jim, you're a moron. And Morris Frost, you're probably a moron, too.
Adam from Cleveland, OH
April 21, 9:17 AM

FROM: Church_Warren@LTDLaw.com
TO: GaryChurch@gmail
SUBJECT: Anybody home?
DATE: April 23, 2009

Hey, Gar—

I know you're busy on the set and all, but I haven't heard
from you in a week. What gives? Shoot me a text or something.

Love,
Warren

FROM: 3105151842@verizon.net
TO: Church_Warren@LTDLaw.com

I'm fine. Don't write me.

SENT FROM MY VERIZON BLACKBERRY

Screw that. (I'd have said "eff" that, but we have a sensitive spam filter.) I'm calling you tonight.

FROM: 3105151842@verizon.net
TO: Church_Warren@LTDLaw.com

I'M FINE. DON'T CALL ME.

SENT FROM MY VERIZON BLACKBERRY

ERICK LAUGHLIN:

I still don't know the exact date in April that it started, and I still don't know most of what happened, and since I'm not the deepest thinker in the world, I don't like going there all that often. Whatever.

What happened was, every night I stayed home—whenever I was in my apartment—I'd fall asleep at exactly 9:33 P.M., and then wake up each morning at 9:33 A.M. When I was at a gig, or a rehearsal, or on a date, or at a movie, I'd stay awake, no problem. But if I was in my crib at 9:33, *boom,* out like a fucking light. Those sleeps were dreamless, and I always woke up tired. What the fuck, right?

Once I figured out the pattern—which took four, maybe five days—I tried to keep myself awake. I'd set my alarm for 9:35 P.M.—two minutes after crash time—and I'd blast that shit at full volume. Didn't work. Slept right through it. I bought two more alarm clocks and set them at staggered times throughout the night. Same thing.

Now, I may not have the ability or desire to examine my inner self, but I'm definitely not one of those guys who'll let things sit. I'm a pragmatist. Like if I see a red splotch on my balls, I'm going to the dong doctor's office, and parking myself in his waiting room, and not leaving until the guy sees me. Having a father who half-assed his cancer treatment until he had one toe in the grave will affect you that way, you know? So on the fourth night of this crap, when I woke up with dirt on the cuffs of my jeans, reeking of sweat socks, I was like, *Screw this, something ain't right. I might be sleepwalking all over the damn place. I'm getting a sleep study.*

DR. JOSEPH HOLLANDER *(director, Austin American Sleep Diagnostic Center):*

Erick Laughlin came to the center on April 30, 2009, complaining of what was, in effect, a case of narcolepsy. Most people have the misconception that having narcolepsy means you fall asleep at random times, and while that is one of the symptoms, the disorder is, unfortunately, far more debilitating. Among other symptoms, narcoleptics can also experience sleep paralysis, hallucinations, and, worst of all, cataplexy, which is similar to an epileptic seizure in that the patient is conscious but unable to speak, or move, or feel.

Mr. Laughlin's sleep study took place on the nights of May 2 and May 3, and it proved nothing. On the first night, he fell asleep just before midnight and awoke at seven A.M.; the second, he slept from eleven P.M. to eight A.M. His test readings both nights were normal.

At our May 5 consultation, he insisted that we take our equipment to his residence and conduct the study there. Unfortunately, that would have been prohibitively expensive, and his insurance didn't cover a remote study, so we had to refuse. It was at that point he became argumentative and physically aggressive. Security escorted him from the building, and I never heard from him again.

I should note that some narcolepsy sufferers are prone to violence.

ERICK LAUGHLIN:

After Dr. Hollander told me they couldn't haul their equipment to my pad, something snapped, and I jumped over his desk, grabbed him by the lapels of his lab coat, and shook him, and shook him, and shook him, and I couldn't stop. I had no control of my limbs. It was like I was standing outside of my body. Apparently that might've been caused by my narcolepsy that, according to Hollander, wasn't really narcolepsy, but whatever. It happened. Nobody got hurt. Badly.

Since the center wouldn't do a study, I decided to do one myself. My apartment became the Erick Laughlin Clinic for Weird-Ass Sleep Disorders. It wasn't the most high-tech setup: We're talking a microphone fed into my Mac and a sweet video camera I borrowed from my drummer, Theo. After years of being a film critic, I was making my very own movie. Sort of.

So three days after my two bullshit nights at the center, I got into bed at 9:00, pressed Record on my computer, turned on the camera, and stared at the clock. The last thing I remember was seeing 9:32.

The next morning, I woke up at 9:33, put on some coffee, pulled the DVD-R out of the camera, stuck it into my computer, synced it up with the sound, and hit *play*.

And then I disappeared.

THEO MORRISON (*drummer, Massacre This*):
Yeah, I totally remember when Erick called about the whole disappearing thing. He was like, "Dude, get over here now."

I was like, "I'm on my way to the shop, man." I worked at Friends of Sound over on South Congress Street. My manager didn't like it when I was late, and I was *always* late, so when I had the chance to be on time, I took it.

He was like, "Call in sick, man. I need you. I'm fucked-up, Theo."

Me and Erick met in freshman year of high school, and we've been tight ever since. We've been through a lot of shit together, but he never told me that he needed me, so I knew something was up. I was like, "Okay, bro. Be over in fifteen." My boss at the store was pissed until I told him it was a family emergency. Because that's what it was. Laughlin was family, man.

I got to his crib in, like, five minutes. He buzzed me in, and I went up the stairs, and he looked a mess . . . at least for him. Unless he was wasted or hungover—or both—Erick was one put-together cat, like with his hair always in the right place, and his face always all shaven, et cetera. Not that morning. That morning, he looked . . . wild. Animalistic. Kind of creepy.

I was like, "What's wrong, bro?"

He was like, "It's this sleep thing."

I was like, "What about it? How'd the camera work out?"

He goes, "It's fucked-up."

I was like, "Dude, tell me you didn't fuck up that camera. That shit was expensive."

He says, "The camera isn't fucked-up. The whole *thing* is fucked-up. Dig this."

And then he showed me the video. It was him sitting there reading, then him falling asleep, then him disappearing. Poof. Gone.

I go, "Dude, that was some awesome editing!"

He was like, "I don't have any video editing programs on my computer. What you see is what happened. I . . . fucking . . . disappeared."

I was like, "Well, you're back now. Did you look at the end?"

He goes, "Shit, no. I freaked. I didn't want to watch alone. That's why you're here."

I go, "Hell yeah, that's why I'm here. Fire that shit up again."

So he drags the cursor to the end of the recording, and *poof*, he reappears in the exact same position he was in when he disappeared. I was like, "WTF?"

He goes, "Yeah. WTF. Bro, you're staying with me tonight."

I was like, "Shit."

ERICK LAUGHLIN:

Theo was not psyched. I can't say that I blame him. I know if one of my friends was evaporating and asked me to babysit him, I'd probably be a little, um, let's say trepidatious.

THEO MORRISON:

I couldn't say no. He'd have done it for me.

So fast-forward to 9:33 that night. We're sitting there yammering about John Bonham, and right in the middle of a sentence, the dude falls asleep, right on schedule, and then, right before my fucking eyes, the dude disappears. WTF, right?

I go to the bed and feel around, and yeah, sure e-fucking-nough, that bastard was gone. Gone, gone, gone, clothes and all. I grab his keys from his desk and go for a walk to see if I can track his invisible ass down. I didn't know where to start. I mean, where the fuck was I supposed to go? His mom's house? Our rehearsal space? A cemetery? No clue, so I went back to his crib, and lay down on his bed, and waited for 9:33.

Now that I think about it, it's weird that we never discussed *why* this was happening to him, only how we could fix it. Hunh.

ERICK LAUGHLIN:

I opened my eyes at 9:33—of course—and there was good old Theo, crashed out right next to me. He rolled over, then said, "Yo. Welcome home, dude. Sleep well?"

I said, "Did I disappear?"

He said, "Yeah. You disappeared like a motherfucker. But I have an idea."

THEO MORRISON:

I didn't sleep for shit that night. I mean, would you? Your best bud disappears, and you're supposed to be able to crash? No way, man. So I thought, and thought, and thought—what else was I going to do?—and came up with the best idea *ever*.

ERICK LAUGHLIN:

He said, "We're going to use the camera."

I said, "We already used the camera."

He said, "No, we're going to put the camera on you."

I said, "We already put the camera on me."

He said, "No, we're going to put the camera *on* you."

I said, "What're you talking about?"

He said, "Dig it: Your clothes went with you when you pulled your fade, so maybe if we duct-tape the camera to your chest, it'll go with you, too. We'll hit the Record button before you go beddy-bye, and we're good to go. It'll pick up *something*."

Theo was right about that. It sure as shit picked up something.

THEO MORRISON:

That camera weighed like fifty pounds, and it took an entire roll of duct tape to get that thing secure. It was probably uncomfortable as shit for Eric, but, you know, the dude wasn't having trouble falling asleep, so that wasn't an issue.

So he disappears at 9:33 at night *again,* and he comes back at 9:33 in the morning *again,* and when he gets up, I pull out a box cutter and start cutting off all the tape. He's like, "Dude, slow down. My skin is under this tape." So I slowed down, and I got the camera off, and I managed to cut him only once.

I've got to tell you, man, we were not psyched to watch the video. But we watched it.

ERICK LAUGHLIN:

Based on what we saw, I wasn't disappearing, exactly. It was more that I became invisible and moved really fast.

At first, the picture was kind of a blur, but we could tell I was going down my stairs and out of my building, and then I made a left, which meant I was heading west. Beyond that, it was impossible to even guess where the fuck I was going.

About half an hour into my invisible run, or sprint, or whatever the hell it was, I came to a sudden stop in front of a mall, and it was light outside. Maybe that was a trick of the camera. Or maybe I went so far west that I caught up with the sunset. No clue.

I clearly still wasn't visible to the world at large, because nobody looked directly at me, and if you saw some guy in the middle of a mall wandering around with a video camera duct-taped to his chest, you'd stare.

No staring. No nothing.

I was gliding smoothly through the mall—the picture never once became shaky; it was almost like the camera was on a dolly. The angle of the shot was relatively high, and since the camera had been strapped onto my chest, and I'm only five foot ten, it seemed like I was floating.

And then people started falling.

THEO MORRISON:

There were these red things shooting *out* of Erick, or from *behind* Erick, and when one would hit somebody, they'd stumble onto the ground, then they'd get right back up again, like nothing happened. It was totally random who was getting zitzed: some dudes, some chicks, some grown-ups, some kids, some African Americans, some white peeps, and some Asian folks. Wait, now that I think about it, it wasn't *totally* random: All the people getting shot were alone. The only zitz-ees were wandering the mall all by their lonesome. Weird. Or weird*er.*

After about an hour at the mall, Invisible Erick took off and glided along for another forty-five minutes. He ended up at a movie theater—no surprise there; Erick's a film nerd, and that's the way he rolls . . . even when he's invisible, I guess—and then he went shooting that weird red shit at the loners again. That was when things got weird. Or weird*er.*

ERICK LAUGHLIN:

I didn't know where the hell I was, so I didn't know what the hell the local time was. It could've been ten, it could've been midnight, it could've been four A.M. No way to tell.

So I'm walking up and down the aisle of the movie theater, and that red stuff is still shooting out—still no idea where it was coming from—and unlike what was going on in the mall, the people who are getting shot have these brief seizures, then fall asleep. I don't know when they woke up, because I went from theater to theater without hanging out for the aftermath.

And then the battery died.

And then, nothing.

EARTHQUAKE BY MOVIE THEATER INJURES 300-PLUS

FIRST EARTHQUAKE IN SANTA FE IN OVER A CENTURY

BY MAUREEN FRANZEN

MAY 5, 2009

An earthquake measuring 6.1 on the Richter scale shook the Miller Keresotes Fifteenplex at 152 Cerritos Road. No casualties were reported, but officials estimate that over 300 were injured.

The earthquake, which is the most serious such incident reported in Santa Fe since 1918, appears to have been extremely centralized.

Dr. Roman Zetterberg of the United States Geological Survey said, "The quake did zero property damage to the general vicinity. Even the restaurants adjacent to the building seemed unaffected. This is odd behavior for an event such as this, but far from unprecedented."

No aftershocks have been reported, but Zetterberg will not rule them out. "If there are aftershocks, the chances of them being as centralized are minimal."

TOBE HOOPER WITH ALAN GOLDSHER

Police are asking local residents to take precautions. For more information on how to prepare for an earthquake, please visit http://www.sfreporter.com/QuakePrep.

FROM: DianeDee123@yahoo.com
TO: HottieMcHottie1993@gmail.com
SUBJECT: the quake
DATE: May 5, 2009

Hey, Gwennie—

You were at the theater last night, weren't you? You okay?

xox,
Dee

FROM: HottieMcHottie1993@gmail.com
TO: DianeDee123@yahoo.com
SUBJECT: re: the quake
DATE: May 5, 2009

Hey, Dee—

You won't believe what happened.

So me and Kerrie and Melissa go to see STAR TREK. Why would
I want to see STAR TREK? Well, I didn't. Kerrie only wanted
to go because she thought Neal was going to be there, and
Melissa wanted to go because if Neal was there, then Steven
would be there, and I only wanted to go because I had nothing better to do.

So we get into the theater, and a half hour in, I knew I was
right that it SUCKED. So we were bored, and we started looking around, and Melissa saw Steven and Neal, so we tiptoed
over. On the way down the aisle, I tripped and fell on my
face, and I think I knocked myself out for a second, but Kerrie and Melissa didn't even notice, because they were totally
running to get to the guys.

So I catch up to them, and they're already sitting next to the
guys, and there weren't any seats by them, so I took a seat
on the end next to this supercute guy who was with his supercute friends. He and his friends looked OLD, like they were
thiry or something.

I was wearing a short skirt, and I could have sworn I saw
him checking out my legs, so just for the fun of it, I kind of
touched my THIGH against his. I'm such a dork sometimes.

But I guess I was wrong about him looking at me, because when my leg touched his, he didn't even flinch. I don't think he noticed.

That's when the earthquake started. At first I thought it was an explosion, because the ground didn't start shaking right away. It was just a loud BOOM, and then the movie stopped, and then everybody started screaming (I screamed too), and THEN the ground started shaking. I went to meet the girls, but it turned out that the old guy next to me had accidentally sat on my skirt, so I couldn't stand up. I yelled at him, I'M STUCK, and he said he was sorry, and he stood up, and sort of handed me my skirt back, and his fingers touched my leg, and all of a sudden, the world disappeared, and it was just the two of us. I know you think that sounds weird, but it's TRUE.

We kissed, and it was CRAZY! I don't know how long it went on for, but it seemed like forever. My legs started trembling, and I fell down on the floor, and the old guy fell right on top of me, and then he rolled off of me, and we were on our sides, face-to-face. And then I touched him DOWN THERE through his pants. I couldn't help it. And the second I touched him, he came, and there was so much stuff that it leaked through his pants. It got on my hands, and it was gross and sticky. I had a paper cut on my index finger, and that stung BAD.

Suddenly, everybody's running around and screaming their heads off, but I look behind me, and there's another girl with another guy and they're in the exact same position as I'm in, and the girl's wiping her hand on the floor like she'd gotten something nasty on it. I was just about to say something to her when this guy who was running down the aisle tripped over me. He said he was sorry, then he stood up and offered his hand. Without even thinking, I gave him the hand that had the old guy's stuff all over it, but I don't think he noticed, because that's when the walls started falling apart.

I don't remember much of what happened after that. I think I went into shock or something. I kind of remember dragging Kerrie and Melissa out of the theater, but that may have been my imagination.

Mom's taking me to the doctor today to make sure I'm okay. I told her I'm fine (WHICH I AM), but you know my mom. Overprotective. I'll tell you how it goes.

xox,
Gwennie

FROM: DianeDee123@yahoo.com
TO: HottieMcHottie1993@gmail.com
SUBJECT: re: re: the quake
DATE: May 5, 2009

What is your problem? You gave an old guy a hand job during an earthquake, and you think you're okay? YOU ARE NOT OKAY! We need to talk about this. Call me when you can. If you need me, I'm here for you. I'm ALWAYS here for you.

xox,
Dee

FROM: HottieMcHottie1993@gmail.com
TO: DianeDee123@yahoo.com
SUBJECT: re: re: re: the quake
DATE: May 5, 2009

Dee—

I need you. Do you think your mom would let you sleep over tonight? I'm scared.

So we go to the doctor, and she gives me the once-over, and says that I was probably right, and that I went into a little bit of shock. Then she took some blood tests and she made me give her a urine sample. So I went to the bathroom, but I didn't really have to pee, so I sat there and started thinking about last night, and what it was like kissing the old guy, and I started getting excited down there, which wasn't help-ing with the peeing. So I wiped myself off, because I didn't want that stuff mixing with my pee, and here's the scary part.

The toilet paper came away red and blue.

I screamed. I couldn't help it. One of the nurses banged on the door and asked if I was okay. Part of me wanted to tell her that there was some blue stuff coming out of my hoo-hah, but the other part of me wanted to keep it quiet, because after all that stuff that happened with Willy last year, I HATE hospitals. But I looked at the toilet paper again and decided that since I was already there, I'd better say something.

The doctor made me go right to my gynecologist, and I'll spare you the details, because she ran about a MILLION tests, and they all hurt SO badly, and I don't want to think about it anymore. I just want to stay here in bed, and I want you to come and keep me company, because I hurt, and I'm scared, and I can't stop thinking about the old guy no matter how hard I try, and my sheets are getting stained blue. Come over ASAP.

xox,
Gwennie

May 7, 2009—I am in, and it could not have been simpler.
It is an offshoot of an offshoot of an offshoot. In typical
fashion, they do not even know what group they are
splintered from, and, also in typical fashion, they do not
care. Their only concern is the cause.

They knew who I was, but that was not a surprise.
Most of these field generals take themselves and their
work quite seriously, and they do their research. The
leader, who goes by the name Brian, told me that I was far
from the first Homeland Security agent to "turn." Upper
management keeps us all isolated from one another, so it
was little surprise that I was not aware of that.

Brian has refused to give me specifics about the
mission, which I believe is because he does not have
all the specifics himself. So all we have done is train
and procure. It appears that is how it will be for the
foreseeable future.

We train right by Lake Michigan in Evanston, a suburb
just north of Chicago, right out in plain sight. But we
have nothing to hide. We are simply exercising: yoga,
running, tai chi. We must remain in tip-top shape. We do
not know why. That is simply the fact.

They would prefer that I live with them in their
compound, which is actually a modest house on a quiet
side street in an affluent neighborhood, but I prefer to
sleep in my own bed. They realize that I bring a wealth of
knowledge to the table, so they have compromised: sixteen
hours with them, eight hours away.

They are quite paranoid. I have told them time and again that, due to our edict of plausible deniability, nobody at the department knows of their existence, other than me. They do not believe me, which is understandable, but they will come to. Numerous times, I have demonstrated that I know more about their world than they do. They are impressed. They like having me around.

They are also taken with my ability to build weaponry. I brought along a pipe bomb recipe that Brian called the finest he had ever seen. My concoction for a fertilizer bomb is far less expensive than theirs, and I am confident that it will be equally powerful, if not more so. Much to my surprise, they did not know what a barometric bomb is. I doubt we will ever use one, but it is good to have them available.

One thing that was quite disappointing to me was their lack of respect for their firearms. They have a Stinger FIM-92A missile in the basement that has never been fired, but they do not realize they must keep it clean whether or not it has been used. I spent almost an entire day wiping off the layer of dust that had covered the weapon, both inside and out.

Two days after they let me into their inner circle, I took them to an underground shooting range on the South Side of Chicago that they did not know about. It is things like that that help me ingratiate myself. Sooner or later, they will trust me in full. I hope it is sooner.

I do not even have a clue what my mission is. All I know is that if I have anything to say about it, it will involve bloodshed, and pain, and destruction, and, if all goes well, a body count for the ages.

Andi-Licious

The Useless Musings of Sophomoric Sophomore Andrea Daltrey

MAY 11

MY WARDROBE

My clothes don't work for me because they cover too much. Like if you can't see my NIPPLES through my shirt, then that shirt has to go. If you can't see the CRACK OF MY ASS peeking out of my pants, those pants have to go. If you can't see my CLEAVAGE, that's unacceptable, because if I walk down the street and a guy doesn't stare at me then something's wrong.

I want every guy to stare at me. I want every guy to want me, even though I don't want every guy. But if I want a guy, he has to WANT me, and I don't want to work at it like last night. I went to the Beauty Bar and wore a white baby-doll tee without a bra, so my nipples were all out there. I wore a short skirt without PANTIES, and while I was sitting at the bar, I spread my LEGS apart a couple of times just for fun. I don't remember the name of the headlining band, but it was a good thing I wore what I did, because the second I saw the drummer, I wanted his cock in my MOUTH.

After they were done playing, I went backstage and grabbed him by the back of his neck and gave him one of those new KISSES that seem to put guys under my spell or something. After I pulled away, I stuck my hand down his pants and squeezed and he came immediately all over the place, and it was blue just like it always is. I LICKED my hand clean, then wiped the rest of it onto a guitar case, then I went home and rubbed myself until I feel asleep.

Good night sweet dreams dream of me getting you HARD AND SUCKING you dry and turning you blue.

LOS ANGELES COUNTY PROSECUTOR'S OFFICE

1. INCIDENT: Missing Person Investigation	2. DATE OF REPORT: May 14, 2009
3. INVESTIGATING OFFICER: Detective Omar Saxton	4. FILE NUMBER: 10K1-462192-LA260

5. SUBJECT (NATURE OF INVESTIGATION/NAME AND ADDRESS OF INDIVIDUAL):

Missing Persons Investigation—Gary Church, 1424 S. Swall, Los Angeles

6. INSTRUCTIONS: Report Will Be Prepared in the Following Order

a. Reason for Investigation

b. Synopsis of Investigation

c. Conclusion

d. Recommendation and Comment (When Appropriate)

e. List of Attachments (If Any)

a: The undersigned investigator was assigned to assist in the investigation of a missing person (Gary Samuel Church, sixty-four-year-old white male of Swall St. in Los Angeles, May 14, 2009).

b: The subject was reported missing by his brother, Warren Roderick Church of Seventh Ave. in Brooklyn, NY. Warren Church last had contact with the subject on April 23, 2009, via a text message. Warren Church says that Gary Church had been "acting weird" for several weeks before the disappearance. Warren Church says that the last individual to see Gary Church was Donna Nathan, a key grip on the film that Gary Church was shooting at the Twentieth Century Fox Studio (10201 Pico Blvd.) until his disappearance. The date was May 2, 2009. Warren Church claims that Donna Nathan has expressed her willingness to submit to an interview. On May 10, Warren Church examined Gary Church's house for information and did not uncover anything "useful." Between May 10 and 13, Warren Church approached several of Gary Church's neighbors, who could offer no suggestions. Warren Church has also called numerous local hospitals, to no avail.

c: No definitive conclusion can be made at this time.

d: It is my recommendation that we do a second sweep of the local hospitals and interview as many individuals who worked with Gary Church on the Fox lot as possible. According to Warren Church, Gary Church had never displayed any suicidal tendencies, but considering that Warren Church emphasized that Gary Church had been "acting weird," suicide is not being ruled out. As Gary Church is well-off, it is also recommended that we conduct an airline search, both local and domestic, to see if he simply left his home without telling anybody. A secondary search of the house is also essential.

e: —8" x 10" photo of Gary Church

—Keys to 1424 S. Swall

JANINE DALTREY:

I was laid up in the hospital for a month, and at first, my friends were wonderful. I had visitors coming in and out of my room, and everybody had a present for me: books, stuffed animals, pizza, DVDs, pretty much anything I wanted. My professors were also terrific. They all stopped by with lecture notes, and homework, and lots of bad jokes that made me laugh despite myself. Andi came by, all slutted up in her new sexy-time outfits. She was her usual self, just . . . sluttier. I tried to grill her about this new look and attitude of hers, but she'd always change the subject. Honestly, I was too tired to push it. I regret that to this day, and probably will for the rest of my life.

As the days progressed, the visits kind of dwindled. I guess I can understand. I had some decent friends in Austin, but they weren't the kind of friends you'd keep in touch with after graduation. You'd become Facebook buddies and maybe get together when you were in the same town, maybe not, but we're not talking lifelongers here. It was kind of like they did their duty, then they moved on.

Naturally, I watched a lot of TV—a lot of CNN, to be precise, because my hospital roommate would kick and scream if I even thought about putting on VH1 or something—and by the end of my stay at Chez Sickbed, the news was driving . . . me . . . fucking . . . crazy. Terrorists blowing up shit in Chicago; a mini-riot in Atlanta; earthquakes in San Diego, Baja, Tijuana, and New Mexico; and, of course, the rash of fires in Austin . . . I think there'd been almost three dozen at that point, and some of them were really bad, like five-alarm bad. The only good news was that the Dallas Stars might make the playoffs.

When they sprung me, Andi came to pick me up, and she was off in the ozone. I said to her, "You look tingly. Did you find a boy or something?"

She shrugged, gave me this weird, cockeyed smile, and said, "Kind of."

I said, "He's a lucky guy, what with your boobs all hanging out like that."

She said, "It's funny, I never realized how easy it is to get a man with these things. I mean, they're just boobs. But if I push them up, or if they can see my nipples, it's like they're my slave or something."

I said, "How's it going with the doctor?"

She said, "Which one?"

I said, "What do you mean 'which one'? The one who you were fucking on my hospital bed."

She said, "Oh, right, Cyrus. Yeah, I'm done with him. I fucked him out."

I said, "Jesus, I never thought I'd be hearing this from Ms. Prim and Proper."

She said, "Screw prim and proper. I'm on a mission."

I said, "Just be careful."

She said, "I don't need to be."

I said, "What're you talking about?"

She said, "Don't worry about it. What about you? What's your boy situation like?"

I said, "Honey, I'll be happy when I can stand up without my joints creaking. No sex in the champagne room for Janine."

She said, "Great! More for me."

I wondered what the hell happened to her. But again, I didn't ask.

Welcome to the Truth About Zombies

May 20, 2009

We've been dicking around with this zombie stuff for, what, three years now, and it's all been in good fun. Until now. To that end, a quick Q & A . . .

Q: Do we believe that undead roam the earth?
A: Maybe in Haiti, but not the United States.

Q: Have any of you actually seen a zombie in person?
A: No.

Q: What would you do if you did encounter a zombie?
A: Have a mental meltdown.

Which leads to this: <u>**CLICK HERE TO SEE WHAT IS PROB-**</u>
<u>**ABLY A ZOMBIE**</u>

I saw this thing. I smelled this thing. I heard this thing. And I survived this thing. Right. Now let me tell you what happened. And it's straight out of a shitty horror movie.

Ironically, my pal Dave-o and I had just gotten out of a shitty horror movie, and I was craving an In-n-Out burger, so we picked up some grub, brought it outside, sat on the hood of my car, and shoved down burgers while railing on that piece-of-shit flick. I hadn't even gotten to my fries yet when a car pulled up, and the driver opened his window. He was ugly as hell, and twice as smelly, and at first I thought it was a homeless guy, but then I wondered, *What would a homeless guy be doing driving a Mercedes M-Class?*

I yelled out to him, "You need some help with something?" Because he looked like he could use a serious hand. He shook his head and mumbled something I couldn't make out. While all this was going on, Dave-o pulled out his cell phone and snapped a picture—the very picture you see **HERE**—and that got the dude riled up like a motherfucker. He opened his door, then—and I swear to God this is the 100 percent honest truth—ripped off the car door with his bare hands and threw it to the other side of the parking lot.

At this point, Dave-o said, "We're out."

I said, "Wait, I think this guy needs help."

To which Dave-o responded, "Get in the car, moron. He has a gun."

I looked back at him and saw that Dave-o was wrong. He didn't have a gun. He had pulled off his own arm and was cocking it at me like it was a rifle. I raised my arms above my head and said, "We're cool, man. You want money? We got money. I'm going to reach into my back pocket and get my wallet. Don't shoot. We're cool."

And then he let out a moan that literally made my eardrums bleed, which I'll share with you now. **CLICK HERE TO SEE MY BLEEDING EARDRUM**

Right then, Dave-o fell onto the pavement. I don't know whether he tripped or whether his brain was blown away by the guy's moan—my ears were bleeding, for fuck's sake, so anything was possible—and then the guy (who, believe it or not, looked familiar to me) jumped over both me and the car and landed on Dave-o's chest. Then he took his dismembered arm and smacked Dave-o upside his head. I heard Dave-o's nose crunch, and saw four of his teeth fly out of his mouth. The guy then stepped on Dave-o's kneecap. Dave-o started screaming, and the guy kept moaning, and then the guy fell on top of Dave-o and bit his ear. Then he went to work on me, and he didn't stop chewing until people started coming out of the restaurant, at which point he got into his Mercedes and speeded away.

We're both in the hospital right now. I'll survive, but they're giving Dave-o only a 50/50 chance. So I'm done with this web-site. Our attacker may or may not have been a zombie, but regardless, I've lost my taste for this. You can keep posting your comments, but I'm finito. I mean, look at me: **CLICK HERE TO SEE ME IN A FUCKING WHEELCHAIR, WITH ONE LEG RIPPED OFF**

As you might imagine, horror has lost its appeal.

COMMENTS

Swell story, asshole, but I have two words: Photoshop, bitch.
Brew 'n' View from San Francisco, CA
May 20, 9:33 AM

Awesome!!!!!
Martin from Miami, FL
May 20, 11:42 AM

MIDNIGHT MOVIE

HOLY SHIT. I CAN'T BELIEVE THAT. THE SAME THING SORT OF HAPPENED TO ME AND MY BOYFRIEND. IT WAS LIKE THREE IN THE MORNING AND WE WERE AT OUR 24-HOUR STARBUCKS. WE WERE DRINKING OUR DRINKS AND THERE WAS NOBODY AROUND. A CAR PULLED UP AND IT MIGHT HAVE BEEN A MERCEDES BUT I DON'T KNOW FOR SURE. A MAN JUMPED OUT AND HE WAS CARRYING A TIRE IRON. HE SWUNG AND HIT MY BOYFRIEND IN THE NECK AND HE WAS MOVING SO FAST THAT I DIDN'T HAVE TIME TO DO ANYTHING. HE YANKED OFF MY BOYFRIEND'S HEAD AND SUCKED ON THE NECK STUMP. I SCREAMED AND SCREAMED AND THE BARISTA CAME RUNNING OUT OF THE STARBUCKS AND CALLED 911 ON HIS CELL PHONE. I DON'T REMEMBER WHAT HAPPENED NEXT BUT I WAS TOLD LATER THAT THE COPS SHOWED UP ALMOST IMMEDIATELY AND TOOK A BUNCH OF SHOTS AT THE GUY BUT HE DIDN'T DIE OR BLEED OR ANYTHING. HE LIFTED UP THE TABLE AND THREW IT AT POLICE CARS THEN GOT INTO HIS OWN CAR AND DROVE AWAY. HE DIDN'T GET A CHANCE TO EAT ME BUT MY BOYFRIEND IS DEAD. HIS FUNERAL IS TOMORROW BUT I'M NOT GOING TO BE ABLE TO GO BECAUSE I'M REALLY SICK. I'M ALL ITCHY AND I'M GETTING ZITS. MY DOCTORS SAYS IT'S EITHER CHICKEN POX OR STRESS. WHATEVER IT IS I'M SAD AND SCARED AND I HOPE THAT YOU AND DAVE-O ARE OKAY SOON.
LOVE . . .
Cherie from Los Angeles, CA
May 20, 2:18 PM

MAY 21, 2009

ZOMBIES SIGHTED IN SOUTHERN CALIFORNIA

LOS ANGELES—First they took over the multiplex, then they took over the bookstores, now they're taking over the West Coast!

Packs of zombies, the monster du jour, have been spotted throughout Southern California, specifically in Los Angeles, La Quinta, Arcadia, Rancho Cucamonga, Thousand Oaks, and Glendale.

A UCLA physics professor, who wishes to remain anonymous, said, "It's possible!" A doctor at Cedars-Sinai, who apparently treated several victims of attacks, agreed, saying, "Yes, it's possible!" The Los Angeles Police Department refused to discuss the matter.

A relative of one victim, however, was brave enough to speak on the record. Bella Napoli, 25, of Los Angeles County, claims that her sister was attacked in a mall parking lot by four undead gentlemen. Napoli says that after the zombies subdued her sister, Gina, 22, they removed her limbs and "did something weird," after which they reattached the limbs and carried Gina away.

"I haven't heard from her since," Bella said with tears rolling down her cheeks, "and I don't think I'll ever hear from her again."

So, dear readers, please stay alert when you're in those mall parking lots, because you never know what's out there!

twitter.com

 ScaryBarry tweaking like a motherfucker. better than ever. who wants in?
May 22 2:14 PM **via** web

 BorisDSpider @ScaryBarry Where u at, bro?
May 22 2:18 PM **via** web

 ScaryBarry @BorisDSpider tejas. the big a.
May 22 2:22 PM **via** web

 BorisDSpider @ScaryBarry Big A? R u the guy?
May 22 2:32 PM **via** web

 ScaryBarry @BorisDSpider word bitch.
May 22 2:39 PM **via** web

 StinkyCat @ScaryBarry THE guy? PM me. Please.
May 22 2:48 PM **via** web

 TheFakeShaqO @ScaryBarry Ur a legend. PM me too, pleez.
May 22 2:50 PM **via** web

 Supergirl1491 @ScaryBarry Are you this guy?
http://21521.tinyurl.com
May 22 2:58 PM **via** web

ScaryBarry @Supergirl1491 @TheFakeShaqO
@StinkyCat @BorisDSpider that article is b.s. none of
that piddly crap here.
May 22 3:03 PM **via** web

 Supergirl1491 @ScaryBarry What do you mean "piddly
crap"?
May 22 3:14 PM **via** web

 ScaryBarry @Supergirl1491 @TheFakeShaqO
@StinkyCat @BorisDSpider my shit is five alarm,
bitches. they'll never find me though. but y'all will.
come & get it
May 22 3:20 PM **via** web

ERICK LAUGHLIN:

Needless to say, after Theo and I watched the video, I made it a point to never be in my apartment after 9:30, which meant crashing on couches throughout Austin and a lot of worn-out welcomes. My friends were as cool as they could be about it, but having houseguests is a pain in the ass, especially a guy like me who was ranting and raving about all kinds of supernatural bullshit.

I tried to go about life normally—you know, write my articles, rehearse with the band, get my fill of Internet porn . . . kidding about the porn—but it was impossible. I couldn't stop thinking about it. Would you have been able to? Would you have been able to get it out of your brain that you turned invisible, then ran or floated into another time zone, then shot red bullets out of *some* part of your body? Good luck not obsessing over that.

No wonder I got baked every night.

I was turning into such a space cadet wasteoid that Theo dragged me to see his general practitioner so I could get a full physical workup. I'd been poked and prodded enough at the sleep center, but my health insurance at the newspaper was okay, and this guy was in our network, so I figured, *Why not, it won't cost you anything except time.*

So we're sitting in the waiting room, and I'm reading a three-month-old issue of *Sports Illustrated,* and somebody taps me on the shoulder. It was Janine Daltrey, who I hadn't seen since the Tobe Hooper screening. The poor girl looked terrible. Her sister, Andi, however, looked smashing, so smashing that when I asked Janine what was wrong, and she told me about getting beaten by her ex, I couldn't look away from Andi, which made me feel like a lame-o. I've always considered myself a gentleman, and I've never been the guy who gawks. But if you saw Andi that day, there's absolutely no way you wouldn't have stared. I mean, she had on a tight, strappy tank top that pushed her breasts together and gave her some death-defying cleavage. Her jeans had big holes in the knees, so you could see the fishnet stockings she was wearing underneath. Andi Daltrey was a walking pheromone, and it took all of my restraint to not lick the back of her neck.

But my gentlemanliness trumped my lust, and I managed to focus on Janine. I told her about my disappearing act, and she kind of freaked. She said, "We had ghosts one summer when I was in high school."

Andi said, "We did?"

Janine said, "You were at overnight camp."

Andi asked, "Why didn't you tell me?"

Janine said, "What good would it have done? They went away before you got home."

Andi said, "You're bullshitting me." Then she turned to me and said, "She's bullshitting me, right? It's the twenty-first century. They don't make ghosts anymore."

I said, "Andi, you're talking to a guy who has filmed evidence of himself disappearing. There're ghosts." Then I asked Janine what happened.

She said, "It wasn't as sinister as it sounds. The woman who owned the house next door to us died when I was a kid. Her name was Mrs. Pupe—spelled P-U-P-E, but pronounced 'poopy.' You can imagine how much crap she took from us kids in the 'hood."

Andi said, "Oh, I kind of remember her."

Janine said, "I'm not surprised. She loved you. She thought you were the cutest little girl. She used to give you candy all the time. Me, not so much."

Andi batted her eyelashes and said, "I was pretty cute. Still am." Then she rubbed her fingernail on my knee and said, "Right, Erick?"

Back when I was in junior high, I thought about sex so often that I'd get a boner if a leaf fell off a tree and landed on my head. If a girl accidentally brushed her arm against me, forget it, I'd be in a daze of lust for forty-five minutes. But that was junior high.

Now that I'm a semi-adult, it takes me a minute or three to get an erection, but when Andi Daltrey's finger grazed my leg, I swear I almost came. A bit disconcerting, I have to say. I excused myself, and went to the men's room, and, if I may be crude, finished myself off in the stall.

When I got back, Janine was struggling to get to her feet. I gave her a hand standing up, then asked her what happened with Mrs. Pupe. She said, "Long story. Call me." Then she gave me her number and went to see her doctor.

JANINE DALTREY:

My arms were still pretty bruised up, and my eyes were still rainbowed, and my ankle wasn't all that much better, and Dr. Finnegan was concerned that my wounds weren't healing faster. He wanted to take some blood and run tests to make sure I wasn't anemic or something.

I walked over to the lab, and Andi said she wanted to ask the doctor a few questions. I hate having blood drawn—I hate needles in general—so I asked her to come with me and hold my hand. She said, "No, sis." Then she touched the doctor on the chest—a doctor who, I should mention, was probably in his mid-fifties and was, if I may be rude, pretty damn fugly—and said all whispery, "I have a few questions for the physician." I swear, he shivered.

Long story short, I wasn't anemic. They couldn't find anything. I was at wit's end. And I wanted to hurt somebody.

ERICK LAUGHLIN:

They found nothing. I was pissed. Times ten. And I didn't know what to do. I mean, where do you go when your friends, in spite of their best efforts, can't help you, and your doctors are useless?

Outside of Theo, there wasn't anybody in my life who'd take this seriously.

TOBE HOOPER:

All the shit with the Game was raining down—the fires and the bombings and whatnot—but at the time, I wasn't following it. My television was permanently tuned to American Movie Classics, and the only two things I ever did on my computer were write and answer e-mail, so unless the news was happening right in my front yard, I wasn't aware. And that was just the way I liked it.

Random chitter-chatter from the outside world wasn't good for my career—hell, most of the outside world wasn't good for my career, but that's for another book. Seriously, all I needed was a keyboard, a screen, some food, and a few libations, and I was good to go. It was when I had to deal with the general public that things got hairy. Like, for example, pitching projects.

If you put a gun to my head and asked, "What's worse, a zombie attack or a pitch meeting with a studio head? Answer quick or die," I'd probably be dead, because that's a question that merits much pondering. If a zombie attacks you, you'll fight the good fight, and if you go down, you'll go down with dignity. But when a dude from the studio attacks you, or your script, or your ideas, you get defensive, and you start to beg. You beg for money, or you beg for an audience with the next fellow on the food chain, or you beg for a second chance, a third chance, a tenth chance. They cut you to pieces, but they do it so politely that you don't even realize you're gushing blood until you're in your car and halfway home.

I liked to go into these things with a small pile of scripts and a big pile of ideas; that way, if they chopped off my leg, I'd still have another ten or so to stand on. So if somebody asked me, "Tobe, what were you doing during the beginning of the Game?" I'd tell them, "I was prepping for one epic motherfucking pitch meeting."

May 27, 2009—Still quiet on the eastern front. Brian's
runner, who went by the megalomaniacal moniker of the
Lord, had not initiated contact in months.

They brought me in and embraced me as best they
could, but there was always the distance, likely because I
chose to sleep at home. Going in, I had a hunch that might
happen, so I came armed. Not with weapons. With a plan.

All I wanted to do was prove myself. And if I
exterminated a few people in the process, so much the
better.

One thing I have learned over the years is that it
is as important to cover your tracks as it is to devise
quality weaponry. Look at those idiots who tried to blow
up the World Trade Center in 1993, or that so-called bomb
factory that was raided in Park Slope, Brooklyn, in 1997.
The bombs were not good, but their planning was worse.

There had not been any significant terrorist action
in Chicago period (strange, I always thought, because it
was not a well-protected city), so I thought that blowing
up the Excalibur nightclub—which would at once be
catastrophic and endear me to the Lord—would not prove
to be a problem.

FROM: HottieMcHottie1993@gmail.com
TO: DianeDee123@yahoo.com
SUBJECT: HE FOUND ME!!!!!
DATE: May 27, 2009

Dee—

Where have you been? I haven't heard from you in a few days.
I miss you.

That old guy from the earthquake night found me.

It was lunch period, and I was craving Taco Hell, and I
wanted to be left the hell alone, so I snuck out to the parking lot and got in my car. I drove out the exit, and all of a
sudden, I felt something cold on the back of my neck, and a
voice said, "I missed you, Gwennie."

I screamed, and he yelled, "I'M NOT GOING TO HURT YOU, I'M
NOT GOING TO HURT YOU!!!"

I said, "THEN WHY ARE YOU HOLDING A GUN ON MY NECK?"
He started laughing, and I said, "Why are you laughing? This
isn't funny! I'm calling the cops."

He crawled into the front seat, then grabbed my purse (which
is where my cell was) and said, "No, no, don't call." Then he
showed me the biggest, most beautiful diamond necklace I'd
ever seen and said, "It wasn't a gun, Gwennie. It was this."

I kind of gasped. You would have too, it was so beautiful. I
said, "Is it real?"

He said, "Do I look like the kind of guy who would show up with a cubic zirconia?"

I looked him over, and he most definitely was NOT the kind of guy who would show up with a cubic zirconia. He had thick, black hair that he'd gelled into a cute fauxhawk, and his eyes were penetrating green, and he was skinny, but not too skinny. He was wearing a brown designer suit with a sharp striped shirt and a really cute tie. He looked like an older version of Robert Pattinson. I said, "No. You look pretty good. How did you know my name?"

He laughed, then said, "It came to me in a dream." And then he kissed my cheek gently, and it was over.

I don't want to tell you exactly what we did. I want to keep that to myself. I will say that we didn't have actual sex, but we did almost everything else. But here's the weird part. I gave him a blow job, and he came all over the place, even in my eyes a little bit. And it was that blue, that same blue I saw in my period last month. I got my period this morning, and there wasn't any more red. It was all blue. I was bleeding blue. The same blue as the old guy's come.

But that's not the weird part. The weird part is, I don't care.

xox,
Gwennie

FROM: DianeDee123@yahoo.com
TO: HottieMcHottie1993@gmail.com
SUBJECT: re: HE FOUND ME!!!!!
DATE: May 27, 2009

I had my period too. I'm bleeding blue. And unlike you, I fucking care.

I'm transferring schools, and I'm not telling you where. Don't call or write me anymore. If I see you on the street, I'm going to hurt you, and you can save this e-mail to show to the police. I hate you, and I will hate you until one of us dies.

Fuck you fuck you fuck you fuck you fuck you.

May 28, 2009—I gave them the plan. They loved it, all
except for Brian. That is not true, exactly. Brian loved
the concept, but he did not want to execute it, as he was
nervous about doing anything to "advance the cause"
without his runner's approval.

I wanted to make Brian angry, so angry that he
would make a decision that went against his masters.
He had come to respect me, and he felt that my opinion
of him counted for something, so I called him a coward.
I insulted his mother. I questioned his masculinity.
For hours. In my experience, this is the kind of thing that
can put a Middle Eastern male over the edge. But Brian, to
his credit, would not be swayed by name-calling. He simply
laughed.

The other men, who had been held down for two-plus
years, were itching to kill, maim, and destroy. (Bully
for them!) They believed I had hit on the perfect way
to simultaneously make a statement and cause some
considerable civilian damage, so they went to work on
Brian. After hours and hours of what I believed were
some quite convincing arguments, Brian would not bend, so
they told their soon-to-be-deposed leader that if he was
not with them, he was against them, and if he remained
against them, they would inform the runner that Brian was
a double agent who moonlighted with Mossad. He saw they
were serious, and he gave in. Blackmail is never elegant,
but it is effective. And besides, like all of us, he wanted
some blood on his hands.

Before I came aboard, they had procured four nondescript vans that, as far as the Department of Motor Vehicles was concerned, did not exist. Brian had explicit instructions to save them for future action. Much to my eternal gratitude, he allowed me to use two of them.

At this point, we had a goodly number of homemade explosive devices at our disposal, including several dozen pipe bombs, five suitcase bombs, and, the keynote to my plan, a cyanide bomb.

When I refer to my "plan" as a plan, it makes it sound much more grandiose than it actually was. In reality, all we were going to do was load van #1 with twenty pipe bombs and five canisters of gasoline, set it on fire, and leave it behind the Excalibur, where it would kill somewhere between twenty-five and fifty people, and send the remaining two hundred or so clubgoers out the front door, where they would be met by van #2, which would house the gas bomb. The timer on that particular explosive, as well as the compound, was a masterwork.

It could not have been easier. I drove the pipe bomb van, and Brian took the cyanide vehicle. We arrived at the Excalibur at precisely midnight, when it was at its most crowded. I got out of the van and made a bonfire in the back, then jumped into a car we had planted earlier and drove off. Simultaneously, Brian parked his van across the street from the club, turned on the timer, calmly left the van, and retreated to the subway.

It went off without a hitch. My only regret is that I was not able to see the aftermath.

CHICAGO SUN-TIMES

EXCALIBUR STILL OFF-LIMITS

HOMELAND SECURITY: "NO END IN SIGHT"; CDC CITES CYANIDE

JUNE 4, 2009

BY DONNA WONG

CHICAGO—Three days after the deadly terrorist attack at the Excalibur, the area surrounding the club is still being quarantined.

Homeland Security press officer Lt. Gregor Montone said, "It is going to be like this for the foreseeable future. There's no end in sight. Despite our best efforts, the air is still deadly. Think of it as Ground Zero. Citizens should avoid downtown like it's the [expletive deleted] plague."

The death toll from the disaster has risen to 93, and there are at least 20 others in critical condition, some with third-degree burns and others with respiratory damage from the bio-weapons.

Marlon Wooten of the Centers for Disease Control in Atlanta believes the chemical used in the attack was a cyanide composite.

"It is possible it was straight cyanide," Wooten said. "Normally, something like that would dissipate in several hours. We have no clue how or when this will scatter. We hope that the chemical fingerprint will

point us in the direction of the solution and the perpe-
trators."

Illinois governor Wilton Jacobs and Chicago mayor
Elvin Washington will tour the event zone this afternoon.

Andi-Licious

The Useless Musings of Sophomoric Sophomore Andrea Daltrey

JUNE 8

PSOA

I haven't slept in I don't know how long and I'm exhausted
but it's okay because I'm happy for that matter happier than
I've ever been because I walk around in what I've decided
to call a Perpetual State of Arousal or PSOA and this PSOA
is amazing and I wish that everybody could feel what I feel
and I'm trying to get everybody to feel what I feel but it's getting
tiring like I sometimes think my pussy is getting destroyed by all
the cock it's been getting but I'm not sure because it feels fine
while I'm fucking but it hurts when I'm walking around but it's
kind of a nice hurt and once in a while I even have an orgasm
while it's hurting which is why PSOA is sometimes difficult so I
thought it would be a good idea to give it a rest but I needed to
come and it's not the same when I do it myself so I decided to
find a girl because it never hurts to experiment so I called my
friend jennifer and asked her to come over and she said it's after
midnight and I hadn't even noticed so I apologized and told her I
was going to visit her and she tried to talk me out of it but I told
her it was important and I needed her and she said she'd never
heard me sound scared like that so I should come on over so I
get over there about twenty minutes later and she's wearing a

robe and slippers with nothing underneath and before we got in
I told her how pretty she looked and she thanked me then asked
me what was wrong and I told her to give me a hug and she did
and then I kissed her and then the same thing happened that
had been happening which was she melted into me and I think
she came right away and then I pulled her into her apartment
and threw her down on the sofa and took her robe off and I was
right she wasn't wearing anything underneath and I licked her
tits and they tasted like candy and then I licked her pussy and
I'd never tasted a pussy before and it tasted like blueberries
and then after she came like three more times I sat on her face
and she licked and licked and licked and I came and came and
came and then I got up off of her and her face was covered
with blue stuff and she looked so pretty and I kissed her on the
cheek and then she stopped breathing and I got the fuck out
of there and I called 911 and I hid in the bushes by her house
and I watched the ambulance take her away and then I called
the hospital when I got home to find out how she was doing
and they asked me if I was family and I told them that I was her
cousin and they told me that she died and I started screaming
and crying and I couldn't stop so I called janine's doctor and told
him I needed him and he came over because they all come over
after I've fucked them and I fucked him and he came forever
and his come was blue and then his face turned blue and then
he died and I couldn't help it but I bit off his ear and ate it and I
threw up all over the place and when I was done throwing up I
ate his other ear and I can't believe I'm writing this all down and
for some reason I can't stop but it doesn't really matter because
nobody's going to think this is real anyhow and I have to make
myself come again or else I'm going to die so I'm going to jerk
off then I'm going to call that guy I met at coyote ugly and I'm
going to fuck him until I kill him and I can't wait because it will
be the most beautiful thing in the world

http://www .thetruthaboutzombies.com

Welcome to the Truth About Zombies

COMMENTS

To all the other folks out there who think they're going crazy . . .
You're not.

I haven't slept in like a week. I'm afraid to. I've guzzled about a zillion cans of Red Bull because nobody sells speed around here anymore. You can get all the weed you want, but good luck finding a handful of pills. As much as I'd love to get baked, I'm afraid that if I fall asleep, I'll stay asleep. If you could call it sleep.

I'm at an all-night Internet café right now. They say there's safety in numbers, but based on what I've seen, it's not about where you are or who you're with. It's about paying attention. It's about using all of your senses, especially hearing and smell. Because those fuckers aren't subtle.

I didn't know jack about zombie mythology until last week. After you see your brother get attacked and eaten by a gray guy with exploding boils on his face, and after you hear that you aren't the only one who lost a family member or a friend, you kind of want to see what you're up against. So I read what Wikipedia had to say about it, and I went to a bunch of horror chat boards, and I skimmed through a Brian Keene book, and I even watched the remake of *Dawn of the Dead*, and I came to one conclusion:

None of these people know shit about zombies.

First of all, they don't all shuffle. Some of those fuckers can move fast, like Usain Bolt fast. The one that got my brother came after me, and if he hadn't tripped over the curb, and fallen into an oncoming bus, and gotten his head crushed like a grape, I'd be one of them.

Second of all, they function at a higher level than you'd think. It's not like they wander around with their arms out in front of them and moan, "Braaaaaaains! Braaaaaaaains! Braaaaaaaains!" No, they come after you, and even though they aren't exactly Einsteins, they can track you down.

Third of all, some of them are scared of us. This is why I stay awake. This is why I swill down all that nasty-ass Red Bull. If you're awake, you can defend yourself, and if you can defend yourself, that'll keep at least half of them away from you.

Fourth of all, they can be killed, and it's not like you have to do it in any special way. If you get them in either the head or the heart, they're toast. And you don't have to use a platinum axe or a silver bullet to do it.

So if you're in the Denver area and you're having problems with zombies, please e-mail me at JohnZee1911@yahoo.com, or call my cell: (303) 846-****. Let's get a bunch of us together and figure this shit out.

John from Denver, CO
June 8, 12:10 AM

John, I'm outside of Phoenix, and I'm dealing with the same stuff as you.

She didn't come after me, because I ran away after she turned my parents. How do I know my parents were turned? Because when I got home an hour later, they were gone, and from what I've seen, the creatures don't carry around their victims, so Mommy and Daddy must have left on their own. So I grabbed my Daddy's Winchester from the box under his bed, took some food and water from the kitchen, went into my bedroom, and locked the door. Great plan, right?

Then I read your posting, and I figured it was time to do my part. It's not like I had anything to lose. So I put every bullet I could find inside my backpack (and there were a lot, because Daddy was kind of paranoid) and hit the streets.

I took down twelve of them, and it felt great. I'm back home now, but I don't know what to do. Should I go out and keep killing them? Should I stay at home until it blows over? Will it blow over? The stories on the news are dismissive and barely detailed, so I don't know if it's only happening in a few places or if it's happening everywhere and they're covering it up.

My e-mail address is LissieLiss@msn.com, and my cell is (480) 481-****. And don't call me just to be an asshole. Call me if you can help, or if I can help you.

Alyssa from Mesa, AZ

June 9, 2:16 PM

ROLLING STONE

6.18.2009

Speed Kills, Now More Than Ever

How Texas Has Become the New Hell

BY KATHLEEN NESBIT

Like most high schoolers, Corky Davidson has facial issues.
The craters are a good three millimeters deep. His scars and
scabs could've been the result of chicken pox, or measles, or
a wasp attack. Then there're the purplish splotches, and the
reddish scratches, and those thumbprint-sized yellow things
on his cheek that defy description.

I'm going to just go ahead and say it: Corky Davidson's
complexion is fucked.

Now, I'm not the kind of writer to pass judgment on a
subject. In 2003, I even wrote an article about the Bush ad-
ministration that didn't contain a single discouraging word.
(Okay, maybe there were a few discouraging words, but
nothing so bad that it required a trip to the principal's, er, the
editor's office.) So why, you may ask, am I dumping on this
poor high school kid from Austin? Why am I using the kind
of language and attitude you'd normally only get from the
sophomore-class bully? Why, why, why?

Because Corky Davidson is an idiot who deserves to be
ridiculed by his favorite magazine. And quit laughing. I'm
not kidding.

Corky is 16, the youngest of three. His 20-year-old brother,
Craig, is off in Iraq, and his 18-year-old sister, Danielle,
is getting ready for her freshman year at the University of

Miami. Corky's parents are as all-American as you can get: Mel Davidson is a history teacher, and his wife, Jori, makes fresh fruit pies at the local bakery. So how did Corky—"the Corkster" to his friends—become such a douchebag?

Simple: drugs.

Now, I have no issues with illegal drugs in general. I've done my fair share—a little weed here, a little X there—and I like them. I like them a lot. I think we should legalize the hell out of them.

Well, *most* of them.

The one mind-alterer that should be eradicated from the face of the earth is methamphetamine, a.k.a. dextromethamphetamine, a.k.a. methylamphetamine, a.k.a. N-methylamphetamine, a.k.a. desoxyephedrine, a.k.a. the douchebag drug, a.k.a. crystal meth.

I can speak with authority on this. I've tried meth. Several times. More than several times. Like maybe several dozen times. And each time I smoked it, or snorted it, or stuck it in a brownie, I became a raging jerk. I screwed over my friends, I stole from my parents, my writing became horrible (some would say it didn't have far to fall), and I had lots and lots of idiotic sex.

The weird thing about meth is that even though you know it's turning you into a piece of trash, you want to share it with your friends. Or, at the very least, sell it to your friends, so you can have some extra pocket change to buy some of your own.

Corky—who, it should be noted, is an athlete and used to be considered one of the big men on campus—first smoked meth after a basketball game in which he was held to six points and two rebounds. (He averaged 10.2 points and five boards. What a traumatic comedown that must've been for him. The perfect time to spark it up.) The story then becomes familiar and, frankly, a bit tired: He tried it again, and again, and again; then he got kicked off the basketball team; then his grades took a nosedive; then he started missing classes, then entire days; then his parents threatened to put him in rehab, but, like many addicts, he charmed his way out of that; and so on, and so on, and so on.

Here's where things went off the rails.

After Corkscrew got canned from his job at Pizza Hut, he met a 20-year-old meth head known only as "Scary Barry" and fell into the manufacturing end of things. Meth is easy to make, and even though his brain was becoming further eroded each day, Corky managed to put together batch after batch, which he sold. Then he used the profits to do whatever it is that moronic meth heads like to do.

One sunny Monday afternoon, Scary Barry—who sounds like a real piece of work himself—brought Corkenheimer a new recipe. Corky says, "I was like, 'What the fuck, dude, the other stuff was working fine.'"

According to Corky, Scary Barry said, "Use this, or, I swear to sunny Jesus in heaven, I will kill you. And I'll have fun doing it."

Corky was a follower, a spineless weenie who'd do whatever his meth guru told him. So on May 4, Corky toodled over to the apartment of fellow meth dork and Scary Barry acolyte Al Darnell, mixed up a batch of the stuff, and boom goes the dynamite. The ensuing fire burned down Darnell's entire apartment building. Three people were killed, 12 were injured, and the property damage was ugly. Even a month later, the place still reeks.

But here's the weird part. There was no evidence of a meth fire.

Austin, Texas's chief fire officer, Dennis Leary—and yes, that's Dennis Leary like the fireman-worshipping comic, except with an additional "n" in Dennis—says that meth fires are almost always easy to detect. "They have a distinct odor, almost like human hair, and that smell stays around for a good long time. Additionally, the people who cause these sorts of fires aren't generally the brightest bulbs in the chandelier, so they tend to leave evidence everywhere."

The investigators who checked Darnell's building after the fire came away with the belief that the conflagration was caused by faulty wiring. The investigation ended about 45 minutes after it started, and Cork-A-Doodle-Doo went right back to work.

Davidson took his wandering minstrel show over to his

girlfriend Antonia Beresford's house. (Antonia is 25. The only reason she dated Corky is that she, too, was a tweaker. I didn't have a boyfriend when I was 16, nor when I was 25. Some meth heads have all the luck.) Same recipe, same result, except this time, lives were lost, specifically those of Beresford's two roommates. Beresford, who was on the other side of the room when the meth "lab" went kerflooey, suffered only minor burns. Corky, however, ended up with his first dose of pizza face.

But that didn't stop him. His hair was still smoking when he went back to work the next week.

At this point in our tale, you may be asking, *Why would this kid, this tweaker, this dipshit, keep cooking his junk?*

Simple: It was some good shit. According to the locals, it was the *best* shit.

Tweaker #1, female, 21: "It was so much mellower than the stuff we'd been getting in the 'hood. It sped you up while slowing you down."

Tweaker #2, male, 28: "The best thing about it was there was no hangover, and meth hangovers can be, like, *crippling.*"

Tweaker #3, female, 20: "Not only was it good, but it was cheap. They were practically giving it away."

Fantastic. Just fan-fucking-tastic.

Turns out that Corky wasn't the only person using Scary Barry's recipe. Fires raged across town—Chief Leary said there were 47 of them, and those were the ones that were reported; he's convinced there were more—and the local fire experts were baffled. Their theory was that it was the work of a very clever pack of arsonists, but they didn't have any evidence to support that. They brought government experts from Washington, DC, and civilian experts from New York, and came up with bupkus.

So how did they catch Corky? Here, I now offer you the reason that I keep referring to Corka-Cola as a moron.

Corky wasn't a moron because he did drugs, although tweaking is pretty moronic.

Corky wasn't a moron because he made drugs. After all,

Pizza Hut wasn't going to rehire him—would you?—and the guy had to somehow bring in *some* money.

Corky wasn't a moron because he burned down four buildings, killing two people and causing several thousand dollars' worth of damage. Sometimes, y'know, shit happens.

No, Corky was a moron because he bragged about it on Twitter.

This Tweet from Corky to Scary Barry: *Burn baby burn disco inferno!*

This Tweet from Scary Barry to Corky: *you do well my son. keep up the good work. newer and better recipe to follow.*

This Tweet from Corky to Scary Barry: *To quote Beavis and/or Butt-Head: FIRE FIRE FIRE. Man, I'm good at this stuff!*

This Tweet from somebody called GTownRepresent to Corky: *Was that apartment deal yours?*

This Tweet from Corky to GTownRepresent: *Hell to the yeah! E me at CorkyDeeTX (at) msn for deets.*

And there it is. An e-mail address. Give it up for Corky Davidson, ladies and gentlemen, a genius for the ages.

The FBI hunted down Corky. The five agents I spoke with refused to discuss how, and I have no problem with that, although I'd bet that whatever they did involved some computer tracking and would have some folks kvetching about that whole personal rights thing. If that's the case, I have no problem with it. If the Feds want to track *my* Tweets, fine, I have nothing to hide.

The bad news is that they haven't found Scary Barry, and that's becoming a problem, because Barry is clearly the mastermind, and Austin continues to burn. Sixth Street has all but closed up, and to my mind, Sixth Street *is* Austin. Without Sixth Street, Austin is Texas, and Texas is, well, it's Texas. Nuff said.

From his cell at the Gardner Betts Juvenile Center in Austin, Corky told me they'll never catch Barry. "The dude's practically invisible. I met him once, but to be honest,

I probably wouldn't even recognize him if I tripped on him. But even if I did, I wouldn't turn him in or anything. I think what he's doing is great. I wish *everybody* could take a hit of his stuff, because it makes you feel like you're kissing God or something. And as soon as I get out of here, I'm going to find Barry and help him. We can change the world, one tweaker at a time."

Seriously, what an idiot.

June 18, 2009—Brian is obsessive about American
television. CNN is on in our little headquarters
99 percent of the time, and the other 1 percent is
split between MSNBC and Fox News. Brian finds CNN
the most neutral. I have no feelings one way or the
other. Up until recently, it was merely background
noise to me.

Over the last week, however, I have been paying
close attention, in part because I want to find out if my
friends at Homeland Security are as clueless as they
usually are, and my answer is an unequivocal yes. The
authorities have zero idea as to our identities. Or if
they do, they are not talking, which I have found is quite
unlike them. When they find a clue, they tend to trumpet
at least a hint of it from the mountaintops. After all, Joe
Taxpayer must be appeased.

This is all so easy. Enjoyable, even.

The other reason I have been viewing the television
so much is that I seem to have started a trend. And I
could not be prouder.

In Miami, a twenty-two-year-old white male drove
his car into a club called Club Play. The crude explosive
device strapped to his front bumper blew up upon impact.
Only two people were killed, but there were countless
injuries. The footage that CNN ran was gruesome.

In Atlanta, at a club called Masquerade, somebody put
a trace amount of sarin in the ventilation system. It was

MIDNIGHT MOVIE

not enough to cause any fatalities, but several hundred people had to be taken to the hospital.

Here in Chicago, somebody set off a nail gun on the first floor of Water Tower Place. Again, no fatalities, but plenty of injuries.

Nobody has claimed responsibility for any of these incidents, which I find delicious. If you do not know where the violence has originated, it is that much more terrifying. Let us say that Hamas sent out a communiqué that they were responsible for the sarin attack. People in Georgia would be sure to cross the street whenever they came across a Middle Eastern male. But since the attacker (or attackers) has remained silent, the locals must fear everybody. For all they know, it was a white supremacist— which is actually a possibility, as Masquerade is a predominantly black club—or a gang member, or a former club employee hell-bent on revenge for his dismissal. What a way to create terror!

If I were to venture a guess, I would say these are all copycat crimes. There is something in the air, something wonderful and horrible, something magical and frightening, something on the brink of chaos and renewal.

NEW YORK TIMES MAGAZINE

THE SPRING OF OUR DISCONTENT

JUNE 18, 2009

BY JESSICA BRANDEIS

People are scared.

People are angry.

People are depressed.

People are sweaty.

People are burning.

People are exploding.

People are broke.

Welcome to the spring of 2009, a spring replete with suicide bombers, burning cities, an inordinate number of missing persons, and a new strain of STD that has doctors baffled. To paraphrase classic British rockers the Zombies, it's the time of the season of misery.

Dr. Stavros Alexander, a social sciences professor at Columbia University, claims that this outbreak of what he calls "negativity" is far from unprecedented. "If you'll recall, the New York City of 1977 was an unequivocal mess. You had David Berkowitz's murder spree; you had a massive blackout that led to massive looting and an almost-riot; there was a rash of arson in both the Bronx and Brooklyn; there was a garbage strike that turned the Manhattan streets into a junkyard, a problem that was particularly galling because there

MIDNIGHT MOVIE

was a subway strike that forced people to walk more than they ever had before.

"We live in different times now," Dr. Alexander says, continuing, "so the incidences are more drastic and violent. For instance, the fires in Austin, Texas, are being attributed to incompetent methamphetamine labs, whereas the 1977 Brooklyn and Bronx fires were simply the work of a firebug. You see, nobody was mixing crystal meth in their basement in '77, nor did we have terrorists who had access to professional-strength bombs and chemical weapons, and the only sexually transmitted diseases that the general public had to deal with were syphilis, herpes, and gonorrhea. Modern times bring us a modern negativity."

The issue of the missing individuals appears to be most troublesome in the western and southwestern United States. Phoenix police chief Russell Crosbie believes that the issue is being blown out of proportion. "It's a sad fact of our society that people disappear all the time, and it's generally nothing sinister. Mostly it's a person who wants to get away from their life for whatever reason, and they'll usually turn back up in a day, or a week, or a month. As everybody is aware, the Internet has turned this world into a global village, so if a family member or a loved one goes missing, it's easier to alert the world. I don't think more people are disappearing. I think it's just being more widely reported."

Dr. Christian Wade, chief of urology at Johns Hopkins Hospital in Baltimore, agrees with Alexander and Crosbie about the public's misguided take on the spring of 2009. However, he is concerned about the new STD strain. "It's difficult to study," Wade says, "because so few people have acquired it. The primary symptom in both men and women is an oddly colored discharge. If you notice something out of the ordinary, it is recommended that you see your doctor immediately."

Even though none of these incidents are related, online wags have cited the cause of the country's woes as "the Game," a moniker that seems to be edging its way into the mainstream, and in a way, it's a perfect encapsulation of the weirdness that is the spring of 2009.

THE NEW ENGLAND JOURNAL OF MEDICINE

June 20, 2009

The Emerging Risk of a Sexually Transmitted Disease Involving Discolored Discharge and Heightened Desire

BY CHANDAHAR ZOONI, PHD, MPH; CORNELIUS REMAR, MD, MPH; MARY GRIFFIN-WATTS, PHD, MPH

Context: Transmission of sexually transmitted disease that can be passed via genital and oral sexual engagement.

TOBE HOOPER WITH ALAN GOLDSHER

Design: Cross-sectional survey conducted May 12, 2009, to June 12, 2009.

Setting and Participants: A total of 20 clients of the Denver Public Health HIV Counseling and Testing Site in Colorado.

Main Outcome Measures: Self-report of heightened sexual desire, increasing pain in the genital area, and a blue discharge in both men and women.

Results: Of the 20 clients, 16 were male (80%); all were white (100%), heterosexual (100%), and aged 20 to 50 years (100%). Of those, 16 (80%) had had multiple sexual partners over the 14 days prior to the test. Of those, 10 (50%) had 2–4 such partners; 6 (30%) had 5–10 such partners, and 4 (20%) had 11–20 such partners. All (100%) reported the blue discharge; 18 (90%) reported painful and swollen genitals. All (100%) reported increased, painful sexual desire.

Conclusions: The strain is completely debilitating, as it renders the sufferer unable to function without repeated sexual encounters through their waking hours. It appears the strain can be passed via either penetration (vaginal, oral, or anal) or physical exposure to either male or female discharge. It is a possibility that it can also be transmitted via saliva, but the testing period did not allow for sufficient time to draw any meaningful conclusions in that venue. Additional testing will be required before a treatment protocol is recommended. As it is vital that this remain contained, it is advised to quarantine any patient who demonstrates a symptom.

Pre-publication Notes:

- Just prior to publication, a female lab technician at the Denver Public Health HIV Counseling and Testing Site in Colorado was exposed to the virus via saliva transmitted by Patient #3 (white, male, heterosexual, age 32). Symptoms were detected in 52 minutes. The lab technician requested she be quarantined. As of deadline, she has exhibited acute sexual desire and blue discharge.

- Just prior to publication, Patient #13 at the Denver Public Health HIV Counseling and Testing Site in Colorado (white, female, heterosexual, age 21) assaulted a male doctor. Both individuals have since expired.

ERICK LAUGHLIN:

The 9:33 thing stopped. Just like that. And I was fine. Never found out why it started. Never found out why it ended. Never found out what those red things were. Didn't want to dwell on it too much. So I moved on.

Bad call. *Really* bad call.

Truth be told, all of Austin was in a state of denial. What with all the fires—I think there'd been over fifty of them at this point—the city was a mess, but nobody wanted to talk about it, myself included. Everybody I knew went about their business as if nothing was wrong, as if people hadn't been burned beyond recognition, as if you could walk down the street without smelling something smoldering.

Sixth Street had some . . . I guess you could call it *collateral smoke damage,* and a bunch of clubs had to shut their doors. But nobody discussed it. Me, Theo, and our bass player, Jamal, lived for our band, but when we couldn't gig anymore, we were all like, *Whatever, shit happens, things'll pick up again soon enough.*

So I reviewed movies. And visited Janine.

JANINE DALTREY:

I got incompletes in all of my classes. The professors were cool about it. How could they not be? I mean, what're they going to do, tell the girl who'd been beaten within an inch of her life that since she didn't turn in her African history term paper because she was in the hospital, she's getting a big honking F?

I didn't go out much. I knew Dave was in jail, but the vibe in the city was *off,* so I was perfectly content staying parked on the couch. Naturally, just like in the hospital, I watched a whole lot of tube.

Things were pretty messed up, but I was very, I don't know, sanguine about the whole thing. Probably because I was whacked out on Vicodin.

Erick also kept my mind occupied. He was on the make, and I was fine with that, because he was being a sweetie about it. He'd sometimes come over with a big bag of groceries and make me dinner, which was fortunate, because I was unbelievably sick of ordering out. He brought over tons of DVDs—the studios sent him everything weeks before they were in stores—and he'd hang out for a double feature. He probably wouldn't like hearing this, but it felt like he was my father, or my older brother, you know, a family member who was protecting me. And even though on paper it seemed like I had nothing to worry about—I knew that nobody was making meth in my basement, and I didn't think somebody would suicide-bomb my apartment building—it was still nice to know that somebody had my back.

June 21, 2009

All I do is push-ups. Push-up, push-up, push-up. 5, 10, 50, 100, 500. I feel strong. I can see the veins in my biceps. My forearms look like Popeye's. My neck is corded. I see the guys in the shower checking me out, not because they want to rape me. Because they're scared. They can sense my power. I bet Janine would sense my power. I bet she'd want to be my girlfriend again. I bet she'd like it. I'd tear her apart, and she'd beg for more.

June 22, 2009

I'm hungry all the time, and those fuckers don't give us enough food. I ate a rat this morning. I stepped on it, then ate it, bones and all. I couldn't even taste it. It gave me energy. That's good. There are always rats around, so I'll always have energy.

June 23, 2009

It was two in the morning or something, and I couldn't sleep. I was bored, and since I had nothing else to do, I punched the wall. I bled all over the place, but it didn't hurt. Maybe something was broken. Maybe not. But I could still move it. So I beat the shit out of my cell mate. I did it fast, so I could do the job before one of those dickhead guards showed up. It was awesome.

EMERGENCY MEMORANDUM

TO: Federal Bureau of Investigation, Austin Field Office

        Texas Department of Public Safety/Texas Rangers

        Austin Police Department

FROM: Sergeant Wilmer Arb, Austin Police Department

SUBJECT: Escapee

June 24, 2009, 4:13 A.M.

To Whom It May Concern:

Please alert all personnel to be on the lookout for David Cranford (physical description and photograph attached). Cranford escaped from the Austin City Jail at 9:12 P.M. on June 23, 2009.

On the evening in question, Cranford assaulted his cell mate, La-Marcus Jackson, with his bare hands. When guard Gerard Clovis came to Jackson's aid at 8:54 P.M., Cranford assaulted him, then relieved him of his billy club before Clovis could handcuff Cranford. At 9:01, Cranford assaulted and killed Jackson with the billy club, then took Clovis hostage. Personnel could not subdue Cranford, and he exited out the front door. Cranford then dragged Clovis to his personal vehicle and forced him to drive to whereabouts unknown. Cranford threatened to murder Clovis if he was followed, so officers did not immediately pursue.

Pursuit began at 9:21. Clovis's automobile was found on Interstate 35 a ¼ mile north of exit 246 (Howard Lane). Clovis was deceased; cause of death: fractured skull. Cranford was not in the vicinity.

Cranford is considered armed and dangerous, thus the use of force is acceptable in pursuit.

ERICK LAUGHLIN:

Janine and I were watching *Slumdog Millionaire* when David Cranford broke down the door to her apartment with his bare hands. We found out later that one of Janine's neighbors let him into the building. Sometimes southerners are too fucking polite for their own good.

It all happened fast, man. Janine was screaming before I even registered what had happened and who it was, but I guess if your old boyfriend almost kills you, you're on pretty high alert.

There was a little wooden table by Janine's front door, where she kept her keys, and wallet, and sunglasses. Cranford picked it up and threw it across the room at us. She was fine—she ducked—but I got nailed in the shoulder and the face. Gashed up my forehead pretty good.

Now, like I said, I'm not the least bit adept when it comes to fighting, but after Janine jumped behind the sofa and screamed bloody murder, instinct took over.

Cranford picked up a five-foot-high standing lamp, took two steps across the room, and took a baseball-bat swing at my head. I dropped to the ground and rolled toward his legs. I obviously surprised the shit out of him—I'm sure he took one look at me when he busted into the apartment and thought, *I can take this emo pussy*—so he lost his balance and fell over me, face-first on the sofa.

I managed to pull myself to my feet before he did, so I picked up the glass coffee table and dropped it on his head. It broke, and he screamed, and he was gashed up far worse than I was, but he managed to stand up and dive at my chest.

Again, I flopped onto the floor, and again, he missed me, and this time, he ended up face-first on the floor. I grabbed the lamp, reared back, and hit him as hard as I could on the back of his neck. The motherfucker barely even flinched, and stood up like it was nothing, and went after me. He got me in a headlock and punched me in the nose, then threw me on the floor. I landed on my temple, and I passed the fuck out.

JANINE DALTREY:

When I got out of the hospital, my parents insisted I stay at their place until I got healthy, but even though I love them, that was the last thing I wanted to do. Daddy was pissed about my decision, but he seemed to feel better about the whole thing after he lent me two of his handguns. He said, "Y'all keep one in your bedroom and one in the living room, darlin', and don't be afraid to use 'em."

I wasn't afraid at all. I shot David five times, and I killed him, and I don't feel the least bit bad about it. For that matter, I wish somebody would reanimate him so I can kill him again.

ERICK LAUGHLIN:

Seriously, Janine is a superhero. She killed Cranford, she dealt with the police, and she got me to the hospital, all while I was out on my ass with a concussion.

Yeah, I don't remember shit about what happened between the time that Cranford almost killed me and when I woke up in the hospital, feeling like I'd fallen off a cliff. I just know that I was damn glad the first thing I saw was Janine's face.

THE MIAMI HERALD

6.25.2009

BROWNSVILLE FOUR-ALARM FIRE LEADS TO RIOT

BY MOIRA SOAMES

MIAMI—A four-alarm fire in the Brownsville section of Miami at 2:15 A.M. escalated into a full-blown riot.

The fire, which originated on the 5300 block of 23rd Street, is not believed to be related to the rash of crystal methamphetamine fires that have swept through the southern United States.

As firemen, paramedics, and police arrived on the scene, two bystanders engaged in a verbal altercation that led to fisticuffs. Two men, believed to be members of the People Nation street gang, pulled guns and opened fire. Neighbors spilled from the houses and took to the streets, where the fighting became

NEBRASKA CITY NEWS PRESS

JUNE 25, 2009

VIOLENCE BREAKS OUT AT MINOR LEAGUE BASE-BALL GAME

TEN DEAD, 29 HOSPITALIZED

BY LAURENCE SPARKES

OMAHA—Ten were killed and 29 more were injured at Johnny Rosenblatt Stadium during the seventh-inning stretch of the Omaha Royals/Oklahoma City Red-Hawks game last night.

Daniel Martin Brooks, 21, of Omaha assaulted his date, Claire Marie Melvin, 19, of Omaha with a baseball bat he had purchased at the concession area.

Bystanders subdued Brooks after he hit and knocked out Melvin. It was then that Dexter Joe Rayburn, 41, of Omaha removed the bat from Brooks's hands and hit him across the windpipe.

Moments later, it became a full-scale melee. Security guards were unable to keep control, and the fight raged until Omaha police arrived on the scene.

The fight came to an end after over a dozen people were subdued with Tasers.

Brooks and Rayburn are among the deceased. The full list of casualties is available online at the Omaha

THE DETROIT NEWS

JUNE 25, 2009

SNIPER DEATH TOLL ON THE RISE

31 NOW AMONG THE DECEASED

BY NEIL OSWALD

DETROIT—The shooting spree that has terrorized the Warren section of Detroit continues.

Last night, another two murders were attributed to the man authorities now refer to as "the Warren Sniper." The names of the victims will be released pending notification of their respective families.

Detroit police spokesman Ashley Arthur says the department has not ruled out the possibility that there is more than one assailant. "A copycat is not out of the question. The weapon used in all of the murders, a Glock 9 mm, model 26, is a relatively easily accessible gun. It could also be the work of an organized group."

Arthur says police have no leads.

A hotline has been set up. Anybody with information leading to the capture of the assailants should call

June 26, 2009—I have tasted blood. I have tasted blood, and I like it. I have tasted blood, and I realize that tasting food was a waste of time. That law enforcement was a waste of time. That America was a waste of time. That music was a waste of time. That movies were a waste of time. That sex was a waste of time. That love was a waste of time. That family was a waste of time. That life was a waste of time.

The only thing that makes sense is the taste of blood, the taste of suffering, the taste of death. I do not know why I did not realize it sooner.

I despise the fact that I wasted so much of my time on earth. Though this might not seem logical, it is this sense of wasted days, months, and years that leads me to today's farewell.

I am not going out quietly. I refuse to go out quietly. I refuse to go out alone. I will take hundreds with me. Quite possibly thousands.

Two hours ago, I loaded my van with gasoline, propane, fertilizer, nitroglycerine, frozen orange juice, and all of our remaining homemade pipe bombs. At 1:00, I will leave the house and drive to Wrigley Field. When I get to the corner of Addison and Sheffield, I will turn my car onto the sidewalk and put all of my weight on the gas pedal. I will burst through the turnstiles and drive the van as far into the stadium as I possibly can. If it all susses out correctly, I will be able to get close to the box seats. I will then light my single stick of dynamite and place it on top of my pile of explosives. Then I will close my eyes and feel the magnificent heat. I will be incinerated, as will anybody within a 500-yard radius. As Wrigley Field is an older building, I am confident that the explosives will cause extensive structural damage. My ultimate hope is that the upper deck collapses onto the lower deck.

My only regret is that I will be directly on top of the blast, thus I will not be conscious for the aftermath.

Andi-Licious

The Useless Musings of Sophomoric Sophomore Andrea Daltrey

JUNE 27, 2009

It hurts it hurts so bad it won't go away I'm raw down there and it's bleeding red and leaking blue and it's coming out purple and it stings like pins but I need cock I have to have cock I can't go two hours without cock but my magic kisses stopped working and nobody wants to fuck me anymore because I'm ugly and fat and my pussy leaks purple and all my friends hate me now because I stole all their boyfriends and girlfriends but I couldn't help it they don't understand what it's like if they could feel it they'd know how awful and wonderful it is and they'd probably fuck me themselves thank god for janine she's the only one who'll see me and she's with erick all the time but for some reason I don't want erick even though he's pretty cute wait that's not true I wanted erick at one point but it stopped I mean if he said he wanted to fuck me I'd let him and he'd be fucked like he never was fucked before but maybe not because since my magic kisses went away and boys don't like me and I don't like me and I probably don't fuck like I used to so maybe I'd be just another girl to him and the only thing that would make me different is that I'd get his cock covered in purple juice and I didn't tell anybody and I can't believe I'm writing this but I

176

blew my nose yesterday and the snot was blue and I looked
really close at myself in the mirror and I swear that the
whites of my eyes had a blue tint to them and that won't do
that won't do that simply won't do so I'm going to masturbate
then take an ambien and go to sleep so I won't have to think
about sex or blue pussy juice oh my god I hate myself and I
hate my life

FROM: HottieMcHottie1993@gmail.com
TO: DianeDee123@yahoo.com
SUBJECT: re: the quake
DATE: June 28, 2009

Dee—

You probably won't write me back, and that's fine. You're the only person who's been there since the beginning, so I don't have to explain everything. I don't have the time. I need to do this NOW.

So a couple of weeks ago, I stopped feeling. It was like my skin was dead. Like when I showered, I couldn't feel the wet. I stuck my head in the freezer, and I couldn't feel the cold. I put my hand in the oven, and I couldn't feel the hot.

I also don't feel anything on the INSIDE. Nothing's funny. Nothing's sad. Nothing's scary. Nothing's weird. It's all flat. And I don't care that it's flat. I don't care about anything.

A few days ago, I took a piece of paper and gave myself a paper cut on my arm. It didn't hurt at all. I went to the kitchen, and cut open a lemon, and rubbed it all over the cut, and there was nothing. I cut myself 19 more times, and I was still numb. I bled a little bit, and my blood was red.

You might be asking why I'd tell you that my blood was red. Well, because when I did my paper cuts this morning (I've been giving myself between 15 and 20 paper cuts each day when I wake up), I bled blue. It was the same blue that came from DOWN THERE, bright and almost aqua. It didn't bother me, though. And it should have. I should have told somebody.

I should have gone to the hospital. I mean, wouldn't you be bothered by BLUE GOO coming out of DOWN THERE? I'm not. And I should be. Which means I should be gone.

I'm going into the bathroom, and I'm stepping into the shower, and I'm bringing lots of paper and lots of lemons and a knife with me. I'm going to do it slowly, so maybe I can feel something on the way out. That might make the whole thing worth it.

One thing I should tell you. Up until the numbness started, I missed you a lot. Now I don't really care.

Gwennie

http://www .thetruthaboutzombies.com

Welcome to the Truth About Zombies

June 30, 2009

COMMENTS

I don't know how this hasn't made the mainstream news. It's such bullshit. The government or somebody has to be telling the media what to air and what not to air, because if they were doing their jobs, if things were right, CNN would be all up in our asses.

It's the middle of the afternoon, and the streets of Laredo are empty. It's not like Laredo was a bustling metropolis or anything, but there were always people out and about, doing their shopping or whatever. Now, nothing. Everybody's probably hiding in their basement, like they're expecting a tornado. I'm the only moron at street level, but somebody has to report the news, and it may as well be me.

So what have I seen firsthand? Well, last night, right around 11:00, a 5'3" white woman ran up to a 6'5" black man and killed him with her bare hands in probably thirty seconds. Then when he was on the ground, she pulled off his head, also with her bare hands. (I should mention that the spinal column came with it. But after what I've seen over the last two weeks, that didn't even faze me a little bit.) Then she stuck her face in his open neck hole and went to town. I could hear the slurping from down the block. A couple hours later, I saw the black guy shuffling down Northpoint Drive. His head was back on, but at a weird angle. Again, totally not fazed.

What else? Oh, yesterday afternoon, my high school junior-year ethics teacher, Mrs. Crampton, who had to be seventy-four when I took her class in 2000, put her hands through the plate glass window at a clothing store in Mall del Norte and yanked out one of the mannequins, then tried to eat it. Her teeth flew everywhere. One thing I'm realizing is that zombies, while scary, and smelly, and strong as all get-out, aren't particularly bright. I think they can be outfoxed. I haven't figured out how, but when I do, I'll post it here.

If somebody's reading this and they want to communicate, BBM or SMS me at (956) 472-****. But don't reach out if you're going to waste my time.

George from Laredo, TX

June 30, 1:51 PM

I'm almost dead. I can feel it in me. I can feel it taking overrrrr. It's awfu;;;;;l. If you see one of them, ruars awaq. Fasdjsfkl;lkjfadsfjldfjsfjkl.fjkdlsa;jfkdls;afjfkld;saka. HeLP. Afdsjklladfksdfjklslkjfas goodbee goodbye gooooooooooooooooooooo

loewfqhof from Biloxi, MS

June 30, 5:13 PM

TOBE HOOPER WITH ALAN GOLDSHER

Let's start from scratch. Let's tear the roof off this mother. Let's burn baby burn. Let's burn down the house. Let's kick out the jams. Let me hear some of that rock 'n' roll music. The world is my oyster, the world is my bitch, I'm still alive, so scratch my motherfucking itch.

Everybody's dying. All I'm doing is speeding things along.

Back to work. Lots to do.

Charles Starkweather from Everywhere, NY

June 30, 6:02 PM

THIS WEBSITE (WWW.THETRUTHABOUTZOMBIES.COM) HAS BEEN CLOSED UNTIL FURTHER NOTICE. PLEASE COME BACK LATER.

JULY 3, 2009

OBITUARIES
RECENT OBITUARIES AND DEATH NOTICES

Andrea Dale Daltrey, age 20, passed away July 1, 2009. Our baby girl was called home by our Lord and Savior way too soon for those of us who remain. Andi was a vibrant and spirited young lady who lit up any room with her beautiful smile and outgoing personality. She had goals and ambitions for life that she will not achieve, including earning a college degree from the same school from which her mother graduated. Although she was unable to complete her goals and aspirations here on earth, they will be fulfilled in the arms of our Heavenly Father. She'll forever remain a bright light in our memories and will always be her daddy's little girl, her momma's angel princess, and her sister's darling best friend. The family will receive friends from 4:00 P.M. to 7:00 P.M., July 5, 2009, at Harrell Funeral Home, Kyle, TX. Recital of the Holy Rosary will be at 7:00 P.M. Funeral service will be at 2:00 P.M., Thursday, July 6, 2009, at St. Anthony Catholic Church, Kyle, TX, with Father Howard Goertz officiating. Burial will follow at Phillips Cemetery, Dripping Springs, TX. A candlelight vigil will be held at Buda City Park at 9:00 P.M., July 8, 2009.

TOBE HOOPER WITH ALAN GOLDSHER

Farewell, Loves

(Addendum)

by Megan Matthews, Yearbook Editor

July 7, 2009

My Fellow Students—

I begged Mr. Goriczek to stop the presses so I could include this note, because it is important. As awful as it will be, we must keep the horror of the last week in our hearts and minds. You see, as the great philosopher George Santayana said, "Those who cannot remember the past are doomed to repeat it."

On June 28, our dear friend junior Gwenneth Bryer tragically took her own life. Before we could even grieve her loss, another dear friend, junior Diane "Dee" Rockwell, also took her own life. Sadly, heartbreakingly, that was only the beginning.

Over the next week, we lost eight other friends in similar fashions:

Justin Abrams, junior
Robert Beasley, sophomore
Philip Carrison, sophomore
Julia Gorley, junior
Irina Gretzic, senior
Donnell Hardaway, freshman
Francis Quinn, senior
Tucker Smith, junior

MIDNIGHT MOVIE

Up until last week, it was a wonderful year at SFHS, but now it is marred forever by this tragedy. I hope that you can take comfort in the fact that Gwennie, Dee, Justin, Bobby, Phil, Julia, Iree, Donny, Fran, and Tucker are all in a better place, because it was obvious they were hurting.

I know you are all feeling the pain that I feel, but it is very important to remember that no matter how bad things may seem, it will get better. If you feel like you are going to hurt yourself, reach out to a parent, or a friend, or a relative. If you are unable to find anybody, call Crisis Response of Santa Fe at (505) 820-6333. They are there to help.

No matter what, you must stay alive in the face of tragedy and terror. Because somebody, somewhere, loves you. Like me.

Love always,
Megan

twitter.com

 ScaryBarry fires rage. it won't stop. catch me if you can bitches.
July 7 12:00 AM **via** web

 ArtieMess @ScaryBarry You can barely breathe in Waco. Smells like smoke. What else is new?
July 7 12:02 AM **via** web

 TonyStarkWannabe @ScaryBarry @ArtieMess You guys think you have game? Two hours from now, Philadelphia is GONE!!!
July 7 12:04 AM **via** web

 TheRealDorkyMan @ScaryBarry @ArtieMess @TonyStarkWannabe BARRY IS THE MAN! RECIPE RULES! THIRD-DEGREE BURNS TASTE DELICIOUS!
July 7 12:05 AM **via** web

 GrinningFool1987 @TheRealDorkyMan @ScaryBarry @ArtieMess @TonyStarkWannabe Dorky's right. Burnt skin tastes awesome. Like McDonald's. I'm lovin' it.
July 7 12:08 AM **via** web

 BlackBerryDeadOfNight @GrinningFool1987 @TheRealDorkyMan @ScaryBarry @ArtieMess @TonyStarkWannabe I'm soooooooooooooooo fucked up. Never coming down.
July 7 12:10 AM **via** web

ScaryBarry @BlackBerryDeadOfNight
@GrinningFool1987 @TheRealDorkyMan
@ArtieMess @TonyStarkWannabe spread the word,
my children. spread the recipe. spread the flames
July 7 12:13 AM **via** web

ScaryBarry @BlackBerryDeadOfNight
@GrinningFool1987 @TheRealDorkyMan @ArtieMess
@TonyStarkWannabe it won't end, nor should it.
July 7 12:19 AM **via** web

ScaryBarry @BlackBerryDeadOfNight
@GrinningFool1987 @TheRealDorkyMan @ArtieMess
@TonyStarkWannabe forever is now, and now is forever.
July 7 12:20 AM **via** web

ScaryBarry @BlackBerryDeadOfNight
@GrinningFool1987 @TheRealDorkyMan @ArtieMess
@TonyStarkWannabe feel the burn taste the burn smell
the burn.
July 7 12:22 AM **via** web

ScaryBarry @BlackBerryDeadOfNight
@GrinningFool1987 @TheRealDorkyMan @ArtieMess
@TonyStarkWannabe the burn is life and i will never die
July 7 12:30 AM **via** web

ERICK LAUGHLIN:

After Andi's funeral, Janine had a bit of a breakdown, and I can't blame her. She unofficially moved in with me—and I say unofficially because she still kept 90 percent of her crap at her apartment. She wouldn't go back there, though, and whenever she needed stuff, she made me a list, gave me the key, and told me to get to work.

Her parents were awesome. Even though they couldn't really afford it, they gave her a ton of money so she wouldn't have to worry about working. They wanted her to spend the summer resting up her body and mind. At one point, Mr. Daltrey called me and gave me a lecture—a nice lecture, but still a lecture—about taking care of his baby. He said, "I know Cranford's dead, but there are other Cranfords out there. You make sure they stay away from my girl, y'hear?"

I heard.

Austin was still fire central, and Janine didn't want me leaving the apartment any more than absolutely necessary, so we started having band rehearsals at my place, which pissed off most of our neighbors. But, you know, fuck 'em. Desperate times call for desperate measures.

One night after a rehearsal—and this was the same night that that suicide bomber in Seattle drove into Safeco Field and took out most of the lower deck—Jamal said to me, "You know who you should call? You know who'd probably have some sort of insight on all this crap? Your pal Tobe Hooper."

I said, "What do you mean 'all this crap'?"

Theo said, "Dude, shit's blowing up, and shit's burning up, and people are getting the shit kicked out of them, and there's all these people killing themselves, and there's all that shit online about zombies, and shit ain't right."

Jamal said, "And there's that little matter of your sleepwalking. Remember?"

I said, "Barely." And that was almost the truth. I'd done a good job of compartmentalizing that little mess. I focused on fixing Janine's problems, which meant I didn't have to dwell on my own.

Janine, who'd snuck into the room at some point, said, "I'll tell you why you should call him. Because all this crap started after they showed that movie of his."

I said, "You're blaming suicide bombers on Tobe? Give me a break."

She ignored me and said, "Like Andi. She started losing it after the Cove."

I said, "So what? What does *that* have to do with *this*?"

I must've sounded kind of harsh, because she threw up her hands and said, "Don't snap at me, Erick. And I don't know *what* that has to do with this, and I don't know *if* that has to do with this, and I don't know what or if *anything* has *anything* to do with *anything*. I'm just putting it out there. I don't see you putting anything out there." She wiped her eyes—I hadn't noticed she'd started crying until then—then said, "But maybe that's because you didn't get beat within an inch of your life and watch your sister go bat-shit crazy."

I said, "Hey, I had my own problems. Like the nine thirty-three thing—"

She interrupted me: "Which you've conveniently neglected to mention for the last month."

Theo said, "Janine, didn't that douchebag beat you down after the movie?"

I said, "Jesus, Theo, come on. *Beat her down?*"

Janine said, "No, he's right, David beat me down. And yes, it was after the movie." She paused, then said, "Call Tobe Hooper."

I said, "Why? Tobe Hooper could not care less about me. Who am I?"

Jamal said, "Don't say that, man. No self-dissing. I bet he'd at least listen. It's possible he's holed up in his room, working on a script, not even watching the news."

I said, "I'm sure he watches the news. I'm sure he knows what's up. And I'm sure he'd hang up on my ass if I called him, especially if I said that he had anything to do with this."

Janine said, "Even if he thinks you're giving him garbage, you should talk to somebody, just to get it off your chest."

Theo said, "Hells yeah, you should. I've had nightmares about that nine thirty-three business, and I told my shrink about it, and I feel way better."

Jamal said, "You're seeing a shrink?"

Theo said, "Hells yeah. I'm, like, *totally* mentally healthy now. What, you don't notice a difference?"

Jamal said, "Yeah, sure, Theo, I *totally* notice a difference. You're a goddamn *bastion* of mental health."

I said, "Listen, Tobe Hooper is not my pal. I'm a writer, and he's a subject, and generally, never the twain shall meet. Besides, even if I felt right about calling him—which I don't—I don't have his number."

Theo said, "Dude, seriously, J's right. Hooper's probably sitting in his mansion right now, writing a movie about this shit. He probably thinks about it all fucking day."

Janine said, "I think about it all fucking day, too. It's *all* I think about." She turned to me and said, "Erick, when you're not in the room with me, I stare at the TV and cry. You're pretty much the only reason I'm still sane."

It got really quiet and intense in there, and I actually thought *I* was going to cry, but then Theo said, "You may be keeping her sane, but you're driving me *in*sane."

We all laughed, even though it wasn't particularly funny, but in those days, you took your laughs where you could get them . . . even if they were shitty laughs.

Janine said to me, "Jamal's right. You should call Tobe."

Theo said, "Dude, if you don't want to call Hooper, you could *totally* talk to my shrink."

I ignored Theo and said, "I don't know . . ."

Janine said, "I *do* know. Call some of your publicist friends, get Tobe's number, and give him a ring. Or I'll do it myself."

I said, "Okay, fine." Then something dawned on me, and I asked her, "You were at the movie. How come nothing happened to you?"

She said, "I was outside the whole time. I didn't watch it."

TOBE HOOPER:

It was after midnight, and I was lying in bed, sucking down a bottle of some brown, trying to figure out how I could keep the third act of my new script from sucking—which was turning out to be a losing battle—and *ding* fucking *dong*, the doorbell goes off. Now, a postmidnight visitor is weird for anybody, but for me, it was *especially* weird, because my doorbell never even rings during daylight hours, let alone the dead of night. Everybody in Hollywood knows that I don't dig pop-ins. Hell, the UPS and FedEx dudes are well aware that they should always leave my packages on the porch without ringing the bell and without asking for a signature. And believe you me, they never forget. How could they forget? I mean, it's amazing what a memory aid my fake little chainsaw can be.

So while all this *ding* fucking *dong*ing was going on, I reached under the bed for my gun, but, as usual, it wasn't there. Still in my damn office in the coach house, still in my damn safe. But the doorbell didn't care; it kept right on ringing. So without putting on a robe or anything, I walked downstairs, snuck out the back door, and went out back to rescue my firearm. It took me five tries to get the damn combination of that safe dialed in properly, a fact that you might blame on my minor buzz. And sure, the buzz might've had something to do with it, but that little lockbox was a piece of shit—you get what you pay for, man—so you can't put it *all* on the drink.

At any rate, I finally got it open, and I reached in there, and there was *nothing*. Okay, not *strictly* nothing: My emergency five g's were there in a big yellow envelope, but the gun was gone. The doorbell was still dinging and donging, and I was weaponless and wearing only my boxers, and you can imagine how freaked I was.

I ran back upstairs, went into my bedroom, got down on my hands and knees, and dived under the bed, just in case I missed the gun the first time. Nothing. I banged my head while I was crawling out. Raised a pretty good knot. A little trickle of blood, even. But just a little one.

And then it dawned on me: I'd gone to the shooting range the week before. That's a can't-miss, every-other-week thing for me, because you have to stay sharp with the trigger in case you need to protect yourself in a crisis. The thing is, it doesn't matter one goddamn bit how good of a goddamn shooter you are if your goddamn gun is in your goddamn glove compartment.

The bell kept ringing and ringing, and I had a feeling that fucker wasn't leaving, so I called 911 and told the dispatcher what the deal was. I thought I sounded calm, but apparently not: The dude told me to stop screaming at him and to lay low, and they'd have a man there in a few.

I lay on the floor for three or four or five or ten minutes, and nada. No screaming sirens, no tires burning rubber in my driveway, no bullhorns telling the doorbell dude to stand down. Just *ding dong ding dong ding* damn *dong*. Finally I thought, *Screw it, you've had a nice life, Tobe, now go deal with this yourself.* I tiptoed down the stairs; made my way through my living room, twice stubbing the shit out of my toe; then peeked out the front window and was greeted by a vision that weirded me out like a motherfucker.

There, on my porch, pounding my doorbell with both of his fists, was Gary Church, looking like he'd just walked through a minefield. As I walked over to the door, I kind of laughed at how freaked I'd gotten. I mean, just because someone unexpectedly shows up at your doorstep in the middle of the night doesn't mean they're there to kill you.

I opened the door and said, "Gary, what the fuck, man?" He didn't stop punching the doorbell: *ding dong ding dong ding* damn *dong*. I had to yell at the dude: *"Gary, what the fuck?!"*

He didn't answer. He moaned. And I was wrong about his appearance. He didn't look like he'd walked through a minefield. He looked like he'd spent three years in the shit in Saigon.

When your stomach is bothering you, sometimes somebody'll tell you that you're looking a little green. Well, Gary was a *lot* green, like almost olive, the color of army fatigues. His hair—what little of it was left—was matted and clumped; it looked like he'd tried and failed to grow dreadlocks, or maybe like he had on a really shitty Medusa wig. His mouth was wide open, and he was missing most of his teeth, and his tongue appeared to have been, I don't know, *forked* or something, as if he'd had a tongue piercing go really fucking awry. His right ear was dangling by the lobe, and his left arm was hanging off by what looked like a single piece of skin, but that wasn't the worst part, if you can believe it. No, the worst part was the boils on his face. I swear to God, those fuckers were alive. They were erupting, like miniature volcanoes, and the shit that was oozing out of those volcanoes was steaming, and that steam smelled like roadkill to the fiftieth power.

I wanted to invite him in, but I *didn't* want to invite him in, you know what I mean? This *was* Gary Church, but it *wasn't* Gary Church, and I didn't want the not-Gary to bring his bad juju into my living room.

He finally realized I was standing there and stopped ringing the bell. I said all quietly, "Gary, what's happening, brother? Actually, what *happened*?"

He ripped off his arm and pointed it at his face, then moaned again.

I told him, "I don't know what that means, man." I gagged a little bit. The smell was getting to me.

He then hit himself in the head with his arm. Some of his facial ooze splashed onto my drawers, and I jumped out of those boxers quick-like, right before the ooze touched my skin. This made for one hell of a tableau: me, bare-assed at my front door, and my dearest childhood friend holding his dismembered left arm in his right hand, and some sort of molten pus leaking from his cheeks, and forehead, and nose, and chin, and his ear swaying in the wind like a pendulum. *Wonderful*, I thought, *this is what you get for making* Chainsaw, *asshole. Ain't payback a bitch?*

Finally, Gary said something I could make out. Kind of: "Shoooooooot me."

I said, "Um, pardon me? Could you repeat that?"

He did, except louder and longer. "*Shooooooooooooooooooot meeeeeeeeeeeee.*"

I said, "Brother, I don't get what you're saying." I actually got what he was saying loud and clear, but I didn't want to tell him that. I then continued. "Nine-one-one's on the way, man. They'll get you to the hospital. We'll get you fixed up." I didn't know if Cedars-Sinai had a treatment center for explosive face goop and leprous limbs, but they'd sure as shit be able to do more than I could.

Before I could go on, Gary tore off his own left leg and, while hopping on one foot, started beating himself on the chest with that damn leg. Each time he hit it, he'd say, "*Shoot me.*" He sounded like an Indian chanting around a campfire: "*Shoo*-hoo-hoot me! *Shoo*-hoo-hoot me! *Shoo*-hoo-hoot me!" The pus was flying everywhere, so I said, "Screw this, man," and ran out to the car to get my gun. I mean, who am I to refuse a friend's dying request?

Naturally, right at that moment, who rolls into my driveway? You guessed it: a police car and an ambulance. Great timing, right?

Two cops ran up to the front door, a big Asian dude and a bigger black dude, and what a scene they came upon: naked film director and almost-limbless actor. One of the cops pulled his gun—which I can't say I blame him for; I'd have probably done the same thing—and asked to see some ID. I patted my pockets—or where my pockets would've been had I had some damn clothes on—and said, "I seem to have left my wallet in my other pants, detective."

Before I could tell them who I was, Gary hopped over to the cops and, blurry-fast, used his dismembered leg to break both of their necks—two quick swings, *pow, pow.* After they fell to the ground, Gary decapitated the black cop with his bare hands, then stuck his tongue up through the cop's neck and slurped, and slurped, and slurped.

My dude was eating the other dude's brains. My dude was a zombie. A motherfucking zombie.

I wanted to run. I wanted to hide. I wanted to get a video camera. But mostly, I wanted to put on some clothes. As it turned out, I did none of the above.

While Gary was pigging out on the second cop, I said as calmly as I possibly could, "So, um, Gary. How long you been undead?"

He tossed the black cop's head across the lawn, leaned over, ripped off the Asian officer's noggin, and again said, "*Shoo*-hoo-hoot me! *Shoo*-hoo-hoot me! *Shoo*-hoo-hoot me!"

I noticed that the dudes in the ambulance were staying put; I hoped they were calling for backup, or maybe somebody who could do an exorcism, or maybe my pal Stephen King, because if anybody on earth could figure a way out of this mess, it'd be Uncle Stevie.

I *really* wanted to shoot him, but *really* I *didn't* want to, you know what I mean? I told Gary, "That's asking a lot, man."

He said it again: "*Shoo*-hoo-hoot me! *Shoo*-hoo-hoot me! *Shoo*-hoo-hoot me!" Yeah, man, it was a goddamn Indian chant.

I wanted to put him out of his misery, but it was still Gary's face, and, well, shit, you try shooting your oldest friend. It's a bitch to pull that trigger, even if he is a motherfucking zombie. I said, "I can't. Can't do it. Nope. No way. No how. We'll get somebody to help you." I pointed at the ambulance. "Those guys are on the case." I didn't believe they were on the case—my guess was that they were hiding under the dashboard, which is the same thing I would've done—but I had to say something to make him feel better.

It didn't make him feel better, not one bit. Hell, at that point, he probably didn't even have any feelings. He finished up with the second cop, then fell to his knee, lifted his dismembered leg to the sky, and bayed at the moon. I thought, *Great, now he's a werewolf zombie.*

But he was my friend, and I had to at least try to help out, and going to the car, pulling the gun out of the glove compartment, and plugging him in the brain stem would've been the easiest and probably the most merciful way out. I said, "Okay, Gary, settle down. We can fix this. I promise."

He got up, hopped over to the ambulance, and banged his face against the front windshield. Then he did it again. And again. And again, until the thing finally shattered. The whole time he was yelling, "*Shoo*-hoo-hoot me! *Shoo*-hoo-hoot me! *Shoo*-hoo-hoot me!"

At this point, I figured it was time. It would be best to put us both out of his living hell. So I went to the car, pulled out my pistola, and put one bullet through my oldest friend's heart and another through what I hoped was his brain stem.

My aim wasn't too good. After all, I was crying the entire time.

One of the paramedics poked his head out of the broken window and said, "Can we help you?"

Right then, I heard the phone ringing from back in the house. I told the paramedic, "If you can come up with some way to help me right now, you are a saint. I'm going to grab this call."

If rule number one in the Hooper household is "No visitors," rule number two is "No phone calls after ten o'clock." If you call at 10:01, you're getting the machine. But there were all kinds of rules being broken that night, so I picked it up and said, "What?" And I said it *loud.* Some would say I even barked it.

I heard a second of heavy breathing, then a guy's voice: "Toeb?"

I said, "It's Toe-*bee,* you dildo, not Toeb. Who's this?"

"I don't know if you remember me. Dude McGee. Via Austin, Texas. The *Destiny Express* guy. And I'm pretty sure it's Toeb, not To-bee."

Before I could get out a single word, the smell of rancid luncheon meat filled my nose, and I passed the fuck out.

PART
THREE

TOBE HOOPER:

When I came to, I had one of those it-must've-been-a-dream moments. There was no way that I shot and killed a zombied, rancid, pus-covered version of Gary Church in my driveway . . . and while I was naked, yet. Then I looked down at myself and realized I was indeed naked, and I was lying on the floor, and the telephone was right next to my shoulder, and the earpiece was alive, and it was all real.

The phone started yelling at me: "Hello?! Hellooooo?! Mr. Hoopster? Helllllllllooooooooo?!"

I said, "It's Hooper. Not Hoopster."

The voice said, "No, I'm pretty sure it's Hoopster."

Then I remembered: Dude McGee. I said, "Why in the name of fuck are you calling me at who-knows-what-time-it-is A.M.? It's the dead of morning in Austin, asshole."

McGee said, "Oh, I'm not in Texas anymore. It smells something awful down there. Too many fires." I chuckled despite myself. When you hear a guy who smelled as bad as Dude McGee complaining about the air quality, you can't help but laugh, no matter how many zombies are decomposing in your front yard. He said, "I'm up in Vegas now."

I said, "Why Vegas?" I didn't really care why Vegas, but, like I mentioned before, us southerners are polite even when we don't want to be.

He said, "It's one of the only cities west of the Mississippi that seems to be completely virus free."

I said, "What do you mean 'virus free'?" I wasn't being polite this time. I'm not a fan of germs, so when the topic of pandemics comes up, I'm all ears.

He said, "What do you mean 'what do you mean'? Don't you surf online? Don't you like crackpot websites? Don't you like conspiracy theories? Don't you pay attention to the world around you? You're a filmmaker. How can you make movies for the people if you don't know what the people are doing?"

I said, "I've been busy."

He said, "You've been so busy that you didn't know our country was falling apart at the seams?" And then he laughed, like a high-pitched giggle. I smelled salami again and felt woozy, so, not so gently, I flicked my balls with my middle finger. That woke me right on up.

I said, "Brother, our country is *always* falling apart."

He said, "Not like this." And then he went on to tell me about the hundreds of crystal meth fires, and the suicide cults, and the Blue Spew—which was particularly horrifying, because, well, suffice it to say that the thought of blue crap coming out of my private parts was particularly unappetizing—and the zombies.

I said, "Wait a minute, zombies?"

He said, "Yeah. But nobody's reporting that on the real news. You can't hardly find stuff online about it anymore. Somebody somewhere shut that shit right on down." And then he giggled again. Not sure why. This wasn't the least bit humorous. He said, "Maybe because nobody believes it."

I told him, "I believe it. I saw one of them."

He said, "You *did*?!" He sounded almost happy about it.

I said, "Yep. Up close and personal, even."

He said, "Tell me about it, Mr. Hoopster."

I said, "No way, Dude. No. Fucking. Way." I wasn't ready to relive that moment yet, especially with a salami-smelling giggler like him.

He said, "You aren't alone, Toeb. Thousands of people see zombie attacks, and only a few have discussed it. Personally, I don't get it. Me, if I saw one of those rotters, I'd take a million pictures, secure a million URLs, and put it right up online for the world to see, and whenever one of my websites got shut down, I'd put another one right on up. It'd be . . . beautiful."

I stood up, walked over to the front door, and took a peek at Gary's corpse. He was turning into mulch before my eyes. The EMTs were gone. I said, "It would most definitely *not* be beautiful."

McGee said, "Beauty is in the eye of the beholder."

I said, "Unless the beholder is a moron. Now, why the hell are you calling?"

He said, "Oh. Right. That's the important thing." Again: *giggle, giggle, giggle.* Moron. He continued. "You might want to know that the Game is all your fault."

ERICK LAUGHLIN:

Tracking down Tobe's number was easier than I thought; I knew a guy who knew a guy who knew a guy. Once in a rare while, my limited power as a film critic in a tertiary market is of use. Once in a *rare* while.

I wanted to call Tobe first thing in the morning, but Janine said, "No. No way. You call him now. If you don't call him now, you'll wuss out and come up with a zillion excuses."

I said, "Why the rush? What's the big deal if I *do* put it off?"

She walked over to me, put a gentle hand on my cheek, and said, "Nobody's talking about it *for real.* Nobody's *questioning.* Everybody's just letting it happen. Maybe Tobe knows somebody who'll have some ideas, and maybe that person will know somebody, and that person will know ten somebodies, and we can get some answers."

I said, "What if there aren't any answers?

She said, "Erick, it's a goddamn phone call." She grabbed my cell from the top of my amplifier, threw it at my chest, and said, "Make it."

I checked my watch and told her, "It's three in the morning here, which means it's one in the morning in California.

Ten o'clock is the cutoff time for nighttime phone calls. Everybody knows that."

The entire room hammered at me for probably another half an hour: *What have you got to lose? . . . What's the big deal? . . . It'll be cool . . . Maybe he knows something you don't . . . Who the hell else do you know that can look at this from a slanted angle? . . . What have you got to lose? . . . What have you got to lose? . . .*

They wore me down. Finally, just to shut them the hell up, I dialed.

TOBE HOOPER:

Right as Dude McGee was going to tell me how I, Tobe Hooper—or, in his little salami mind, Toeb Hoopster—personally had shredded the fabric of America, my call waiting beeped in.

Another post-midnight caller. For the love of God.

I told Dude to hold on and jabbed the star button to find out who it was. I said, "Yeah?"

"Tobe?"

"Yeah?"

"My name is Erick Laughlin. We met at the *Destiny Express* screening. I don't know if you remember me."

I said, "Yeah. Listen, I have to be honest, brother: I don't really recall *most* of that night." That was only partly true. There was one thing I remembered: that chick who kissed me. My Lord. I got hot just thinking about it.

He said, "That's okay. So listen, I know it's late, and I'm sure I woke you up—"

"My night's sleep went out the window when I shot one of my oldest friends in the brain," I said.

He laughed and said, "Yeah, um, sure, um, right." Of course he thought I was kidding. Who wouldn't have? I'm Chainsaw Boy.

I said, "Listen, man, can I buzz you back? I'm on another call."

He said, "Really?"

I said, "Yeah."

He said, "At *this* hour?"

I said, "*You* called me at this hour."

He said, "Ah. Right. Good point. So in an hour?"

I said, "Sure, an hour. But listen, why're you calling anyhow?"

He said, "I wanted to talk about . . . well . . . it's weird."

I said, "Brother, '*weird*' is my middle name. What's the deal?"

He said, "My girlfriend thinks you might offer us some insight into the Game."

I said, "Funny you mention that, Erick. Apparently I'm about thirty seconds away from having some insight."

He said, "Apparently?"

I said, "Yeah. Got to run." Then I clicked back to McGee. "So. Mr. McGee. You were about to tell me how I destroyed the world."

Dude said, "I was."

I said, "Details, please."

He said, "Okay. Remember that movie you did? *Destiny Express?*"

I said, "Vaguely." All sarcastic-like.

He said, "That was Ground Zero. That was the birth. That was the rebirth. That was the afterbirth. That was the launching pad. That was—"

I had a hunch that little freak could've gone on all night with the metaphors, so I finally interrupted him. I said, again, "*Details, please.*"

He said, "It started there, To-*beeeeee*. If you work your way backward, you can trace it to that screening. Everything. The Chicago suicide bomber was there. I think the Blue Spew started there—and you're lucky you didn't catch it, from what I understand. And Scary Barry was there—"

I said, "Scary Barry?"

He said, "The first of the meth arsonists." *Meth arsonists.* Jesus Christ suntanning on a cross. He continued. "I'm pretty sure the suicide cult started there, but I can't prove that for sure. Quite the impressive flick, To-*beeeeee*. Go online and see what havoc you hath wrought."

I said, "Mr. McGee, this is intriguing and all, but I think you're utterly full of shit." And I did. But the fact that Erick called gave me a bit of pause, so I said, "I do have a few questions."

He said, "I can imagine you do. What say I drive up to L.A. and we have a chin-wag? Put our heads together. Smash our heads together. Bash our heads together. Togetherness is what it's all about. Togetherness is the buzzword. Togetherness can make this country whole again. Together, we can fix this. Together, we can save the world. How'd you like to save the world, Mr. Tony Hoobler?"

Tony Hoobler? *Seriously?* I said, "I tried to save the world in the sixties. Didn't work. May as well give it another shot."

He said, "That's the spirit. Jerry's Deli at noon tomorrow?"

I said, "I'll be counting down the seconds." And then I hung up, went upstairs, put on some clothes, and went about the business of burying what was left of my pal. All that other shit—specifically, the dead cops—that would be somebody else's problem. After I did my business, I was gonna blow the scene. I didn't know where I'd go, and I didn't know how I'd get there without getting stopped *some*where by *some* cop, but that's the way it was gonna go down, *period.*

Turned out the cops didn't give a good goddamn about me, but as I found out later, they *couldn't* give a good goddamn about me, because Hell-Lay was a bastion of fucked-up-ed-ness. My guess is that the paramedics filled them in, and since the situation had, shall we say, resolved itself, they left it alone. And that's probably why I never heard a single "official" word about Gary

Church. And you make sure you tell your readers that I'm doing finger quotes around "official."

ERICK LAUGHLIN:
Tobe called me back two minutes before I was going to call him.

The first thing I asked him was, "How'd you get my number?"

He said, "I star-sixty-nined you, man. Hope your girlfriend doesn't take that the wrong way. She's probably the only one who wants to sixty-nine you."

I laughed and said, "So, about this Game business . . ."

He said, "We'll talk about it tomorrow at lunch. There's a six o'clock flight from Austin to L.A. Spell your name out for me."

I said, "Why?"

He said, "Because I'm putting you on it."

I again said, "Why?"

He said, "Because I don't want to meet with that little freak on my own."

I said, "What little freak?"

He said, "Dude McGee."

I said, "You're meeting with that *moron*?"

Tobe sighed, then said, "Yeah. *That* moron."

I said, "Why?"

Tobe said, "He thinks I'm the bad guy. He thinks I'm the villain. And I need to make sure he's wrong."

TOBE HOOPER:
Jerry's was the ideal place to meet McGee, because his bologna BO would be less noticeable in a room filled with deli meat.

McGee was waiting for me when I showed up—and I was right on time for a change, thank you very much. He gave me a too-enthusiastic handshake, then dived right back into his monolithic sandwich. He said, with his mouth full of challah, "I hope you don't mind. I ordered an appetizer."

I said, "Whatever, man. Finish your food. I don't want to start rapping about this shit until my backup shows."

He swallowed—mercifully, because half-chewed food reminds me of a certain nightmarish actor I once worked with, whom I will not name—then said, "Backup?"

I said, "Yeah. Backup. One of the kids who was at the screening. Far as I know, he doesn't have the Blue Spew or anything."

Dude said, "Might you be talking about Erick Laughlin? Erick Laugh-In? Erick Laughing Boy? Erick Idle? Erick's Idol? Erick—"

I interrupted him. "Yeah. That guy. How'd you know?"

He said, "I just do."

I said, "You just do?"

He said, "Erick lives where I live. I live where Erick lives. Us Texans, we know what's happening with our own."

I said, "I'm a Texan, and I don't know a goddamn thing about any of you whack jobs."

He said, "Oh, but you will, Mr. Hooker."

Until Erick wandered in twenty minutes later, the only sound that could be heard at our table was that of Dude McGee murdering two sandwiches. My appetite went right into the shitter, as you can imagine.

ERICK LAUGHLIN:

The positivity of seeing Tobe Hooper was nearly offset by the negativity of seeing Dude McGee.

Before I could even shake Tobe's hand, Dude said, "*You* know about the Game, don't you, Erick Laughing Boy? An oh-so-connected newsie such as yourself is in touch with the outside world, isn't he?" This was all said with max sarcasm.

My hands automatically closed into fists. Steam must've been coming out of my ears, because Tobe touched me on the forearm and said, "I know what you want to do, brother, and I'm telling you not to do it. Too many witnesses. It's not worth it."

I said, "I'm cool, Tobe. Thanks." Then I said to Dude, "Yes, McGee, I know about the Game."

Dude said, "Of course you do. Have you caught a dose? Do you have the Blue Spew? Are you a stinking, rotting zombie?"

No way I was telling that stink bomb about the 9:33 business. I said, "I'm good. My girlfriend was attacked by an old boyfriend, and she thinks he might've been in an, um, *altered state* when it happened, but I don't know about that."

Dude said, "Ah. Yes. David Cranberry."

I said, "Cranford."

Dude said, "Right. Cranberry. Another man who rode the *Destiny Express*."

Tobe said, "What do you mean 'rode the *Destiny Express*'?"

Dude said, "He was there. He was in the house. He was, as the kids say, in the heezay."

Tobe polished off a glass of water in one gulp and said, "McGee, you'd better start making sense, or me and Erick here are going to make ourselves scarce. So talk. But swallow your lunch first."

I said, "I couldn't have put it better myself."

Dude actually looked hurt. He said, "You guys are mean. I bet you were both bullies in high school."

Tobe said, "I wasn't. But you would've made me one. Now . . . please . . . fucking . . . *talk*!"

Dude cleared his throat, lifted his arms above his head and brought them back down as if he was doing a sun salutation, then said, "That movie of yours, To-*beeeeee*. That was quite an impressive film. It was an amateurish piece of celluloid dung, of course—"

Tobe mumbled, "Yeah, I know."

Dude went on. "—but impressive nonetheless. I haven't seen it all the way through, which is why I'm here today. Because I suspect if I had seen it, if I'd have watched it from beginning to end, I'd be . . . *susceptible.*"

I asked, "Susceptible to what?"

He said, "Laughing Boy, *Destiny Express* started the Game."

I said, "Yeah, I've heard that one before."

Tobe said, "Give me a fucking break, both of you." He grabbed me roughly by the shoulder and said, "Let's go."

I said, "Let's hear him out." Naturally, I thought about that horrible video of me zipping through who-knows-where with those red dots shooting out of my stomach, or my chest, or wherever. Was *that* the Game? Did I spread the Game? Did somebody blow up a building because of me? Did Dave Cranford beat the crap out of Janine because of me? *Fuck.* I asked Dude, "Okay, why do you think a movie started this whole thing?"

He said, "Didn't you see *The Ring*? It's possible. Very, very possible."

I said, "*The Ring* is fiction, dickhead. You know, somebody made it up."

He said, "But it rang true to me."

Tobe said, "I'm sure it did."

I said, "Answer the question, Dude. Why do you say this had anything to do with Tobe's flick?"

Dude said, "Oh, I did the research. See, I had the guest list. I know *everybody* who was at that club, and I know what happened to them, and I know what they did. Or most of them. For instance, I know about your sleep study, Erick Laugh-In."

I felt like I was going to throw up. Janine, Theo, and Jamal were the only people I'd told about that. I asked, "How'd you find out, Dude? How the *fuck* did you find out?"

He said, "You may not believe it, but I'm kinda smart. And you may not believe this either, but some people like me, and sometimes when I ask them questions, they answer. Would you care to tell me why you had the sleep study?"

I said, "No, McGee, I would not care to tell you."

He said, "Fine. Then I'll tell you something else I know. I know that To-*beeeeee*'s pal Gary Church disappeared."

Tobe mumbled, "He didn't disappear."

Dude shrugged, then said, "Maybe he did, maybe he didn't, but according to the LAPD, he's a missing person. I also know that Andrea Daltrey died a horrible, tortured death. If the men in black haven't taken it down yet, you should read her blog, Laughing Boy. Quite eye-opening. And boner producing."

I again tensed up, and again, Tobe touched my forearm and said, "Don't do it, man."

I took a deep breath, told Tobe, "I'm cool," then said to Dude, "None of this really proves anything."

Dude turned to Tobe and asked, "Did you touch anybody during the screening, To-*beeeeee*?"

I said, "What the fuck, McGee? What kind of question is that?"

Tobe ignored me and said, "Um, not really."

Dude asked, "Are you sure?"

Frankly, Tobe looked and sounded anything *but* sure. He said, "Not really."

Dude said, "Tell us what happened, To-*beeeeee*. Whatever it was, we won't judge you. At least *I* won't. Laughing Boy here might."

Tobe mopped his brow with a napkin, then said, "It's kind of embarrassing."

Dude said, "Don't worry. We're all friends."

I said, "No, we're not."

Tobe said, "I kissed a girl."

Dude grinned like a fucking shark and said, "Now we're getting somewhere. Now we're cooking with gas. Now we're getting to the meat of things. Spill, To-*beeeeee*."

He took a deep breath and said, "Not much to spill, really. About halfway through the movie, I'm standing at the bar, and this girl walks over, and says something, and kisses me. And that kiss was . . . epic."

Dude said, "I bet it was, I bet it was. Details."

Tobe said, "Jesus, McGee, let it go."

Dude said, "It's important. People are dying from kissing. Maybe we can fix it."

The guy was insane, pure and simple. I asked him, "What makes you think we can fix it?" I tried to sound as condescending as I possibly could. I wanted him to feel like the kid who claimed there was a fantasy world at the other end of his bedroom closet. *The Lion, the Witch, the Wardrobe, and the Moron,* you know?

Dude said, "I don't, really. It's a long shot, really. But I think we should try, really. If there's even the teeniest, tiniest, ittiest, bittiest chance we can make a difference, we should research, really."

I said, "Really." Again, I shot for condescending.

McGee caught it. He glared at me and flatly said, "Really." He took a sip of his water, belched, then said, "Do you want to be *that guy,* Earache? Do you want to be the guy who had a chance to do something other than write shitty reviews and gig—or, as is usually the case, *not* gig—with a shitty band but blew it off? I know you think I'm a fat slob—*everybody* thinks I'm a fat slob—but at least I'm *trying.* At least I'm *doing something.* At least I give a damn about what's happening outside of my apartment." He belched again, then said, "I don't care if you don't care, but I *do* care, and I thought Hoopster here might have some insight. I didn't invite *you,* you know, just him. If you want to leave, then leave. I. Really. Don't. Care."

Tobe sighed, then said to me, "Kid, relax. Let's let this play out." Then he said to McGee, "Fine. I remember falling down and laying on the floor—"

Dude said, "You were on the ground at the Cove, and you lived to tell the tale? Impressive, Hoobner. If my face was that close to that floor, I'd have killed myself on the spot."

Tobe said, "But that's the thing. I didn't care. I didn't care about *anything*. Epic kiss, man. I almost . . . you-knowed."

Dude said, "You mean you almost achieved orgasm? Almost ejaculated? Almost spurted? Almost spooged? Almost came like a mother-humping madman?"

I said, "You are an utter asshole, McGee."

Tobe told Dude, "You *are* an asshole. But you're right. I'd never experienced anything like that. *Anything*."

Dude asked, "Do you have the Blue Spew, To-*beeeeee*?"

I said, "Okay, Dude, since you know so much, why don't you tell us *exactly* what the Blue Spew is? Because nobody else in the country seems to have any idea."

Dude said, "That's the million-dollar question. Well, one of the million-dollar questions, anyway. But you're right; nobody knows exactly what it is, just the symptoms. In men, the seminal discharge is blue. In women, their lubrication is blue. In some cases, the sufferer's blood becomes blue. And in all cases, it's transmitted via fluids of any sort, kissing included."

I asked, "What happens if you have it?"

Dude belched again, then said, "The predominant outcome is death."

Tobe asked, "What, these people just up and die?"

Dude said, "From what patient zero said in her blog, it's less of an up-and-dying kind of thing and more of a killing-yourself-because-you've-been-driven-nuts-by-your-insane-sexual-desires kind of thing." He shook his head, then said, "Poor patient zero. You must be very sad, Earache."

I asked him, "What do you mean?"

He said, "Goodness, you're not very smart, are you?"

I said, "Apparently not."

He said, "Andrea Daltrey was patient zero. In not so many words, she fucked herself to death."

I wanted to tell him he was full of shit, that Andi wasn't that kind of girl. Thing is, based on both what I'd seen and what Janine had told me, she'd *totally* become that kind of girl. All I could bring myself to say was, "Go on."

Dude said, "Not much to say after that. She fucked one man, and he fucked two friends, and they fucked two friends, and so on, and so on, and so on. Just like any other STD." He did that weird giggle again and said, "Except maybe more fun."

Tobe said, "So what you're telling me here is that this chick got a disease from my movie."

Dude said, "What I'm telling you here is that this chick who watched your movie at the Cove got a disease, and Mr. Suicide Bomber Aaron Gillespie watched your movie at the Cove, and Mr. Crystal Meth Firebug Scary Barry watched your movie at the Cove, and Earache Laughter saw the whole thing at my apartment and look what happened to him."

Tobe said, "What happened to you?"

I said, "Nothing. I'm fine."

Dude said, "Sure you are. Tell me that at nine thirty-three." He turned to Tobe and said, "So. To-*beeeeee*. Is this a coincidence? Or is this your handiwork? And most importantly, are you proud of yourself?"

TOBE HOOPER:

I thought it was a pile of bull crap, heaped on a hill of rat shit, surrounded by a mound of bat guano. I told McGee, "You know what? It's nice that you're trying to figure out all this Game junk, but did you ever think it's an actual honest-to-goodness virus?"

Dude said, "At first I did. Some people are saying that those geniuses at the government's House of Viruses in Reston, Virginia, dropped the ball, and that sounded pretty right to me. Those chuckleheads almost caused an Ebola outbreak in the eighties, so I wouldn't put it past them. But I have a connection at the CDC—"

Erick said, "You absolutely do *not* have a connection at the CDC."

Dude went on like Erick hadn't said anything. "—and she told me that Reston was clean. Her personal opinion is that it's a bio-weapon launched by this Russian putz they've had their eye on for a while. But then I started seeing all the names, and it clicked."

Erick said, "What do you mean 'seeing all the names'?" He snarled, practically.

Dude said, "It wasn't anything weird, Earache. *Destiny Express* was my event. I put together the screening, and I put together the guest list, and I have a good memory, and I spend a lot of time online, and I have a lot of Google Alerts set up. One fucked-up person from the Cove is an accident. Two fucked-up people from the Cove is a coincidence. Three fucked-up people from the Cove is a trend. Do the math, dipshit."

Erick said, "Okay, fine, for the sake of argument—and to help get us the hell away from you sooner than later—let's say it *is* a virus, and let's say it started in Austin—"

I interrupted him. "Austin would be the *perfect* place to set off a weapon," I said. "Lots of people coming and going in and out of town for the festival, but not *too* many. If somebody wanted to spread something, that's as good a place as any." If I were writing a pandemic flick, I'd *totally* set it in Austin.

Dude said, "That's what I thought at first. But my research was impeccable. There aren't any regular Joe Shmoes who exhibited symptoms at first. Just the Joe Shmoes who were at the movie."

I said, "Okay, for the sake of argument—"

Dude said, "Everything with you guys is for the sake of argument. Let's just argue. It's healthier."

I ignored him, then continued. "Let's say we believe you. Let's say my movie set off some sort of psychic viral bomb. How do you think it happened? Since your research was impeccable, I guess you're the man to ask on this one."

Dude shrugged. "I'm not. I'm not the man to ask. I've told you everything I know. You're smart. I can't do this myself. I need your help, and you need my help, but there's only so much help that we can help with."

Erick said, "What the fuck are you talking about?"

He said, "You're adults. Figure it out for yourself. I just wanted to keep you in the loop-de-loop. You can call me if you have any questions, but I doubt I'll have any answers. I know the whos and whens. I'll work on the whys if you do." He looked at his watch. "Oops, got to run. I'm meeting somebody for lunch."

Erick said, "You just ate lunch."

Dude said, "What's your point?"

Erick said, "My point is, *you just ate lunch.*"

Dude said, "I'm a growing boy, and if one lunch is good, two is better. Now, let's us three fix this shit. Okay? Okay." And then he belched, flipped us the bird, and split.

ERICK LAUGHLIN:
And then he left the deli, but two minutes later, much to my chagrin, he came back. He waddled over to our table, then dropped a heavy square box right in front of me and said, "Almost forgot. You assholes might want this." Then he farted, said, "I'm trying to help you, here. Show some gratitude," and split for good.

I opened up the box, and inside was another box, and inside that box were three film canisters. I asked Tobe, "Is this what I think it is?"

Tobe peered at the canisters and said, "Yeah. *Destiny* fucking *Express.*" He signaled the waitress for the check, then said, "How about you and I go back to my pad and watch ourselves a movie?"

I said, "Fine. But how about you and I discuss Dude McGee first?"

He didn't say anything else until we got into his car. After he fired up the engine, he said, "I'd prefer to not think about Dude McGee any more than I have to. Something ain't right with that boy."

I said, "I couldn't agree with you more, Tobe. But don't you think it's a bit odd that he came to you with this?"

He said, "You came to me with this because you thought I could give you insight, or some such bullshit, and you didn't have jack shit. McGee at least had something tangible."

I said, "What do you mean 'tangible'?"

Tobe said, "He had a guest list."

TOBE HOOPER:

When we got back to my place, we checked out that flick, I don't know, eight or nine more times, and each time, it sucked worse than the last.

We ordered some pizza, and then I went to the bathroom, a place where I've been known to do some of my best thinking. After multiple viewings of that dreck, we came up with exactly nothing, except for headaches from squinting at the screen. Yeah, there were zombies in there, but how the hell could a kid dressed up as a zombie—and dressed up badly, I might add—turn somebody into a zombie? How could a shitty movie from five decades ago cause somebody to shoot blue come? It couldn't.

When I got back to the living room, Erick was laying on the sofa, fast asleep. I flicked his ear, and he popped right up. Once he was coherent, I told him, "You know what, man? This is entirely a bunch of crap."

Erick rubbed his eyes, yawned, and said, "Well, not *entirely*."

ERICK LAUGHLIN:

I welcomed Tobe Hooper into the 9:33 club: I told him about the sleep study, and strapping the camera onto my body, and the red laser beams, and he was barely fazed. All he said was, "Could I borrow that footage from you? Because I'm working on this sci-fi script, and that'd be a *perfect* third act." And then he laughed. He wasn't laughing at me, though, I knew that. Sometimes a laugh is just a laugh.

At that point, I gave mental props to Janine. She was right: Outside of her, Jamal, and Theo, Tobe Hooper was the only person in my circle of acquaintances who wouldn't dismiss me as a delusional nutbag. But that didn't mean I believed a single word that came from Dude McGee's mouth.

TOBE HOOPER:
We didn't say a hell of a lot over dinner. Most of the talk was of the pass-that-napkin-over-here variety. After we threw down several beers, Erick said, "I have a weird-ass idea."

I said, "Talk to me." I slurred a bit. I was buzzed. So was Erick. If you're in a state of buzz, you come up with weird-ass ideas, and sometimes, those weird-ass ideas are the best ones.

He said, "What if it wasn't *you*, exactly? What if the movie launched some sort of paranormal event, but it wasn't your fault?"

I said, "What do you mean?"

He said, "Okay, stay with me here. What if, say, your leading lady Helen Leary was a Wiccan witch? Or what if your cameraman worshipped Aleister Crowley? What if one of your cast or crew people figured out how to curse your film?"

I said, "Yeah, sure, that's an idea, but here's another one: What if *Destiny Express* had *nothing* to do with *anything*? That's *my* theory."

He ignored me and bulled right ahead. It was like he decided that my movie made this mess, period, exclamation mark, end of discussion. He continued on: "Maybe Gary Church did something. I mean, he was on the screen for practically every scene. Maybe we should talk to him."

I said, "Yeah, that might be tough."

He said, "Why?"

I said, "When we pulled into the garage, did you notice that heap of green compost on the side of my driveway?"

He said, "Saw it and smelled it."

I said, "Well, that's Gary." See, I hadn't even gotten a chance to bury him properly. That dude's body decomposed *fast*.

Erick said, "Excuse me?"

I said, "I tell you, brother, the shit that I dealt with last night makes your nine thirty-three problem seem like a walk in the damn park." So I gave him the 411 about the Gary situation. After I was done, he looked like he was going to toss his pizza, his beer, and whatever he had for dinner the night before back in Austin. I said, "You don't look so hot. You want some seltzer to settle your stomach?"

He said, "Only if you put a shit-ton of vodka in it."

ERICK LAUGHLIN:

After a few drinks, apropos of nothing, Tobe asked me, "You like your girl?"

I said, "Yeah, man. She's awesome."

He said, "What do you like about her?"

I didn't even have to think about it: "She's smart as all get-out; and she's amazingly courageous; and she doesn't give a damn what people think about her; and she loves her family; and she calls me on my shit, but not in a mean way; and she's the most gorgeous woman who's ever let me feel her breasts."

Tobe said, "Yeah, man. Yeah. That's beautiful. Very sweet. Very touching. Wish I had something like that. Now, I ask you this: What if one night, you're alone in your house, and it's midnight, and your front doorbell rings, and there stands your girl, but she's not your girl, exactly, she's a zombie version of your girl, a drool-ing, stinking zombie, all green and moaning, and she's asking, no, she's *begging* you to shoot her and put her out of her misery, and then you shoot her because your heart is being torn in two, and then, like, an hour later, right when you're about to bury her, this douchebag guy you know calls you up and says, 'Listen, I might know why your girl became a zombie, and I have a suggestion of a way you can maybe, possibly stop this from happening to any-body ever again, and it's a half-assed theory, but there's a chance, man, a *chance* that you can get, I don't know, some sort of *redemp-tion,* or *revenge,* or *something,* and all you have to do is meet me for lunch,' and you meet him for lunch, and he lays it out there, and it sounds absurd, but it's a starting point, and you want to do *something,* and you've got nothing else in your back pocket? What would you do?" Before I could answer, he said, "I'll tell you what I'd do: *anything.* Even if I couldn't make it right, I could go to my grave knowing that I at least *tried.*"

I said, "I agree, Tobe. Wholeheartedly."

He said, "Glad to hear it, man. So. I like your plan. Let's go round up the *Destiny Express* crew. Such as it is."

ERICK LAUGHLIN:

I said, "Sweet. When? Where? How?"

He said, "It shouldn't be hard. You saw the credits, there were only, what, six people who worked on it? And one of them is me. And one of them is dead."

I asked him, "Are you in touch with any of these folks?"

He said, "Nope. Haven't been for years. Shit. Maybe it *will* be hard."

I said, "Tobe, it took me three phone calls and ten minutes to get your home phone number. Trust me, it won't be hard."

HELEN LEARY *(housewife, Portland, ME):*

I had a little bit of a crush on Tobe Hooper. But just a little bit. It might've been a bigger one, but he was . . . different. And different is sometimes scary.

I think part of the reason I was into Tobe was because he wasn't into me. He was into movies, and there was something *so* cool about that. I also thought his single-mindedness was sexy. Not that I knew much about sexy back then, but you get the point.

We didn't travel in the same circles. I was more of the pro-totypical popular girl, you know, a cheerleader, editor of the yearbook, that sort of thing. Tobe and I never had a serious con-versation—we were always cordial toward one another but not friendly to the point that we'd talk for real. Which is why I was so surprised when he asked me to be in his movie.

TOBE HOOPER:

A million actresses out here ooze sex, but unless you're a casting director who wants to get laid, that doesn't mean much in terms of the creative process, such as it is. But Helen Leary wasn't like that. Helen oozed *it,* an indefinable something that made you want to screw her, then marry her, then have babies with her, then screw her some more. She was the ultimate in Madonna/whore, and brother, back in the day, I wanted a piece of that.

Now, I wasn't what you would call a ladies' man or anything, but I did have one thing to offer: my filmmaking skills. When I was in high school, you didn't have all these little pishers running around with their camcorders like they do today, making their magnum opuses, and inviting their friends along for the ride. Back then, knowing a thing or two about film meant something.

So instead of asking Helen out on a date, I asked her to be in my flick.

HELEN LEARY:

I won't lie to you. I'd dreamed about being an actress. But what teenage girl in Austin, circa 1959, didn't? Who didn't want to get out of stupid Texas and do something with her life other than get married at twenty-one, have a baby at twenty-two, have another one at twenty-three, then one at twenty-four, then hang it up? Who wouldn't want to go to Hollywood and meet Lee Marvin, and Marlon Brando, and Steve McQueen? So when Tobe asked me to do his movie, I didn't hesitate for a second. My thinking was, *Lots of people all over the world make real, true movies. Why not Tobe? He might just be obsessed enough to make it work.*

Even then, he was a pro. He made me feel comfortable, and talented, and pretty, and relaxed, and as I learned during my brief, less-than-successful film career, that's not something that every director brings to the table.

When Tobe reached out to me in the midst of all that Game mess, I sure hoped it was because he wanted me to be in his next movie. If nothing else, seeing him would take my mind off the fact that my oldest son had become a zombie.

TOBE HOOPER:

We flew to Maine the next day. Helen was waiting for us on her doorstep.

She looked beautiful, and she lived in a beautiful house in a beautiful town, and she had a handsome husband, and two handsome sons, and one beautiful daughter. No surprise there.

She seemed happy enough to see me, but she didn't exactly welcome Erick with open arms.

ERICK LAUGHLIN:

Tobe was nervous and tongue-tied—something I never would've imagined from him—so I took the lead. I asked Helen, "Do you remember making a movie with Tobe?"

She snapped, "Of course I do."

I asked her, "Did you ever see it?"

She said, "As a matter of fact, I did not. I wasn't even sure it was actually finished." Still very snippy.

Tobe piped up. "Helen, Erick's a nice dude. Maybe you could answer his questions a little, I don't know, nicer or something."

She seemed to soften, then said, "To be honest, Tobe, I was hoping to spend some time alone with you."

Tobe said, "Helen, I would like nothing better. I mean, back in high school, I'd have crawled over a mile of glass just to get a sniff of your neck."

Helen blushed, then said, "Why, Tobe Hooper, you dog. I have to admit, I had a little thing for you, too."

I said, "Guys, I hate to break up this lovefest, but we're kind of in a rush here."

Helen said, "But I thought you might be able to stay for dinner."

Tobe said, "Sweetheart, I'd like nothing more than to run away with you to an island where none of this Game crap is going down, but me and Erick here, we're on a mission."

Helen said, "What kind of mission?"

I said, "A mission to save the world."

HELEN LEARY:

While Erick gave me the *Destiny Express* backstory and his theory—that maybe the movie somehow launched the Game—Tobe just sat there and stared into my face with an expression that made it clear they weren't messing around with me.

I said, "Why're you coming to me? What do you think I have to offer?"

Tobe said, "No clue. We were hoping you could come up with something."

I said, "What do you mean 'something'?"

Tobe said, "Something about the shoot. Or about me. Or about anything weird."

I said, "Okay, let me think." I closed my eyes, and shut off my brain, and tried to transport myself back to that summer, tried to recall whether anything odd happened during the shoot. And then it came to me. "Remember when we were doing the alligator scene?"

Tobe said, "I don't remember a damn thing about shooting that damn movie."

I said, "Well it was really, really hot out. Gary was covered with makeup, just *covered,* and he kept saying he was going to pass out, and you kept saying, 'You're fine, you're fine, drink some water, you're fine. Next shot, next shot, we're on the clock, we're on the clock.'"

Erick said, "Sounds like you were already in training to be an indie director."

Tobe laughed without humor, then said, "Yeah, that's definitely the kind of thing I'd say on a set, no question."

I said, "That fake alligator was amazing, Tobe. You made it yourself. I remember you stole a bunch of leather jackets from some clothing store or another." Then, out of nowhere, it all came crashing back to me. I hadn't thought about that movie in decades, but all of a sudden, I was back in Austin, sweating, rushing around, and, frankly, a bit frightened. I could practically smell it. "And then you sewed all the jackets together and stuffed it with roadkill."

Tobe said, "I did what, now?"

I said, "You and the cameraman; what was his name?"

Erick said, "Darren Allen."

I said, "Right, Darren, that nerdy kid who lived across the street from you. The quiet one. And there was one other guy who was around sometimes."

Erick said, "William Marron. He did the special effects."

I said, "My God, it's like Old Home Week. Wow. Right. Billy Marron. He was a piece of work." I asked Erick, "How do you know so much about this?"

He said, "Mrs. Leary, I've watched *Destiny Express,* what, ten or eleven times now. And I've only seen *Citizen Kane* twice, if that means anything."

Tobe said, "And at the end of the fifth inning, the score is *Citizen Kane* two, *Citizen Crap* ten or eleven."

Erick ignored him and said, "I know that movie better than Tobe does."

Tobe said to me, "Hell, Helen, this kid knows *The Texas Chainsaw Massacre* better than I do."

I said, "At any rate, it was a Sunday afternoon, and I specifically remember what day it was because I thought it was funny I was going to shoot an alligator attack in a swamp right after I got out of church. I showed up before everybody else, which was weird, because Tobe was always the one waiting. Gary came next, and then here come Tobe and Darren, hauling this fake gator, looking like they were two cats who'd eaten a dozen canaries. They plopped the thing down right in front of me, then Tobe said, 'What do you think?'"

Tobe asked, "What *did* you think, Helen?"

I said, "Looks-wise, it was really impressive. If you were even ten yards away, you might've thought it was real. But good Lord, that thing reeked. I remember I asked why it smelled so bad, and Billy gave me this weird laugh. Then you told me about the roadkill."

Erick said, "Do you remember specifically *what* he told you about the roadkill?"

I laughed a little bit, then said, "Unfortunately, Erick, it's all coming back to me."

Tobe said, "Why's that unfortunate, Helen?"

I said, "Because you two had apparently wandered up and down the highway for five hours, carrying a shovel and five shopping bags and scooping up every dead possum, and raccoon, and rabbit, and squirrel you could find. And then I guess you used that to stuff the leather jackets with."

Tobe said, "Man, I was committed."

I said, "You should've *been* committed."

Erick said, "What could the point of that have possibly been?"

Tobe said, "The point of me being committed?"

Erick said, "No, the point of the roadkill."

I said, "I believe it was actually Billy's idea. I think he said something along the lines of 'The stench of death will add a certain sense of *verisimilitude*.'"

Tobe chuckled, then said, "That sounds like the kind of thing Billy would say. He was always using those fifty-cent words."

Erick said, "Did it? Did the, um, stench of death make it seem more real?"

I said, "Probably, but I can't tell you for sure. My screams were probably louder."

Erick said, "That's important. Fay Wray had been making movies for over ten years before she did *King Kong*. Her screaming probably added another twenty years onto her career."

Tobe said, "Good screams make for good cinema. Sometimes you have to do what you have to do."

Erick asked me, "Do you remember any other weird stuff like that? Like did you shoot a scene on an Indian burial ground or something?"

Tobe snapped his fingers and said, "Now, that's an *excellent* idea. Erick, do you think you can help me find one of those for my next project?"

Erick gave him a funny look and said, "What, a burial ground?"

Tobe said, "Yeah, man, you could be my location scout. Fuck it, I'll even give you an EP credit."

Erick said, "You *are* kidding." When Tobe didn't answer, he said, "Aren't you?"

Tobe just shrugged.

I said, "I guess in some ways, nothing's changed."

Erick said, "What do you mean?"

I said, "I mean that even back then, Tobe was full of weird ideas. And when he got enthusiastic about something, he'd *go for it*. He'd do whatever he could to make it better. And grosser."

Erick asked, "Like what?"

Then Tobe said, "Yeah? Like what?"

It was on the tip of my brain . . . or I guess the tip of my nose. I said, "Okay, I remember you covered Gary with crap."

Tobe gave me a *look* and said, "I did?"

I said, "Yeah, yeah, yeah. We were in Billy's backyard, and we were doing another scene where Gary attacks me, and Billy had done up Gary perfectly. He looked *so* creepy. Like in those old movies, before special effects got all expensive, you could almost always see, I don't know, the zipper in the back of the gorilla costume or something, which would make it seem less scary. But whatever Billy did to Gary was creepy even in person. It probably looked even creepier on the screen."

Erick said, "It did."

I said, "I'm not surprised." Then I turned to Tobe and said, "So Billy'd spent all this time putting on Gary's zombie makeup, and you said it wasn't nasty enough, and you two got into this big argument, right out in the backyard. Poor Gary was sitting there all covered with zombie goop, and you and Billy were going on, and on, and on, and finally you told him you'd take care of it yourself, then you stomped off and disappeared for a half an hour and came back with a big bag of cow shit, and you told him to rub it on his legs."

Erick asked, "What did he say?"

I said, "I don't remember. But he did it. What the heck were you thinking, Tobe?"

Erick said to Tobe, "I bet you wanted your actors to spend the entire movie looking like they were about to puke. Am I right?"

Tobe said, "Who knows what the hell was going on inside of my little fucked-up brain. But it sure sounds like my thought process, doesn't it?"

Erick said, "It kind of does, Tobe. It kind of does."

TOBE HOOPER:

We didn't know what we were looking for from Helen, but then again, if we knew what we were looking for, we wouldn't have been looking in the first place. Frankly, she wasn't of much use; she didn't really remember much beyond the dead animals and the shit. Weird, no doubt, but it didn't explain how my piece-of-crapola movie could've launched an epidemic. We bullshitted for a while, then we split, because we had a flight to catch. I told her I'd be in touch, and she said that would be nice. And she was right. It would.

In the cab on the way to the airport, Erick asked me if I had any thoughts. I said, "Okay, maybe I wasn't the most sympathetic director in the world. But I don't think some feces and some roadkill would cause any problems. Do you?"

Erick said, "Who knows? Let's say, for the sake of argument, that movies can have a negative physical and metaphysical effect on the viewer . . ."

I said, "Which they can't."

Erick said, "Right. Of course. Which they can't. But let's say they can. Has there been anybody in the history of cinema who used shit and roadkill like you did in *Destiny Express*?

I said, "John Waters had one of his actors eat shit in *Pink Flamingos,* and nothing happened."

Erick said, "True. Maybe we should go talk to John."

I said, "Nah. Me and John, we have issues."

Erick said, "Like what?"

I said, "Like Odorama."

Erick said, "What's Odorama?"

I said, "Just an idea I came up with that he used before I did."

Erick asked, "Did he steal it from you?"

I said, "Nah. He just got there first."

Erick said, "Have you ever spoken to him about it?"

I said, "Doesn't matter. Let's focus, here. So in answer to your question, as far as I know, nobody in the history of cinema has used shit and roadkill like I did in *Destiny Express*."

Erick said, "So maybe if you use shit and roadkill in a movie, something'll happen."

I said, "Like it'll cause any man who sees it to come blue? That's insane, man. Can we stop talking about this for a while?"

I must've sounded pissed, because Erick said, "We can stop talking altogether, if you want."

Until we landed at LaGuardia, we said a grand total of six words to each other.

CLAIRE CRAFT *(senior editor, **Vanity Fair** magazine, New York City):*
Tobe Hooper and I weren't friends before I shot that movie with him back when I was sixteen, and we weren't friends after, but I still kept tabs on him throughout the years. Even though he was far from my favorite person in the world, he was still the

hometown boy who made good, so I couldn't help but be, I don't know, *intrigued* is the word. I suppose.

ERICK LAUGHLIN:

Tobe didn't want to speak with Claire on the phone, and when I called her up at her office, I guess I could understand why.

When I finally got through to her, I introduced myself as the film critic for the *Austin Chronicle,* figuring she'd be more willing to speak with a fellow writer than some random dude off the street. When I went on to explain my connection with Tobe, she hissed, "Jesus. That fucker." And yet she agreed to see us right away. Go figure.

CLAIRE CRAFT:

I was in love with Scott Frost, and it wasn't just some little-girl puppy love thing, it was the real deal. He treated me like gold, and he was handsome, and smart, and as fine of a boy as he was, he was going to be that much better of a man. He was young, but he was a good one, and having been through God-knows-how-many pseudo–love affairs with God-knows-how-many bad ones, I can speak with authority on that.

Of course I had no idea at the time that Scott had impregnated a college girl. I didn't find out until five years after I left Austin, and knowing what I knew about him by that point, I can't say I was surprised. Let's just say that Scott liked the ladies.

Intellectually, I realized it wasn't Tobe's fault Scott got killed by that red Corvette. And from what I've learned after many, many years of therapy, it would've been healthier for me to have embraced Tobe right after it happened, to have grieved with him, rather than harbor all that anger and resentment for all those years. But, you know, easier said than done.

I didn't know how I'd react when I saw Tobe. Would I be angry? Forgiving? Ambivalent? Scared? I had no clue, and I was nervous.

TOBE HOOPER:

First of all, Claire looked amazing. She could've passed for forty-five. I'm sure part of it was genetics—I remember her mom was pretty hot—and part of it was many trips to the gym. I'm also damn sure there was some plastic surgery involved.

Second of all, I was pleased as punch that she didn't haul back, slug me, and give me a black eye. I knew she wasn't a fan of yours truly, and I was pretty certain there was no way she would've forgiven or forgotten. Not that she had anything to forgive—it wasn't my fault Scott got killed, and besides, I almost died too. But still.

Third of all, thank God that Erick was with me. She seemed okay with me, but I'm not sure that would've been the case if I were alone.

ERICK LAUGHLIN:

The tension was pretty thick, so I skipped the pleasantries and launched right into my spiel: *Destiny Express,* the Game, Tobe's fault, blah blah blah. I asked her, "Any thoughts?"

She stared at me. *Gawked* is a better word, I guess. Then, to Tobe, she said, "You're insane. You're utterly, totally fucking insane. Tell me why I shouldn't call security right now."

Tobe said, "Oh, gee, I don't know, Claire, maybe because we're trying to save the world, and maybe you can help."

She sighed and said, "Ooh, *save the world,* such drama. Give me a break." She took a swig from her massive water bottle, then said, "Okay. Fine. What can I do? What can I say that'll get you to leave my office sooner than later?"

I said, "Tell us anything you can remember about making the movie."

Claire said, "There's not much to tell. I was there for one day, and"—she pointed to Tobe—"this one bit my ear off."

Tobe said, "I didn't bite your ear off. Gary did."

Claire shook her head, then said, "No, he didn't. Gary was late that day, and you were all pissy and told your weird friend you'd handle it. What was his name, Willy?"

I said, "No. Billy."

She said, "Right, Billy. Billy Marron. Another piece of work."

I asked her, "What do you mean 'piece of work'?"

She took another hit of water, then said, "Tobe was a creep, but at least he was a *talented* creep. Billy was just a creep."

I said, "Did you ever see the movie?"

She shook her head and said, "Tobe never invited me to see it."

Tobe said, "Honey, I never invited *anybody* to see it."

I told Claire, "You aren't missing much, but some of the effects were pretty impressive."

Claire said, "Maybe it was all that shit they used."

Now, *this* was interesting. I asked her, "What do you mean 'shit'? Did they cover you with shit? Because it didn't look like shit. It looked like blood."

Claire gave me a death look. Man, that chick was scary. She said, "Are you serious? It wasn't literally shit. Do you think I'd let *him* cover me with feces? No, they put some stuff on me that was made from I-don't-know-what, but it smelled like, I don't know, maybe a grave."

I asked Tobe, "Do you know what you put on her?"

He said, "Marron might."

I said, "Yeah, that's what I figured." I turned back to Claire and asked her, "Can you remember anything else? Anything at all?"

She said, "There wasn't much to remember. I was there for two hours. I flipped some cue cards. Tobe cut off my fake ear . . . during which he gave me a goddamn scratch on my neck."

I said, "Was the scratch bad?"

She said, "You know what? Now that I think about it, it was. I remember putting a bandage on it when I got home, and then when I took it off the next morning, it was all red, puffy, and hard. I remember thinking that the goo had gotten in there, and I caught some sort of infection. It lasted for a while. The day before I was planning to call the doctor, it started shrinking, and it was completely gone a couple days later." She lifted up her hair to reveal her neck, then pointed right below her left earlobe and said, "It's tiny, but if you look carefully, you can still see it."

Claire was right. I could see it. Easily. It looked like a big zit scar. I think she was in a bit of denial about the size. I asked her, "Does it ever hurt? Or itch?"

She shrugged, then said, "It itches once in a while, but it's nothing to cry about."

Tobe said, "Are you healthy in general?"

She said, "Yes, Tobe, I'm healthy." She checked her watch, then said, "Are we done here? I have a meeting."

Tobe said, "We're done. Do you think I can call you?"

Claire rolled her eyes, then said, "I'm happily married, Tobe Hooper, and even if I wasn't, there's no way I—"

Tobe cut her off, and said, "I have zero interest in fucking you, Claire. We might have some more questions. That's all."

She said, "Tobe, I've told you everything I know. Feel free to see yourselves out. And feel free to lose my phone number."

While we were in the elevator, I said to Tobe, "Now, there's one warm and fuzzy chick."

Tobe nodded. "And to think I actually *did* fuck her. Let's go see Mr. Marron."

CLAIRE CRAFT:

Okay, fine, yes, we had sex. It was heinous.

TOBE HOOPER:

One thing Claire was right about: Back in the day, William Marron was a piece of work.

I felt bad for the dude. He meant well, but nobody realized it, because all those good intentions were buried under several layers of BO, blubber, and bad attitude. I hate to sound mean, here, but that's the only way to describe it. He was fat, and he didn't smell particularly good, so I suppose I could understand why he was such a grouch. But we had a whole lot in common. He was the only cat in the area who was as into the movies as I was.

The funny thing is, we hung out probably once or twice a week, and we periodically ate lunch at school together, but I never felt like we were really pals. Then again, I don't know, maybe getting together those few times a month made us friends. Neither of us was a social butterfly, so it's not like we knew what the hell true friendship was about.

Billy and I hadn't been completely out of touch; we exchanged e-mails once or twice a year. Nothing important. Just letting each other know we were still alive.

He'd started up a software company in, I think, '97, he and one other dude. Two years after they opened shop, they sold some sort of finance program to Microsoft, and they were set for life. Since then, he's mostly farted around with games. He's sent me a bunch of prototypes, but I haven't touched them. I don't do computer games. No time, man. No time.

Billy was cool when I called. Said I should come up to his office in the afternoon, and lunch was on him. Like the Irish say, never refuse a free lunch.

WILLIAM MARRON *(software designer, New York City):*

Destiny Express was one of the defining moments of my childhood. Working with Tobe showed me that I could do something . . . something . . . something . . . I don't know, *interesting*, I guess. It made me believe that I could interact with *everybody*, not just the misfits.

See, I was a misfit, the typical fat kid that you see on corny TV shows. The football players liked to knock all my books out of my hands, and the basketball players enjoyed sticking my head in the toilet and flushing it—I believe the kids these days refer to that as a whirly—and some of the teachers even liked throwing verbal barbs at me. The only person in the whole school who deigned to have anything to do with yours truly was Tobe Hooper.

Despite what Tobe might believe, I didn't particularly care about film. I pretended to dig the medium because I figured it was the best way to keep him as a pal. I grew to appreciate it, and thanks to him, I understood the difference between good movies and bad ones. But honestly, once we drifted apart, I stopped watching them. I have Netflix now, but I use it almost exclusively for documentaries.

I wasn't surprised he called during all this Game mess. That's the kind of mess that'd get even a people-hater like Tobe Hooper to have significant, non-business-related interaction with the world at large.

TOBE HOOPER:

I almost passed out when Billy walked out that door. I said, "Jesus Christ, brother, you got skinny!"

He smiled, then said, "Jesus Christ, brother, you got old!"

I said, "Billy, my man, if you'd been dealing with the Hollywood bullshit that I've been dealing with for the last twenty years, you'd look old, too. How the hell did you get all slim and trim?"

He said, "Exercise, diet, and a healthy dose of gastric bypass surgery. Probably added twenty years onto my life."

I said, "That's cool, man, real cool. But what Erick here is going to tell you will probably take those years right back off again."

Erick said, "I'm going to tell him?"

Tobe said, "That's right. You're going to tell him. Right now."

ERICK LAUGHLIN:
Before we even left the lobby, I launched into the same spiel I gave Helen and Claire: *Destiny Express*, the Game, Tobe's fault, blah blah blah. Billy listened thoughtfully, then said, "Let's go into my office."

While we walked down the hallway, I asked him, "Billy, do you know something? Do you have an idea?"

He said, "Do I know something? No. Am I shocked about this?" He paused for a bit, then repeated, "No."

Billy ushered us into his office, which was much bigger, and much *much* nicer, than my apartment: three sofas, two recliners, two huge flat-screen televisions, a dining table with six high-backed chairs, and a space-age workspace that would probably be a good place from which to rule the world. Billy sat us down on one of the sofas, then his assistant brought us drinks—Diet Coke for me, Maker's Mark for Tobe—and he started right in.

He said, "Guys, believe it or not, I think about *Destiny Express* probably once or twice a month. And I don't mean from a perspective of *Oh, boy, I worked with Tobe Hooper before he became famous.* Being with you, being your friend, being your partner, well, I guess you could say it informed my work."

Tobe said, "If it informed your work, brother, you need some better information."

Billy ignored him and said, "That movie expanded my mind. It opened me up. It helped me overcome my fear of creating. It also taught me what *not* to do. Like for instance, if I were a special effects artist right now, I probably wouldn't cover my male lead with a mixture of applesauce, fish food, chewed broccoli, and dog turds."

Tobe said, "We didn't actually do that. Did we?"

Billy said, "We did."

Tobe said, "Christ, what the hell was I thinking?"

I said, "Pardon me if I'm speaking out of line, but I don't think you *were* thinking."

TOBE HOOPER:

I told him, "You're right. We weren't thinking. We were doing. Or really, *I* was doing. Everybody else was following orders."

Billy laughed, then said, "Following orders? Jesus, Tobe, you make it sound like you were Hitler or something."

I said, "I was a bit of a dictator, Bill. Always have been on the set. I have a vision, and I want to bring it to life, and sometimes I get a bit . . . a bit . . . a bit . . ."

And then Erick came up with the perfect word: "Myopic?"

I said, "Bingo. Myopic."

Erick asked Billy, "Is there anything out-of-the-ordinary you remember? You know, like the alligator."

Billy cracked up and said, "Oh my God, the roadkill alligator. Wow, doesn't that bring you back, Tobe? Good times, good times." He thought about it for a second, then said, "Wait a sec, do you remember the car wreck scene?"

Something tickled me at the back of my head. I fished for it—fished for it pretty hard, actually—but it stayed just out of reach. Shit. I said, "Refresh me."

He said, "You wanted to set it up so you could make a bunch of edits back and forth between the car and Gary's face, so you did Gary's reaction shot from I don't know how many angles. It was weird."

Erick said, "What was weird about it?"

Billy said, "Well, Tobe kept yelling at Darren to circle around Gary faster and faster with the camera. Hey, did you guys speak to Darren yet?"

I said, "He's next."

Erick said, "He's in Houston. We saved him for last."

Billy said, "Give him my best. There was another member in good standing of our merry band of mutants, right, Tobe?"

I said, "Yeah, you could rightly say that."

Billy said, "So Darren was jogging with the camera, and he tripped. Gary managed to catch the camera before it hit the ground. Then Darren stood up and fell right back down. He got a concussion, remember?"

I said, "No. Unfortunately, I don't."

Billy said, "Yep, he got knocked out, and when he came to, you told him to rub some dirt on the bump on his head and to get back to work."

Erick said, "Jesus, Tobe."

I said, "What can I tell you? That's the way us dictators work."

WILLIAM MARRON:

Was I surprised at how little Tobe remembered? Absolutely. But I know that car wreck messed him up pretty badly, so I suppose I shouldn't have been.

I asked Erick—who seemed to be an earthbound fellow—if their talks with me, Helen, and Claire were of any use. He said, "I don't know. I mean, you guys did some weird shit during the filming, but I'm sure Eli Roth has done equally weird shit—if not weirder—and so have Sam Raimi, and John Carpenter, and Wes Craven. I don't even want to imagine what goes on during a Takashi Miike shoot. But none of those caused any problems. *Audition* was, like, the most fucked-up movie ever—*way* more fucked-up than *Destiny Express*—and it didn't make blue stuff shoot out of people's cocks."

I said, "Guys, I don't think *Destiny Express* did either."

Tobe said, "I wish there was a way to find out, man."

I said, "You know what? There is. Possibly."

Erick said, "Yeah? What's that?"

I said, "Make it again."

DICK GREGSON (*head of production, Warner Bros. Pictures*):

My daughter Celia had just graduated from Stanford—a full year early, I should note—and she was getting ready to go to Japan to teach English for a year. I hadn't seen her in a few weeks, but that wasn't unusual; Celia did her own thing, and that was fine. I trusted her to do the right thing. She always had.

Celia committed suicide on July 1, 2009, right when the Game was in full swing, right in the middle of the summer of hell. She was twenty-one. Twenty-fucking-one years old, and all the potential in the world, and she ended her life.

I don't want to discuss identifying her body.

She didn't leave a note, and I wanted some answers, *any* answers, so I hired a private detective. He spoke to a bunch of her friends, and if you're researching the Game, I'm sure you know more or less exactly what he found out.

My wife and I had been divorced for ten years, and our relationship was toxic, so there was no comfort there. My friends were sympathetic, but there was only so much crying on somebody's shoulder I could do before they'd ask for their shoulder back. I needed distraction. I needed an alternate reality, and since Hollywood is the most alternate reality our fine country has to offer, I went back to work.

The Game was quite prevalent in California, so of course it had a tangible effect on the industry. For some reason, we didn't lose much big-name above-the-line talent—some said that Marty Scorsese had become a zombie, but it turned out he was just in Aruba without his cell phone or his laptop—but we lost a lot of below-the-line personnel and behind-the-scenes studio people. My assistant, for example, disappeared two days after I got back to the office, and I never heard from her again. One of the big muckity-mucks at Sony—I won't say who—got a case of the Blue Spew. They caught it early enough that he was institutionalized. He was monitored 24/7. If I may be so crude—and I'm certain you've heard worse, so I probably won't be creeping you out, here—he almost jerked himself off to death. It got to the point that they had to strap his hands onto his bed rails. As I'm sure you know, the doctors never found a cure for the Spew, but this man survived and managed to not infect anybody else.

So many of our employees were sick or unaccounted for that we almost closed up shop. After what seemed like thousands of meetings, we decided to keep moving forward, albeit in a pared-down fashion. At the beginning of April, we had forty-six movies in production; by July, we'd suspended shooting on thirty of them. And the sixteen we kept alive were all comedies or family movies. It wasn't the time for us to dive into *Dawn of the Dead: The Angels of Death,* you know?

Which is why when Tobe Hooper called and asked me for a bucket of money to remake his very first movie, I laughed my ass off.

TOBE HOOPER:

There are few things in life I hate more than begging for money from a film studio. Root canal *sans* Novocain is far more appealing. So's a sharp stick in the eye. So's a sharp stick up the ass.

Before I go into one of those meetings—meetings where I have to pitch a concept until I'm red in the face, then listen to those executive types tear my idea a new asshole, then discuss ways to cut the budget to the point that I can't even feed my cast and crew anything but Domino's pizza, generic soda pop, and peanut butter and jelly sandwiches—I get the sweats something awful, and my stomach gets all fucked up, and I end up in a really, really dark place. I've been known to lose my temper at these shindigs. I've been known to throw a telephone. I've been known to gouge the phrase "FUCK YOU" on a conference room table with the Swiss Army knife I keep on my key chain.

I guess it's possible that's why I haven't gotten any *real* money from a *real* studio since, well, since *ever*. But that's just a guess.

DICK GREGSON:

Tobe Hooper and I are about the same age, and we've been in the industry for almost the same amount of time—since the seventies—but we'd only rarely crossed paths. I respected his work, and he tolerated mine—he was never a fan of working with major studios, that Hooper—so our dealings, such as they were, were always cordial but distant. Typical Hollywood stuff, I suppose: hearty handshakes, big old smiles, effusive praise for the other person's latest project, and subtle boasting about your own latest project. Bullshit makes the world go 'round.

On the phone, I warned Tobe that our purse strings were tight and we weren't going to put any horror flicks into production until the world started getting slightly less horrible, but I told him that if he wanted to, just for the hell of it, he could come in and pitch it to me. I said, "Eventually, things will get back to normal, and the machine will start right on up again, and it'll be business as usual. And when it's business as usual, *anything* can happen."

Actually, there are most definitely some things that *couldn't* happen . . . one of them being Warner Bros. giving Tobe Hooper a single red cent.

TOBE HOOPER:
I told Gregson I'd be at his office in forty-eight hours. I also told him that I wouldn't be coming alone. I was bringing my EP.

ERICK LAUGHLIN:
On the flight out to Houston, Tobe asked me if I wanted to be executive producer of what he was now calling *Destiny Express Redux.* How could I say no? What was the worst that could happen? It's not like I'd have to deal with a roadkill alligator or anything.

TOBE HOOPER:
Ah, Houston. Good old Houston. The nastiest city in the world.
Aside from Hollywood, of course.

DARREN ALLEN (*head curator, Houston Film Preservation Society*):
I wasn't surprised Tobe Hooper called me after over thirty years of silence. I knew he'd be back.

ERICK LAUGHLIN:
Tobe was right. Houston was the nastiest city in the world. What made it worse was that the streets were empty and rancid, because

the undead saturation level—that's what the Net nerds started calling it, the "undead saturation level," and it stuck—was one of the highest in the country. They claimed that at its worst point, one out of every five beings in Houston was undead. It created a whole lot of controversy when some dick on Fox News said that there was no way to tell the difference between a Houston resident and a zombie. But that's why the dude was on Fox News. Because he was a dick.

A few months back, I saw some of the Houston footage from that June on YouTube, and it was brutal, man, just brutal. Imagine the creepiest moment from *Night of the Living Dead*, then multiply that by fifty. Their moans were loud as all get-out, and they all had these oozing sores on their faces—I guess like the ones that Tobe saw on poor old Gary Church—and most of them had a body part or two dangling by a single thread of skin, and you could practically smell them through the computer screen. Fortunately, by the time we got there, the majority of the zombies had migrated to Mexico, but nobody wanted to leave their house, thus the Magnolia City was a ghost town.

So, yeah. Houston sucks.

TOBE HOOPER:

Here's what I recall about Darren Allen: good kid, smart kid, popular kid, handsome kid. I remembered him to be a tagalong, but a tolerable one. Like some tagalongs can be colossal pains in the backside, but Darren, he was okay. If I would've made a prediction back then, I'd have guessed that Darren would be where Billy was: rich, successful, and happy.

Man, was I wrong.

DARREN ALLEN:

It was nice to see Tobe. Reeeeeeeal nice.

TOBE HOOPER:

Before we tracked Darren down, I'd never heard of the Houston goddamn Film Preservation Society. I didn't even know what the hell a film preservation society did. Did they take the actual films and store them so they wouldn't get tarnished? Did they take artifacts from films and display them under glass? Was it like Madame Tussaud's fucking wax museum, with statues of all two of the big-time movie stars who were born in Houston, specifically Patrick Swayze and Shelley Duvall?

Turned out it was kind of all of the above.

ERICK LAUGHLIN:

Darren Allen was a creepy little man. I knew that he was the same age as Tobe, but he could've passed for thirty-nine. His skin was smooth and unlined, and he had a full head of black hair, and he was pasty white, the kind of pasty that you see on a guy who spends most of his waking hours watching movies.

DARREN ALLEN:

I like movies. Lots.

ERICK LAUGHLIN:

He didn't have much to say, though, and Tobe was either exhausted, or depressed, or thinking obsessively about his meeting with Warner Bros. the next day, so I ended up doing all the talking.

I gave Darren the spiel, then asked if he had any recollections that might shed some light on the subject.

He shook his head.

I said, "Do you remember anything weird that went down during *Destiny Express*?"

He shrugged.

I asked him, "Does the roadkill alligator sound familiar?"

He laughed.

DARREN ALLEN:

I like alligators.

ERICK LAUGHLIN:

Finally, after fifteen useless minutes of trying to drag even a single drop of information out of the guy, I asked him, "So do you have any of Tobe's stuff preserved?"

He smiled, and said, "Mmmmmmm-hmmmmm."

And then—and I know this sounds corny and clichéd, but it's the goddamn truth—he gave me a giggle that sent a chill down my spine.

TOBE HOOPER:

I'll say one thing about that little fucker Darren: He was as organized as hell.

I guess you could call the ground floor of Darren's space a museum. There were statues, and vintage film posters, and artifacts, but, to be honest, it wasn't all that impressive. You could tell it was done with love—the displays were subtle and classy, and the joint was pristine—but it was minor league at best. I mean, when your big coup is landing the box of chocolates from *Forrest Gump*, well, that ain't the kind of place that'll impress your average film nerd.

The basement, however, was a different story.

DARREN ALLEN:

Only VIPs in the basement. *Only* VIPs. And only with the bracelet.

TOBE HOOPER:

Before Darren let us in, he made us put on these weird silver bracelets. He didn't tell us what they were about, and I didn't ask. There wasn't time, and it wasn't important.

ERICK LAUGHLIN:

The basement was two floors down, pitch-black, and reeked like a badly kept used book store on a rainy day. Like you could almost taste the paper. We stood at the bottom of the stairs for a good thirty seconds before Darren turned on the light.

Based on the smell, I expected it to look like, well, a badly kept used book store, but I couldn't have been more wrong. It was filled with dozens, if not hundreds, of floor-to-ceiling metal storage lockers. Each locker had an identifying plaque on the door, and it was in perfect alphabetical order: F. Murray Abraham, David Attenborough, Joe Don Baker, Lucille Ball, Tallulah Bankhead, Kim Basinger, Kate Beckinsale, Fanny Brice, George Carlin. Lots of holes, to say the least, which was why I asked Darren, "How do you determine who gets a locker?"

He said, "We don't determine."

I waited for him to elaborate. Nothing. Finally I said, "Who *does* determine?"

Darren said, "If we get stuff, they get a locker."

I knocked on Lucille Ball's door and said, "What kind of Lucy *stuff* do you have?"

Without a word, he pulled a key from his pocket and opened Lucy's front door. Inside this huge locker—which was, I don't know, maybe thirty square feet—sat a single bottle. I said, "Um, so, Darren, what the heck is that?"

He said, "Vitameatavegamin."

I said, "Say *what?*"

Tobe finally piped up and said, "Yeah, man, I remember that. From *I Love Lucy*. Best episode ever, probably."

For the first time since we got there, Darren perked up. He said, "*Best! Episode! Ever!*"

I asked Darren, "Where'd you get it?"

He said, "Stole it. From Desilu Studios. Or what used to be Desilu Studios. Nobody missed it."

I said, "Yeah? How'd you steal it?"

Darren giggled again and said, "Ancient Chinese secret!"

Tobe rolled his eyes, then said, "I take it there's a Tobe Hooper locker down here?" Man, did he sound exasperated.

Darren said, "Right this way."

DARREN ALLEN:

Not enough in the Tobe Hooper locker. Not enough. That makes me sad.

TOBE HOOPER:

My locker was between Darla Hood's and Harry Houdini's. Talk about Murderer's Row: a Little Rascal, Leatherface's daddy, and an escape artist. What the fuck?

Making matters weirder, there was exactly one thing in the locker. A folder. A red folder. And it looked as familiar as all hell.

I said, "What in the name of Jesus is this?"

And then I walked in.

And then I was on my ass.

And the pain was indescribable.

DARREN ALLEN:

Nobody goes in the lockers but me. Nobody, nobody, nobody. *Nobody!*

ERICK LAUGHLIN:

I screamed, "*Tobe?! What the fuck? Talk to me!*"

I took my cell from my pocket to call 911. Opened it up. No signal.

I grabbed Darren by the shoulders and yelled, "*Is there a land-line down here?!*"

Darren said, "No. There isn't. No cell reception in the whole building. Can't have interruptions."

I said, "*Get . . . me . . . to . . . a . . . landline . . . now . . . motherfucker.*"

Darren said, "No need."

DARREN ALLEN:

Three minutes. That's all. Three minutes.

ERICK LAUGHLIN:

Before I kicked the little weirdo in the balls, he tapped the bracelet he'd made me wear and said, "Electrical perimeter. The shock will wear off in three minutes. Give or take."

My knees gave out, and I sat hard on the floor. Actually, "sat" probably isn't the right word. "Collapsed" would be more accurate, really. The last two days had finally caught up to me. Man, did I miss Janine.

I leaned over to shake Tobe awake, and when I was an inch or two away from touching his shoulder, Darren kicked my hand. I said, "What the fuck, dude?" Again, I'm a shitty fighter, but I'd be willing to get into it for Tobe.

He said, "He's electrical. He's dangerous."

DARREN ALLEN:

My electrical perimeter is . . . is . . . is *awesome*. One of only seven in the United States. Worth every bit of my inheritance money. Mommy's death was worth something.

ERICK LAUGHLIN:

Sure enough, Tobe came to two minutes later, only slightly worse for wear. He sat up, then shook his head back and forth and back and forth as if he were a cat, and then he asked me, "Do you smell salami?"

I said, "I smell old books and BO. You okay?"

He said, "Yeah, I'm cool, I'm cool." Then he turned to Darren and said, "Electrical perimeter, right?"

Darren nodded.

Tobe said, "This SFX dude told me about it. I didn't believe it existed, but there it is. Now, that is some good shit, brother, good shit indeed. I should get one of those for my crib. You'll have to give me your guy's number." He peered into the locker, then said, "Now, what's in that little red folder that's so important that you have to guard it with this high-tech crap?"

Darren said, "A script. *The* script."

For the first time since we started our little journey, Tobe smiled. "Man, you have an original *Chainsaw* script. How 'bout that happy crappy? Far as I know, there're only three in existence. If that." His Texas accent had become more pronounced. Maybe because he was happy.

Darren said, "Not that script. *The* script."

And then it dawned on me. I asked him, "That's what I think it is, isn't it?"

DARREN ALLEN:

All aboard, all aboard! It's time to ride the *Destiny Express*! Yay!

TOBE HOOPER:

I asked Darren, "That's the script?"

Darren nodded.

I said, "*The* script?"

He nodded again, then said, "*Theeeeee* script."

I asked him, "How the fuck did you get it?"

He said, "I always had it. I never didn't have it. And it's preserved really good."

Erick said, "Can we see it, please?"

Darren said, "Oh. No. No. No way. No way, no sir, no how."

I said, "Darren, that's my property."

And then Darren lost his shit. He stomped his feet and said, "It's mine, it's mine, it's mine, you gave it to me, and I kept it, and if you wanted it back, you should've asked for it back, and now you come in out of nowhere, and you want it now, and that's not fair, it's not fair, first the print of the movie disappeared—"

I said. "Wait, what do you mean the print of the movie disappeared?"

He ignored my ass, which pissed me off, because A) that's just fucking rude, and B) it would've been nice to know some details of how the movie ended up with Dude McGee. But I got nothing, because Darren kept right on yelling: "—and now I'm supposed to give you the script? Well, I don't think so, Tobe Hooper. That's not going to work one little bit, not at all. No way, no sir, no how."

After he finished, I said, "Don't hold back, brother. Tell us what's really on your mind."

ERICK LAUGHLIN:

We were all silent for a bit. Really, what the hell was there to say? Finally, I said to Darren, "Here's the thing. We're going to remake this movie. And we're going to try to do it shot by shot, *exactly* the way you guys did it. We'd be able to cobble together a screenplay, but if we had the original one, that'd be so much better. And you know what? You'd be doing your part to preserve film. Isn't that what you're about? Preservation?"

His eyes widened, and he gave us a huge smile and said, "Exactly shot by shot?"

I said, "Yep. Exactly."

He said, "That means you need me to shoot it. If you want to be exact."

Tobe said, "That's kind of why we're here."

The thought of spending any extra time with Darren Allen was, at best, unappealing, but I had to suck it up for the greater good. I said, "Hey, Tobe, here's a thought: No matter what, *Redux* won't be exactly the same. Gary's gone."

Darren said, "Good."

DARREN ALLEN:

I never liked that Gary Church. *Never.* Glad he was dead.

TOBE HOOPER:

I said to Erick, "I *know* we can't do an *exact* remake. You can't do an *exact* remake unless all the principals are in the flick, and Gary ain't gonna be in the flick. And I thought about that. And I have an idea."

Erick said, "What?"

I said, "You. If there's even the tiniest chance that us doing this thing is going to clean up some shit, somebody's got to get dirty. And it's you."

He said, "*What?!*" He sounded pissed.

I said, "You were at the Cove, and you're here, so you're in the shit, whether you like it or not. And you have to see it through."

He said, "Thanks, man, but no thanks. I'll stay behind the camera."

I put my hand on his shoulder and squeezed, and said, "Erick, my brother, you have no fucking choice."

ERICK LAUGHLIN:

I told Tobe, "I'm not the guy. Me and Gary have nothing in common."

Tobe said, "You're both from Austin."

I said, "Nope. No way. Not interested."

Tobe gritted his teeth—yes, that's right, gritted his teeth—and said, "Then you *get* interested, motherfucker, or I swear to God on my life that after all this is done, I'll hunt you down and shoot you dead. I killed one of my oldest friends two days ago, so killing you would be easy. *So* easy."

I believed him. But I still wasn't going to be in the flick.

TOBE HOOPER:

No way I would've offed Erick. He was a good kid. If he didn't want to do it, we'd figure something out.

But it's good to know that I still had a few acting chops, because when we got to Dick Gregson's office, I was going to have to act my ass off.

DARREN ALLEN:

They asked me to film the movie. I said okey-dokey. They asked me to borrow the script. I said okey-dokey. They told me they'd call when they had a shooting schedule. I said okey-dokey.

Everything was okey-dokey. Every. Little. Thing.

ERICK LAUGHLIN:

Now, even though I'm such a film dork, and even though I've interviewed a good number of celebrities, and even though I've been on a movie set or two, I'd never been to a studio—hell, I hadn't even been to California until Tobe dragged me out there. I had my preconceptions, but the Warner Bros. lot wasn't what I thought it was going to be. Let me rephrase that: The Warner Bros. lot *looked* exactly like what I thought it was going to be, but it didn't *feel* like a place where dreams were made real.

Why? Because it was, relatively speaking, empty.

There were only a couple of flicks in production: a romantic comedy with Matthew McConaughey and my old pal Jessica Alba—okay, she wasn't my old pal, but I did interview her once, and I bet she'd remember me . . . or maybe not—and a family drama with Jeff Bridges, Meryl Streep, and Michael Cera, which, considering the cast, had a ton of potential. But that was it. No hustle, no bustle, nobody zipping around on golf carts, nobody running from one building to the next balancing five lattes, no assistants getting chewed out by douchebag execs. Just a few people wandering around dazedly, looking bummed.

When we got to Dick Gregson's office, his unbelievably hot assistant told us that Dick was running late. Tobe said, "That's the best news I've heard all day," then plopped down in a chair and promptly dozed off.

I asked the assistant why the lot seemed so dead. She said, "Because everybody's dead." When I didn't answer, she gave me a look, then said, "You *do* know what the Game is, don't you? Or are you one of those screenwriter guys who doesn't get out much?"

I said, "I'm well aware of what the Game is."

I must've accidentally shot her some attitude, because she said, "You know what? Fuck you. My boyfriend is a fucking zombie, and I'm waiting for my pussy juice to turn blue, so there's no need for you to take a tone with me. Got it?"

I said, "Um, yeah. Got it." I gave her what I hoped was a heroic look, then said, "We're here to help."

She said, "Great, sure, fine. Whatever, fella. Good luck with that." Her phone buzzed; she picked it up and said, "Yes," then she gave me a fake smile and said, "Mr. Gregson will see you now."

I couldn't think of anything to say, so I woke Tobe's ass up and dragged him into Gregson's office.

DICK GREGSON:

If you ran into Tobe Hooper at a party or a screening, you wouldn't think, *This guy made one of the bloodiest flicks in movie history*. You'd think, *This guy looks like my high school English lit professor*. He'd generally be wearing a sport coat with a T-shirt, his hair and beard neatly trimmed. He looked the part.

That day, not so much.

He was wearing old, ratty jeans and a wrinkly button-down shirt that I'd wager had been slept in a few times. His eyes were red and baggy, as if he hadn't had a good night's sleep in weeks. His hair was disheveled, and he was exceptionally pale. This didn't bode well for his pitch.

He introduced me to his co-producer, Erick. I said to Erick, "I've never heard your name before. What's your background?"

Erick said, "I don't really have one."

I said, "You don't have a background?"

He said, "Let's just leave it at that." Then he said to Tobe, "Go."

Tobe asked me, "Where the fuck is everybody, Dick? This place is a morgue."

I said, "Gamed."

Tobe said, "I figured. Good news, though. I'm here to help."

I said, "Yeah? How so?"

He said, "Okay. So back when I was a little shit in Austin, I made a movie."

I asked him, "Really? How old were you?"

He said, "Sixteen or fifteen, or fourteen, or seventeen, or something."

I said, "I'd love to see it."

Erick said, "You most definitely do *not* want to see it."

I said, "I wouldn't go in expecting *Casablanca* or anything. I'd be curious for historical purposes. What's it called?"

Tobe said, "*Destiny Express.*"

I said, "Great title." And I meant it.

Tobe said, "I'm glad you dig it. Because you're going to give me the money to remake it. We need cameras. We need sound shit. We need old-school editing equipment. We need transportation money. Hundred grand ought to do it."

I said, "Well, Tobe, right now we're not making anything scary. The marketplace is already scared. Nobody's going to pay fourteen bucks to get freaked out. They can look out their front door to do that. But maybe when things get back to normal, I'll consider it. Send me a print and a screenplay, then we'll talk."

Tobe stood up and roared, "You're not getting a print. You're not getting a screenplay. You're going to give us one hundred thousand dollars to make this movie, and every cent is going toward production, and me and Erick aren't taking a dime for ourselves, and you need to get your numbers assholes to cut the check before we leave here, because we need to get started, like, yesterday, and we're going to have it done in three weeks, and there's going to be one screening and one screening only, and *that's . . . the . . . fucking . . . deal.*"

I said, "Tobe, please sit down, and please stop yelling." I wondered if he'd caught a case of the Game; after all, over-the-top aggression was one of the many symptoms. I opened the middle top drawer of my desk, reached in, and released the safety on the handgun I bought right before I came back to the office, after my daughter's funeral. I didn't like guns, but the times had changed. You have to play it safe.

Tobe said, "Sorry, man. I'm sorry, really." He sat down, then said, "It's been a rough week. But listen, I'm serious, Dick. I'm broke. Erick's broker. You *have* to give us the bread. You *have* to green-light us. This *has* to happen."

I said, "It's not going to. Now I have another meeting. Thanks for coming in, guys."

That Erick kid said, "Bullshit you have another meeting. There's nobody on this fucking lot except for Matthew motherfucking McConaughey, and Jeff motherfucking Bridges, and a bunch of tech people, and none of them want to meet with you. You've got the dude who made one of the greatest, most profitable horror films in history in your office, and he has something important to say, and you'd better damn well listen to him. He deserves that. You owe him that much. Hollywood owes him that much."

Nobody had spoken to me like that since I became head of production, and I didn't appreciate it. I was about to tell this little pisher he'd never have lunch in this town again—I'd always wanted to use that line; thank you, Julia Phillips—but Tobe piped up before I had a chance to talk. He told Erick, "That was really nice of you to say, man. Thank you." Then he turned to me and said, "The kid's right, Dick. You have to listen. And come on, don't bullshit me: You've got nothing else going on. So hear us out. Ten minutes. Fifteen tops."

They were right. I didn't have a meeting. I didn't have jack shit to do, except sit around and try not to burst out into my daily crying jag. So I heard them out.

ERICK LAUGHLIN:
Tobe was tired and frustrated, and it showed in his pitch. Such as it was.

He said, "This movie, this little shitbag movie of mine, this juvenile piece of crap I made before I knew what a shot sheet was, well, there's a possibility that it caused a whole heap of trouble. We showed it in public once—one goddamn time—and that one goddamn time might've caused a catastrophe. It might've caused the Game. Now, if you back us, Dick, if you give us the bread, if you give us your support, we might be able to *unhappen* it. We might be able to fix things." He paused for dramatic effect, then said, "We might be able to change the world, brother."

Dick said, "Tobe, that's a great sentiment, but if I may be blunt, each week, twenty-some-odd people sit where you're sitting and tell me how they're going to change the world. I appreciate that your heart's in the right place, but—"

Tobe cut him off right there and said, "Listen, Gregson, here's the fucking deal: *Destiny Express* started the goddamn Game, and we think that if we remake the goddamn thing, there's a chance—just a goddamn slight chance—that we can figure out how to put this goddamn disease, or syndrome, or whatever you'd goddamn well call it, to bed. Don't you think that's worth a one-hundred-K gamble? Don't you?" He was practically in tears.

Dick said, "Okay, before I shut down this meeting, answer me this: How could you possibly think that a movie could do this? If I may be blunt again, you sound insane."

Tobe sprang out of his chair, then jumped across Gregson's desk, grabbed him by the lapel of his expensive-ass suit jacket, and shook, and shook, and shook. He yelled, "It's narrow-minded assholes like you who are *killing* this industry, just *fucking* killing it. First you're killing art, now you're killing people. How does that feel? Does that feel good knowing that you're the death of dreams, Dickie boy? Does it? *Does it?!*"

I pulled Tobe off Gregson before any serious damage was done. After I calmed him down—which took some doing, I should note—I asked Gregson, "Can I show you something on your laptop?"

I think if Gregson were in a better state, he probably would've told me to fuck off. But Tobe's attack took him off his game, so he motioned for me to come around the desk and said, "Fine. But be quick."

I showed him Andi's blog, which, for some reason, had survived the great Internet sweep. I showed him some stuff about Aaron Gillespie, that psycho suicide bomber. I showed him as many of Scary Barry's tweets as I could find. I told him about Janine getting the shit kicked out of her. I told him about my nighttime strolls. I told him about Gary going zombie. And then I played my trump card: "Each one of these people was at the *Destiny Express* screening. You do the math."

Gregson watched and listened respectfully, and for that, I give him credit. At one point while he was checking out Andi's blog, it even looked like he was about to cry. After a bit, he said, "What guarantee do I have that this project will have any effect on the Game?"

I said, "You don't. Neither do we. But from what I can tell, nobody *anywhere* has been able to come up with a way to fight this thing. I mean, think about all that H1N1 business. There was a vaccine that was being used up faster than they could manufacture it. And it was all over the news, even before it was widely available. I haven't heard shit about a Game vaccine. Have you?"

Gregson said, "Of course I haven't."

I said, "That's right, you haven't. So if there's even the *remotest* possibility this would work, wouldn't it make sense for Warner Bros. to be all over it?"

Gregson didn't move or say a word. Finally, after probably a minute of dead silence, Tobe said, "Listen to me, Dick: If you say no, the second I get out of your office, I'm calling Connie Borelli over at Fox, and me and Erick here are going to give her the exact same pitch we gave you, and if she says yes, and this works—if this redux of mine does what we hope it's going to do—word will get around about you passing on this, and you're going to look like the biggest idiot in Hollywood history. You'll be forever known as the moron who passed on the opportunity to kill a disease. You want that on your record, brother? You want to be the guy who blew off the chance to keep your son, or your cousin, or your best friend from shooting blue shit from his cock? Hunh? Do you?"

Gregson put his head in his hand and said, "Guys, you have to go now."

I said, "Seriously? You're sending us away?"

He said, "Yeah. I don't want you in the room while my boss is tearing me a new asshole for okaying this . . . this . . . this *pipe dream.* Leave your address with my assistant. I'll deliver the check myself."

DICK GREGSON:

My boss indeed tore me a new asshole. That's all you need to know. I don't care to discuss details.

After that meeting, I left the studio, drove to my house, and grabbed my checkbook. When I showed up at Tobe's doorstep and handed him the check, he gave me a bear hug that damn near collapsed my lungs.

I didn't know if I'd be the hero of the story or the fool who pissed away $100,000 of his own money. But if I was going down, I was going down swinging. Celia would've wanted it that way.

CLAIRE CRAFT:

I don't have the kind of job that allows me to up and leave without any significant notice. The buck stops with me. I'm *Vanity Fair*'s final line of defense. If an article has a factual error, it's my fault, even though the author, or a junior editor, or a fact-checker should've caught it. So when Tobe Hooper's friend Erick called and told me there was a first-class plane ticket to Austin waiting for me at LaGuardia for a nine-thirty flight, I laughed. I couldn't help it. The thought of me bailing on my coworkers just like that was, well, *laughable*.

I told him, "Absolutely not. And even if I had sufficient time to prepare, I wouldn't do it. It's ridiculous."

Erick said, "Don't you think it's ridiculous that the undead are wandering around Times Square?"

I said, "There aren't zombies wandering around Times Square. There hasn't been a word about it on the news. And I'm in Times Square every day." I was lying to him, and he knew it. I mean, my car took me through Times Square each morning and each evening. I knew the score. Maybe not the *whole* score—I never looked out the window—but maybe I didn't want the whole score.

He said, "Do me a favor. Are you by your computer?"

I said, "Yes."

He said, "Go to YouTube and do a search on 'zombies' and 'New York City' and 'eating.'"

I asked him, "What will I see?"

He said, "Just do it."

I said, "I really don't have time—"

He interrupted me: "*Just . . . fucking . . . do it*. Please. I'm begging you, here."

I said, "Fine. If it'll get you off the phone," then I surfed over to YouTube and entered Erick's search terms. Fifteen videos came up. I asked him, "Is there any particular one you want me to watch?"

He said, "Do you see one with the header 'Day of the Living Dead'?"

I said, "It's the first one."

He said, "Good. Click on it."

I did. I wish I hadn't. I had the score.

AUTHOR'S NOTE: *I myself never saw the "Day of the Living Dead" video, and all traces of it seem to have disappeared. It remains one of the great mysteries of the Game.*

ERICK LAUGHLIN:

Ah, yes, the legendary "Day of the Living Dead" video. Like everybody else in the world, I thought it was a hoax. I thought that somebody, like Quentin Tarantino or Eli Roth, slapped it together for shits and giggles. But then when the hot chick from MSNBC and the gay dude from CNN interviewed the poor guy whose leg got yanked off, everybody knew it was the real deal.

It was shot with an iPhone, and the quality was clear but not exceptional, which made it look even creepier, even more realistic. Like, you couldn't see the zombie's whole face, but you could make out the shit oozing *from* her face, which practically glowed in the dark. She was moving faster than you'd expect—virtually human speed, for that matter—so she looked, I don't know, *formidable*. Unbeatable, even.

It happened fast, man, really fast. She shuffled into the picture, then bit this young woman in the neck, then the arm, then the leg, then the breast. And when I say "bit," I don't mean nibbles. No, the zombie girl was pulling chunks off the human girl. When the zombie bit the woman's stomach, she went extra deep, so when she came up for air, the girl's intestines fell on the sidewalk. As the girl stumbled away, her guts unraveled like an old garden hose.

A muscular black dude in his teens tried to take down the zombie girl, and she ripped off his leg like it was nothing. His fucking leg ripped off right at the quadriceps. I have no idea how he lived.

The clip was only one minute long, and it would've been longer—possibly *way* longer—had the cop not shot her in the back.

CLAIRE CRAFT:

I told Erick, "That was the most disgusting thing I have ever seen in my life. I'm appalled that somebody would post something that awful, considering everything that's happened. What kind of person would take the time to make that, just to get a rise? Especially *now*."

Erick said, "Claire, no disrespect, but you are in such denial, it's . . . it's . . . it's *insane*. Just fucking insane. You have a research department. Use it. Get the real story. Read up." And then he said something that struck me: "If there's even the slightest chance this is for real, and your participation is key in making our, I don't know, *reversal* work, wouldn't you want to be a part of it?"

I said, "Erick, I suppose your heart is in the right place, but—"

He didn't let me finish. He said, "Jesus Christ, Claire, it's three days of your life. Get your ass out of the office, go to your jillion-dollar condo, pack a bag, get to the airport, and get the fuck down to Texas. Don't be a cunty stuck-up bitch."

TOBE HOOPER:

I told Erick that if she was being difficult and he needed to go DEFCON five, he should call her a cunty stuck-up bitch. Just a hunch.

ERICK LAUGHLIN:

And then she hung up on me. I thought, *Nice job, Tobe. Good piece of advice with the name-calling.*

Gregson went out-of-pocket, so we owed it to him to get moving, with or without Claire Craft. Since she was out, the question was, who the hell do we cast as our cue-card girl? Me, I was rooting for Jennifer Aniston. Yeah, she wasn't age appropriate, but I'd always had a boner for her, and it's part of the producer's job to sleep with actresses, so I figured I'd float it past Tobe.

Kidding. My heart—and my dick—belonged to Janine. Sorry, Ms. Aniston. Your loss.

TOBE HOOPER:

We flew back to Austin, and I checked into the Four Seasons; my thinking was, *Fuck it, if I'm going out, I'm going out in style.* I still have no idea how Claire found out I was staying there.

She showed up at, I don't know, four in the morning or something, and despite her obvious tiredness, she looked all put together just so, exactly like you'd expect a high-powered magazine chick to look.

I stared at her for a second, then said, "You came."

She said, "I did."

CLAIRE CRAFT:

I had to go. What convinced me? Well, Tobe Hooper was just mystical enough to have created this whole mess. Which I'm sure is why everybody else showed up.

WILLIAM MARRON:

I refused Tobe's plane ticket. I didn't give a damn if Jack Warner himself offered to pay for my flight. I wanted to make my own way there. It was the least I could do.

DARREN ALLEN:

I came. I went. I saw. I conquered.

THEO MORRISON:

Erick banged on my door at, what, like five in the morning or something and said, "Dude, you wanna be a zombie in Tobe's new movie? Before you answer, bear in mind that you'll have to wrestle a fake alligator stuffed with dead animals, and you'll have to suck the neck of a sixty-something-year-old woman, and you'll be covered in ooze made from some of the most unbelievably rancid shit in the world, and there's a decent chance that when this movie gets edited and shown for an actual audience, you'll die a horrible death."

I was like, "Bro, nothing would make me happier. Where do I sign?"

ERICK LAUGHLIN:

It didn't make sense for me to be in the flick. Spiritually speaking, Theo was about as close to Gary Church as we could find: Gary had been Tobe's best friend, and Theo was mine. Gary was an aspiring actor and Theo was an aspiring musician. Gary was short, and Theo was short. And, most important, Gary was dead, and Theo was available.

HELEN LEARY:

When Erick Laughlin invited me to Austin, I told him I'd come on one condition: that I could bring my family along. And he went ballistic: "No goddamn way, Helen! No goddamn way! I don't even want *you* to come, for chrissakes! Hell, I don't want *anybody* to come! This could turn out to be a clusterfuck of the highest order! People could get hurt! Seriously goddamn hurt!"

I said, "I understand that. And they understand that. But they believe in Tobe, and they want to be with me."

He was quiet for a second, then he said, "Listen, Helen. You seem like a nice lady. And I'm not a violent person by nature. But I swear to God, if you bring your husband or any of your children with you to Texas, I'm going to drag their asses back to the airport and physically throw them onto the plane myself. And if you don't believe it, well, just try me."

I didn't want to try him. That tone in his voice was deadly. So I kissed my family good-bye and went by myself.

DARREN ALLEN:

I brought the original camera. The *original.* It wasn't in Tobe's locker at the society. It was in my basement at my house. It hadn't been touched in decades. And I had it. In my basement. In my house.

It was mine.

ERICK LAUGHLIN:

We didn't fuck around. We *couldn't* fuck around. The clock was ticking . . . or at least that's how Tobe and I had begun to look at it. We *had* to believe in what we were doing, and *believing* it meant *doing* it, and *doing* it meant doing it *fast*. What were we going to do, sit around and wait for another city to go up in flames? Or until we were 100 percent certain this movie would have *any* effect on *anything*? We had to roll cameras, and we couldn't let anything stop us.

TOBE HOOPER:

A shot-by-shot remake is a colossal pain in the ass, and it almost never works. You want proof? Check out Gus Van Sant's version of *Psycho* that he shot in, what, '98 or something. Gus is a master, but that thing, it wasn't one of his finer moments, probably because, well, because a shot-by-shot remake is a colossal pain in the ass.

But Gus had one thing on his side that I didn't: a clear template to work from. *Destiny Express* was a snafu from top to bottom, and even though I'd watched it ten-ish times—which is ten-ish times too many—I couldn't get a handle on it. Probably because the movie had no point.

See, *Chainsaw* was a story. It wasn't *The Iliad* or anything, but it had an arc, a beginning, middle, and end. Yes, it was about shocking the audience, but they wouldn't have been shocked if it was a random series of attacks and murders, because they wouldn't have been absorbed into the picture. There would've been distance. If there wasn't anything for the viewer to grab on to, they wouldn't have given a good goddamn what happened to good ol' Sally Hardesty.

This isn't to say that I was planning to infuse *Destiny Express Redux* with meaning; we were staying loyal to the original, so that would've been impossible, because the original was meaningless. But I was a different person come remake time. I had almost two dozen films under my belt, and some of them weren't too bad. It was ingrained in me to bring a point of view to the table, so divorcing myself from the true creative process and shooting a series of random zombie attacks felt tepid and unnatural. I wanted to give it some semblance of, I don't know, nonsuckitude. That was my default mode. But a dude's got to do what a dude's got to do, and I had to make it as sucky as the original, so I was going to make 100 percent certain it would suck *exactly* as bad as the original, no more, no less. So before we shot a single frame of film, I sat down with Darren Allen to figure out the perfect schedule for perfect suckage.

And that was more fun than a barrel of bat guano.

DARREN ALLEN:

I had the original schedule. I kept it. Deep down, I knew I'd need it. Deep down. I don't know how. I don't know why. I just did. I did. I did.

TOBE HOOPER:

I have no clue what happened to Darren Allen. Back when we were kids, he was always somewhat of a misfit, but man, present-day, the fellow was a mess. He breathed heavy, and he stared at you a little too tightly, and he was dressed like a homeless man with a good clothing connection.

You know how sometimes a guy is so difficult to talk to that you have trouble making eye contact with him, because it's so goddamn uncomfortable? That was the deal with the 2009 version of Darren. But I had to do it.

DARREN ALLEN:

Tobe liked the original schedule. He thought it was cool.

TOBE HOOPER:

I hated the original schedule. I thought it was fucking creepy.

First, there was my handwriting. I always thought I had pretty neat handwriting, even when I was a kid, but that yellowing piece of paper that Darren was holding on to for dear life was covered with the scrawl of a madman.

DARREN ALLEN:

It was unreadable. But that's why it was cool.

TOBE HOOPER:

Darren couldn't read it, so I asked him why he even bothered to bring the damn thing with him. He kept saying, "Redux, redux, redux." Man, he was one weird dude.

So I threw him out of my room, called Erick, and told him to act like a goddamn producer and produce me a goddamn schedule.

ERICK LAUGHLIN:

I ignored the goddamn schedule. I didn't think the cosmos would mind.

Since I was dealing with a bunch of nonacting actors, a cameraman who had problems communicating with anybody who didn't operate in his bizarre-o orbit—which was everybody—a makeup and effects guy who hadn't made up or effected anything but computers for the last three-some-odd decades, and an over-tired director who, just one week ago, had gunned down and killed his zombified friend, I thought it best to keep things simple.

So. Day one, we'd shoot Tobe's intro, then we'd have Claire do her cue card thing, then Theo would kill her off, then we'd send her on her merry way. And we had a very good reason for doing that first. I don't like using the "C" word, but Tobe was right: That girl was a grade-A cunt.

Then that night, William, Theo, and I would gather up the roadkill, and Tobe and Helen would steal some leather jackets, then we'd converge at Tobe's room at the Four Seasons and make ourselves a gator. That was the only thing I was looking forward to: bringing a pile of dead animals in and out of a four-star hotel.

Day two, the alligator scene. That was going to be a logistical nightmare, no two ways about it. I expected it to be an eighteen-hour day. Good thing nobody on the crew was union.

Day three I planned to keep somewhat flexible, because there was a chance we'd have to finish off the alligator scene. After that, it would be all Theo and Helen. Attack, after attack, after attack.

Day four, the car wreck. I hoped Darren could handle all the moving around with the camera. I hoped.

Day five, establishing shots and actual human interaction. I saved that for last, because by that point, I was sure we'd need an easy day, and since there were only about five minutes of real dialogue in the entire movie, we could knock that out on the quick.

Day six through who-knows-when, edit this damn thing as fast as possible. Why the need for speed? Because thanks to a sympathetic movie theater manager named Marcus Frost, *Destiny Express Redux* was premiering at the Regal Arbor Cinema on September 1.

I took care of all that—the schedule, booking the theater, and some other logistical crap that I don't remember—in about four hours. Turns out that doing the producing thing wasn't all that difficult. I don't know what Scott Rudin's always complaining about.

TOBE HOOPER:

My primary concern about the end product was the gore factor. Even though it was a piece of rat dung, *Destiny Express* was solidly disgusting. I know I have the ability and intestinal fortitude to be as repulsive as Tarantino or Roth, but we were on a budget, and it wasn't like we had the luxury of watching dailies or anything. So I put on my blinders, shot it, and hoped it'd look properly gross on the big screen.

WILLIAM MARRON:

Listen, I love Tobe, and I think he's a true artist, but *Destiny Express* stunk, and *Destiny Express Redux* wasn't going to be any better.

The first thing we shot was Claire's cue card intro, and even though she was a beautiful woman, and even though I did the best I could with what I had to work with, she looked ridiculous in that Catholic schoolgirl outfit. Sixtysomething women, no matter how well preserved they might be, should never wear plaid skirts with thigh-high stockings.

Claire then cooled her jets—which, frankly, needed cooling—while I turned young Theo into a zombie. That was . . . interesting.

THEO MORRISON:

So after Billy put on my ratty-ass zombie clothes and my nasty-ass zombie scars, he tells me to close my eyes and hold my nose, then he dumps a bucket of I-don't-know-what over my head, and that shit stank to high heaven.

I was like, "Yo, what's in this? I'm going to hurl, here. Seriously."

He said, "Theo, you don't want to know."

Now, Billy was a nice dude, so I didn't want to go off on him, but if I was going to have to be covered in this slop for the next week, I had to be aware. So I was like, "Yeah, dude, I *totally* want to know."

He was quiet for a sec, then he was like, "Okay, fine. But trust me, you won't get sick."

I was like, "I don't know, dude. This stuff smells like crotch, and I seriously feel like I'm going to blorch."

He was all like, "Yeah, but blorching from crotch smell doesn't mean you're sick."

I was like, "I see your point. So what in holy hell am I wearing?"

Billy gave me a big sigh, then was like, "Grape jelly, petroleum jelly, pickle juice, tomato juice, mashed-up bananas, and . . ."

He didn't say anything, and I was like, "And what?"

He was like, "And a bit of animal excrement."

I was like, "What the fuck, dude?! You covered me with shit?!"

He was like, "Yes. But it's safe shit."

I was like, "How the hell do you make shit safe?"

He was like, "You, um, you boil it."

I was like, "So you're telling me that I'm wearing hot diarrhea."

Billy was like, "Well, not exactly. After all, it's not hot."

I was like, "But it *was* hot at one time in the not-too-distant past."

He goes, "Yeah. But it's cold now."

I was like, "But it's still diarrhea."

He was like, "But it's *safe* diarrhea."

I go, "I don't know if I necessarily believe that, Bill. Do you have any scientific data to back that shit up?"

He goes, "No. But Gary Church wore it during the original, and he lived."

I was like, "Yeah. But he also died."

Then Tobe and Erick came over, and Tobe was like, "Theo, my brother, you smell like ass. Perfect. Let's shoot this fucker."

TOBE HOOPER:

We banged out the first part of Claire's section in seven takes. If I were *trying* to make it look good, I would've nailed it the first time through—I mean, how hard is it to shoot somebody flipping cue cards, right? But I'd done so many films that shooting a quality shot was *ingrained* in me. It took all that extra time to make it feel amateurish.

It would've been even more difficult if I'd had a professional, experienced cameraman. Fortunately, Darren was a rank amateur.

DARREN ALLEN:

I shot it. And I shot it perfectly. I *always* shoot perfectly.

TOBE HOOPER:

Then Erick's boy Theo slimed his way onto the set, so he could kill Claire for the closing scene. To be honest, if I had the opportunity, I would've killed her myself. My Lord, what a pain in the backside she was.

CLAIRE CRAFT:

I'm sorry if Tobe felt I was a distraction, but this wasn't exactly a walk in the park. First, they put me in these ridiculous-looking slut clothes, then they had me attacked by a kid who was dressed in a ridiculous-looking zombie costume and was stinking like a sewer. It was hideous. While the kid was attacking me, he accidentally scratched my arm, and I think some of that crap he was covered with oozed into my bloodstream. Billy assured me that I shouldn't worry, but the second I was done for the day, I called my doctor in New York and told him to have a tetanus shot ready to go.

THEO MORRISON:

I didn't *attack* her, for fuck's sake. I did exactly what Tobe told me to do, which was circle around her, pretend to hit her, and moan. He said he'd edit it so it'd look badass. I believed him.

WILLIAM MARRON:

The fake arm, the spurting blood, making Claire's death look convincing: It was all easy. It was like riding a bike. It was a blast, and for a brief moment, I thought about taking a leave of absence and trying to get some work in Hollywood. But then I remembered what Tobe had told me—that Hollywood was a ghost town—so forget that.

TOBE HOOPER:

And then it was my turn. And I was not psyched. Not one bit.

Some directors like to see themselves on the screen—Woody Allen and Alfred Hitchcock come to mind—but not me. Me, I like to be safe and sound in my cocoon behind the camera.

The dialogue was inane: "Good afternoon, dear viewers. My name is Tobe Hooper. You don't know me. I could be a nice guy. I could be a liar and a thief. I could even be a killer. You can believe everything I tell you. Or you can ignore every word that I say. Or you can burn this film into a pile of ashes. But if I were you, I'd listen carefully. Because I have the camera. And I know the truth." Come *on*, man.

After I wrapped up all that gobbledygook, Theo went after me. I guess I could see why Claire was so bitchy when she said good-bye.

ERICK LAUGHLIN:

Tobe was bitchier about the whole thing than Claire was. It was all, "Marron, you'd best de-stink this motherfucker *now*," and "Who's the idjit that wrote this shit . . . oh, wait, it was me," and "Erick, be my body double." It's amazing we finally got it in the can and finished the day without anybody killing anybody else.

HELEN LEARY:

I wish I could describe to you exactly what happened, but it was a blur. I remember getting off the airplane, I remember getting to the hotel, then I remember getting back onto the plane. The four days I was in Austin are a blank.

The day after I got home, I started seeing a shrink. She believes that I blocked out the whole thing. She said—and these are her exact words—"It was a traumatic experience that recalled another traumatic experience. There's no reason for you to recall any of it, because you'll learn nothing about yourself. Put it away inside a safe, lock it up, throw away the key, and move on with your life."

So that's what I did. I never saw the finished product—I had no desire to—and I never spoke to Tobe Hooper again.

BILLY MARRON:

Honestly, I didn't believe it.

I didn't believe that Tobe's childhood movie caused any kind of virus, and I didn't believe that Tobe's adult movie would cure *anything*.

At least at first.

When I got back to New York and I couldn't remember a damn thing about the shoot after I put together that stinking alligator, I believed.

A little.

DARREN ALLEN:

I came. I went. I saw. I conquered.

At least I thought I did.

I made it home. My camera and the screenplay didn't. I was mad. And sad.

THEO MORRISON:

Yeah, I don't remember a damn thing after day two, but I credit that to the fact that I smoked a shit-ton of pot that week.

TOBE HOOPER:

It was weird, man. One second, I've got Theo making out with Helen, and the next, I'm in my hotel, futzing with the footage on the makeshift editing bay that Dick Gregson so graciously paid for.

And that footage was putrid, somehow worse than the original. Watching it actually sickened me. That's probably why I don't remember the specifics about cutting that fucker together. But that was okay, actually. If my brain decided to kick into denial mode, what better time than that?

ERICK LAUGHLIN:

I was so wrapped up with the movie that I didn't notice until August 31—the night before the international debut of *Destiny*

Express—that the streets of Austin were empty. Actually, they weren't totally empty: There were a bunch of guys in hazmat suits wandering around with these scary-ass guns.

I wondered, *When the hell did this happen? And how the hell did I miss it?*

JANINE DALTREY:
It happened quickly, so Erick can't be blamed for not catching it right away. One day, it's business as usual, and the next, everybody's hiding in their house, and all these military guys are patrolling the streets. There weren't a lot of them—maybe one or two teams of two positioned every few blocks—but they were *there*. We called it the Great Austin Takeover. On the plus side, the fires stopped. It was a trade-off, I guess.

Austin wasn't the only city that was on its deathbed. We weren't completely alone. Erick told me that Tobe told him that Los Angeles was unbelievably quiet. But there was nothing about it online or on television, absolutely nothing, so I didn't know for sure.

There was some info out there. Based on a *very* detailed blog by somebody in Albuquerque that somehow hadn't been shut down by whatever entity was shutting down huge chunks of the web, they were dealing with the fires, and explosions, and sex crimes, and apparent zombie attacks—and I say "apparent" because I wasn't totally convinced about the zombie thing at that point—and a heck of a lot of violence. There were hazmat guys on the street, but it sounded like the military presence hadn't quite reached the level that we were at. But it was getting close.

I sent an e-mail to the contact address at the bottom of the Albuquerque blog, but it bounced. That didn't make me feel so hot.

It was more than a little bit disconcerting that the government, or some powers that be, had the ability to completely shut off a story, and it made me wonder what the hell we were missing . . . but I didn't wonder that hard. The fact of the matter was, I was scared, and my body was still hurting, and my heart was broken—you can't imagine how much I missed my little sister—and I wasn't in the mood to play investigative journalist. All I wanted to do was cuddle in the sack with Erick and hide under the covers until this all went away.

And if it didn't go away, what better place was there to be than in bed? If we were going to die, at least we'd die comfortably . . . which is more than I can say for my sister.

ERICK LAUGHLIN:

From the outside, the Regal Arbor Cinema looked like any other multiplex: a ticket taker, a marquee, and a couple of posters on the wall. Nothing special. The inside wasn't much to write home about, either: It was slightly dilapidated, the floors were sticky with months-old soda spills, the bathrooms were in need of some serious updating, and most of the seats creaked when you sat down. Probably the ideal place to show our little flick.

We didn't advertise it or anything. We frankly didn't want anybody to see it. We didn't want to see it ourselves.

Oh. Right. I suppose I should mention that we hadn't seen it yet.

TOBE HOOPER:

Let's do a checklist here: We've got the goddamn zombies, and we've got the goddamn Blue Spew, and we've got goddamn cities burning, and we've got goddamn psychotics beating the crap out of whoever they want to beat the crap out of, and we've got hundreds of people killing themselves in some pretty goddamn imaginative ways. Pretty goddamn weird, right? Right.

But believe it or not, for me, for yours truly, for Tobe Hooper, for the dude who might've started this mess, that wasn't the weirdest.

No, the weirdest was waking up on the morning of August 31 with a film sitting on my nightstand. Right there on the canister, in my own handwriting: *Destiny Express Redux.*

See, I didn't remember finishing it.

ERICK LAUGHLIN:
Naturally we'd planned to show the flick at midnight. We had to.

At noon, my cell phone rang. Unknown number. I screened it. Whoever it was didn't leave a message, so I figured it was a wrong number. Then they called again two minutes later, and the same deal. Then, two minutes later, again. I couldn't turn my phone off, because I needed to be accessible to Janine, so finally, after the sixth call, I picked it up and yelled, "*What?!*"

It was a guy. He said, "Is this Erick?"

I said, "Yeah. Who's this?"

The guy said, "Erick Laughlin? Erick Laughing Boy? Erick the Half a Bee? Erick the Earache?"

Fuck. Dude McGee. I said, "How did you get my number, McGee?"

He said, "You're not hard to find, Laughing Boy. You're not that important. It's not like anybody's protecting your whereabouts."

I said, "So somebody at the newspaper gave it to you."

Dude said, "Oh. No. They wouldn't. Bastards. I have other means. Don't worry about it. So how'd the movie turn out? Better than the first one, I'd hope."

I said, "I'm in a bit of a rush. What do you want?"

He said, "I'd like to see To-*beeeee* Hoopster."

I said, "Hooper."

He said, "Right. Hoopster."

What a dick. I said, "He's incommunicado. Can I help you with something?"

He said, "I'd like to come to the screening."

I thought, *What the fuck?* We hadn't told a single person about it. Our plan was to show it to the empty theater and hope for the best. I said, "How did you find out about it?"

Dude said, "A mutual friend told me. Darren. Darren Allen. Darren Baron Allen. Darren Gallon Allen. Baron Gallon."

I desperately wanted to get off the phone, but I had to ask: "How do you know Darren Allen?"

Dude said, "Oh, I've known about Darren Allen Baron Gallon for a while. He's huge in Houston. Do you want to hear something funny about Darren Allen Baron Gallon? Do you want to know why Darren Allen Baron Gallon is kind of . . . off?"

Tobe had insisted that back in the day, Darren was considerably less weird than he was when he was shuffling around our sets, seemingly barely able to hold the camera, so I actually was a little bit curious. I said, "Sure, Dude. Tell me why Darren is kind of off."

He said, "The poor man was in a terrible car accident a few years back. It almost crushed his head. He doesn't like to discuss it."

I said, "I can imagine."

Dude said, "No. You can't. You can't imagine. It was awful."

I said, "How would you know?"

He said, "Why would you care?"

I said, "I don't."

He said, "I didn't think so. But you should. I did. I helped him. I helped make him feel better. Or at least feel different. See, nobody cared about Darren Allen Baron Gallon. But I did. I helped him, and he helped me. Would you like to know how?"

I didn't have the time or the energy for this, so I said, "Frankly, Dude, I wouldn't."

He said, "None of this would've happened without Darren Allen Baron Gallon. He was the catalyst."

I said, "That's great, Dude."

He said, "His preservation skills are simply marvelous."

Again, I said, "That's great, Dude."

He said, "He's a magician with that camera. Did you like the way he shot your little movie, Earache Laughing Boy?"

I said, "I don't know. I haven't seen it yet."

He said, "I thought you might say that. So. Will your Mr. Hoopster see me after the show, or what?"

I didn't bother correcting him on the name. He was either being his usual moronic self or being willfully douchebaggy, so why waste my breath? I said, "You know what, McGee? Fuck it. If this works, you get some credit. It was kind of your idea to get the band back together, so come on down. I can't guarantee Tobe will want to talk to you, though. That's up to him."

He said, "He'll talk to me. Oh yes he will, Earache, Ache Ear, Ache Ache."

Christ, what a moron.

JANINE DALTREY:
The argument lasted for, I don't know, ninety minutes or so, and it was the kind of argument that a stubborn boyfriend has with his stubborn girlfriend: Each party makes the same point over and over, just restating it in a million different ways. The winner is usually the one who outlasts the other.

My position: *I'm coming to the goddamn screening.*

Erick's position: *No goddamn way. It might not be safe.*

My position: *If it's not safe, then you shouldn't go.*

His position: *I have to go.*

Long story short, he didn't want me anywhere near the place, because he didn't know what was going to happen, and I didn't want him anywhere near the place for the exact same reason, but if something was going to happen to him, then I thought it may as well happen to me.

I thought it was romantic, in an insane way. But at that point, I was a little insane. Wouldn't you be? I mean, practically everybody else was.

ERICK LAUGHLIN:

I wore her down, pure and simple. That's the only way I ever win any argument with her, because she's considerably smarter than me.

JANINE DALTREY:

When Erick told me that Dude McGee was going to be there, I didn't feel so bad about staying home.

TOBE HOOPER:

I told Erick that I was going to get to the theater at around eleven o'clock, and I didn't want him there until right before midnight. I didn't want *anybody* there until right before midnight. Hell, I didn't want anybody there *at all*, but I had a gut feeling that for this thing to work, *somebody* had to check out the damn thing, and if that somebody had to be me, so be it.

The front door was open when I showed, and the lights were off, and there was nobody to be seen. I wandered around the lobby calling, "Hello? Hello? Hello?" I felt like a goddamn horror flick cliché, like Wes Craven or Guillermo del Toro was directing the story of my life. Wes would've had some dude in a mask and gown tackle me from behind and jam a scythe in my back, and Guillermo would've had some sort of vampire materialize out of nowhere. Me, I would've cut right to the chase and had a naked woman chop my head off with an axe. But that's neither here nor there.

I eventually found the light switch and walked in a few circles until I tracked down the stairway up to the projection booth. The booth was just like any other booth, and the projector was just like any other projector. I looked out the projector hole, and the theater looked like it did the last time I was there: just like any other theater. There wasn't anything mystical or magical. It was just a big, dark room where people congregated to share the experience of watching a film together. I suppose that's mystical and magical in a way, but I doubted it was mystical and magical enough to cure a virus.

But fuck it. We made the movie. I figured we may as well show it. I took the film out of the canister, threaded up the projector, sat down on the floor, and stared at the wall.

Then there was a knock at the door.

August 31, 2009

To Whom It May Concern:

I write this of sound mind and fat body.

You don't know me.

I could be a nice guy.

I could be a liar and a thief.

I could even be a killer.

You can believe everything I tell you.

Or you can ignore every word that I say.

Or you can burn this paper into a pile of ashes.

But if I were you, I'd read carefully.

Because I have the pen.

And I know the truth.

On June 8, 1958, Scott James Frost and William Tobe Hooper were the victims of a hit-and-run car accident.

Frost was killed upon impact.

Hooper lived.

Frost was survived by his mother, his father, his sister, and his girlfriend.

Frost's girlfriend was pregnant at the time of the accident.

She had the baby in 1959.

She named him Xavier Frost.

Xavier got married in 1982 to a woman named Rebecca McGee.

They had a child in 1984.

It was a boy.

They named him Marcus.

I am Marcus.

Marcus is me.

And my father was my father.

Some might call my father a lost soul.

Some might call him a mess.

Some might call him angry.

Some might call him an asshole.

Me, I called him Daddy.

And he never answered.

I take that back.

He sometimes answered.

And when he answered, it was usually with his fists.

Sometimes it was with a belt.

Sometimes a wet towel.

On one memorable occasion, a straight razor.

Now, you might be saying, Boo-hoo, boo-hoo, boo-fucking-hoo, lots of people had it rough.

And you'd be right.

You might be asking, Do you still see Xavier?

Never.

Xavier is dead.

My father is dead.

But I do see the scar that runs from my hip to my knee.

And I still see the bruises, even though they're probably not there.

And in my dreams, I still see the pain in my father's eyes.

Pain from not having a father.

I know that pain.

And I need to share that pain.

Had Xavier Frost had a father, his pain might not have existed.

Had Xavier Frost's pain not existed, Marcus Frost's pain might not have existed.

I am Marcus Frost.

So my thinking has always been, Somebody should share the pain.

My thinking has always been, Lots of people should share the pain.

Sharing is the polite thing to do.

And since sharing is the polite thing to do, maybe if I shared, I would feel better.

But how to share.

Here's where things get odd.

I was twenty.

I saw a movie.

The movie was released ten years to the day before I was born.

The movie was called The Texas Chainsaw Massacre.

The guy who made that movie knew pain.

The guy who made that movie knew how to share pain.

So I did some research.

The guy who made the movie was named William Tobe Hooper.

The same William Tobe Hooper who was on the scene when my grandfather was killed.

How many William Tobe Hoopers are there in this world?

So I researched.

And I experimented.

And I figured out how to bring the pain.

There were failures along the way.

And successes.

And casualties.

How did I do it?

How did I create a virus that could be transmitted by film?

How did I create a biological weapon that could end humanity as we know it?

How did I create a disease that has so many divergent symptoms?

I could give you the recipe, but you wouldn't understand it.

And even if you understood it, you couldn't replicate it.

Because you're not me.

And I am part of the process.

My blood is part of the process.

My snot is part of the process.

My shit is part of the process.

My cum is part of the process.

The pain that is on the film itself is part of the process.

Mix it all together, run it all through a hot film projector, and you have the Game.

Pain was felt all over the nation.

William Tobe Hooper was especially pained, pained to the nth degree.

Thus, my personal pain was sort of relieved.

Enough so that all of humanity didn't need to suffer anymore for my sake.

After a bit more suffering, it will end.

That is, if one person makes the ultimate sacrifice.

And I don't think anybody has the courage.

But I do.

I have the courage.

I can make the sacrifice.

That's life.

And death.

And pain.

Adieu.

Marcus Frost-McGee

TOBE HOOPER:

I opened the door, and it was Dude McGee, the man who got both *Destiny Express* and *Destiny Express Redux* rolling.

I said, "Why, Mr. McGee, this is a surprise." He was a large, odiferous man, and his attitude was terrible, and the name-mispronouncing thing got old, but for some reason, I was glad to see him. If this worked, if *Redux* reversed the curse, McGee would get an assist.

Then again, I probably would've been glad to see anybody. See, in retrospect, I realized I'd made a mistake by coming alone to the theater. That was some creepy shit, man, being alone in a dark movie theater, but what with the hazmat brigade and the tumbleweeded streets, *all* of Austin was creepy.

Dude said, "I wouldn't have missed this for the world, To-*beeeeee*. So how did it come out? How's the redux? How's the restoration?"

I said, "You know what, McGee? I have no fucking idea."

He said, "I thought you might say that."

ERICK LAUGHLIN:

I showed up to the theater at quarter to midnight, and who's waiting for me at the front entrance, looking like the fattest ticket taker in the world? That's right, the man, the myth, the legend, Dude McGee.

I tried to walk through the door without engaging him, but he wasn't having it. He said, "Earache Laughing Boy, a pleasure as always. You're the first person here. Wait, no, you're the second person here. To-*beeeeee* is upstairs getting ready for the show. He likes his Maker's Mark, that Mr. Hoover does."

I said, "I have to find him." Again, I tried to get past McGee, but he grabbed my bicep. He was surprisingly strong.

He said, "I have a piece of advice for you, Eerie Laugh Man.

Leave before the ending. Leave before the last scene. Beat the traffic."

I pointed to the empty street and said, "What traffic?"

He said, "I was making a funny. I do that once in a while."

I said, "Whatever," then took a peek over his shoulder to see if anybody was inside. "Quite a crowd we have here."

Dude looked at his watch and said, "Oh, your crowd is right on time."

I said, "There isn't going to be a crowd."

McGee said, "Sure there is."

He pointed over my shoulder. I turned around, and walking almost in lockstep were three dozen zombies.

He said, "That Marcus Frost sure managed to get the word out to the right people, didn't he?"

TOBE HOOPER:

Before he split to go grab a seat, Dude asked me to do him a favor. I wasn't really in a favor-giving headspace but figured that since he was the one who jumpstarted this campaign to save the world, I'd at least hear him out.

He said, "Leave before the movie ends."

I said, "No way, man. I have to see if the guy gets the girl in the end."

Dude said, "He doesn't. Just go. Go home to California. You've done enough. The world has suffered enough. The Game is over."

I said, "I'm staying, brother. I might be the only one."

He shrugged, then said, "Okay, Tobe Hooper. I tried."

I think that was the first time that motherfucker got my name right.

ERICK LAUGHLIN:

I hadn't seen any of the Game zombies up close and personal, only on television and from a far distance. Now, you'd think that since Tobe gave me such an in-depth description of his encounter with Gary Church, I'd have been prepared.

Listen, man, nothing can prepare you for that. Nothing.

On the plus side, they weren't being the least bit violent. They were shuffling to the theater with a purpose, as if they'd been summoned. When they got to the theater, they walked right past me and Dude as if we weren't even there.

On the minus side—and this is a very large fucking minus side—their stench was ghastly. Take the roadkill alligator, cover it with skunk spray, then vomit on it, and multiply that times fifty, and you've got it. You could *see* the smell, too. It was like they were all Pigpen from the Peanuts.

And their skin, Jesus Christ. It was green—olive drab, to be precise. And they all had these sores that were about an inch or so in diameter. Some of them were oozing white shit, and some of them were oozing blue shit, and all of them were bubbling and steaming.

I can't even bring myself to discuss the leprosy.

TOBE HOOPER:

The theater filled up. Erick told me it was going to be an empty theater. Guess he was wrong.

I tried to get a gander at what kind of crowd we were looking at, but it was dark, and the lights were off, and I couldn't see shit from the projection booth.

My only hope was that these people would leave the theater in the same state they'd arrived in.

ERICK LAUGHLIN:

And then, midnight. Roll film.

TOBE HOOPER:

My God, *Destiny Express Redux* was one majorly fucked-up piece of celluloid.

But it was still better than the first one.

ERICK LAUGHLIN:

I stood against the back, right by the exit. No way I was sitting next to any of those undead fuckers.

The zombies stopped their moaning the second the movie started. That made the theater smell slightly less rancid. Slightly.

The first thing we saw was Claire holding the cue cards. And the first cue card said, "DIE." Now, I wrote those cards out myself, and I sure as hell don't remember writing "DIE." But then again, I don't remember much of anything.

The second card: "TOBE."

The third card: "HOOPER."

The fourth card: "A PAINFUL."

The fifth card: "DEATH."

The next five cards: "DIE." "DIE." "DIE." "DIE." "DIE."

The last card: "BURN IN HELL."

Jesus. You'd think that an executive producer would remember such a deviation from the script.

TOBE HOOPER:

That was, without a doubt, the biggest what-the-fuck moment of my entire life. Yeah, I didn't remember shit about the shoot, but you'd think that a pile of cue cards wishing me eternal damnation would ring a bell.

ERICK LAUGHLIN:

And then Theo roared into the screen and cuts off Claire's arm. And that shit looked realer than real. Especially when Claire stared at her gushing shoulder, then passed out face-first on the concrete.

And then we saw Tobe, looking handsome and vibrant. He went into his spiel about being a liar and a thief, and then Theo came in and bit off both of his arms, then sucked on the stump as if he was giving Tobe's shoulder a blow job. Tobe then started chewing his own lips until they began bleeding. And then he screamed. And then Theo pulled down Tobe's pants and gave him a karate chop to the balls. Tobe passed out face-first, just like Claire.

Again, not in the original script. Again, not in the original movie.

It was at this point that the repulsive creatures populating our little movie theater came to life. They stayed calm and quiet, however, which made it that much worse to see them pulling off their own legs.

I threw up on my shoes when they started beating themselves on their own heads with their dismembered limbs.

TOBE HOOPER:

I knew Claire wasn't my biggest fan, but did she really have to tell me to die a painful death? And to go off script without telling anybody? Christ.

I have to give credit to Billy Marron. The dude spends thirty years dicking around with computers, and he manages to come up with better effects than Industrial Light and Magic, at one-ten-thousandth of the price.

The rest of *Redux* was as disjointed as the original but considerably more gruesome. Like, the alligator scene was unreal. I mean, the fucker bit a chunk out of Helen's neck, and you could see gristle.

And then there was Theo. Theo, Theo, Theo, holy mother of God, did he look revolting. What with the roiling warts, and the pointy teeth, and the festering scratches running up and down his face and arms, he made poor Gary Church seem like the picture of health.

I even covered my eyes when he castrated himself with a hammer and a chisel.

ERICK LAUGHLIN:

The smoke started coming from the screen about forty-five minutes in, and if *Redux* was true to the original, we only had fifteen minutes left until the movie was over. I hoped nobody asphyxiated before then. Hell, I hoped *I* didn't asphyxiate before then.

Somebody—or some*thing*—tapped me on the shoulder, and, without thinking, purely on reflex, I slugged him. Not that slugging a zombie would've done a damn bit of good—from what I'd gathered, they could be killed only with something potent like a gun or a knife—but I was on a hair trigger.

Turned out I'd cracked Dude McGee.

He rubbed his jaw, then said, "Get out of here, Erick. Leave. Seriously. Go. It's done. You're done. I've had enough. My point is made. I'm putting an end to this."

I thought, *Weird, he called me by my actual name,* then I said, "What point?"

He said, "Don't worry about it. Just go."

I said, "I have to see how this damn thing turns out."

Dude said, "I'm giving it away. Here's the spoiler: It's a happy ending. Now, go up to that projection booth, grab Tobe, and get the fuck out of here. By any means necessary."

Suddenly, he didn't seem like a moron. Suddenly, he seemed respectable. Suddenly, he seemed like a force to be reckoned with.

Suddenly, I wanted to get the hell out of that theater.

TOBE HOOPER:

Right as Theo and Helen are about to fuck their brains out on the screen, Erick bursts into the booth, grabs me by the back of my collar, and says, "We're going. *Now.*"

I said, "The hell we are. I've got to see the rest of this thing."

He said, "Tobe, right now there are thirty-some-odd undead fuckers down there ripping off their own legs. There's smoke shooting out of their bodies, and I don't know whether it's coming from their warts, or their stumps, or what, but I don't like it, and it smells like an electrical fire and burning hair, and the edges of the screen are smoking, and I really, really, *really* don't think we're meant to be here."

I said, "What do you mean 'meant to be here'?"

He said, "At the risk of sounding cheesy, it's time for us to get our asses off the *Destiny Express.*"

I said, "Brother, listen: Destiny is bullshit. Was I destined to be in a damn car wreck and lose my childhood and my best friend? Was the piddly little *Chainsaw* movie I made for eighty thousand dollars destined to make millions? Was I destined to kill my only friend from when I was a kid? Was I destined to unleash a motherfucking virus on the world? No way, no how, no sir. I've done what I've done, and I'm going to do what I'm going to do, and it's not going to make a damn bit of difference in anybody's life whether or not I stay here or split. Got it?"

He shook his head for a bit, then said, "Again, at the risk of sounding cheesy, it'd make a difference in *my* life."

I said, "What? Why? How? What?" I was babbling.

He said, "Tobe, my relatives suck ass. You're like my cool uncle."

I have to admit, I was touched. I'm not what you would call a people person, so I didn't hear that sort of stuff all that often.

But I was still staying.

He said, "Fine. It was nice knowing you. Good luck, man. You dumbass."

I never saw Erick Laughlin again. And that still makes me sad. He was a helluva kid.

ERICK LAUGHLIN:

I left the booth and went down the stairs two at a time—that is, until the bottom, when I accidentally took three and twisted the shit out of my left ankle.

Right then, I didn't know if it was broken, or sprained, or strained, or what, but it hurt like a bitch. I fell onto my ass and leaned my head against the wall. I don't know whether it was the pain making me woozy or the zombie stench, but I was damn close to passing out. That wouldn't do, so I pinched my cheek as hard as I could—I even drew blood—and that woke me right on up.

I crawled to the door and pulled myself up using the knob, then hobbled my way into the lobby. The smoke was seeping out through the doors, and if I wasn't freaking the fuck out, I probably would've stayed to watch it.

You see, it was a rainbow.

Reds, yellows, oranges, blues, purples, greens, all swirling together. Funnels, and puffy clouds, and streams, and billows, and it was all very, I don't know, *uplifting*. It still smelled like skunk farts, but my oh my, it was beautiful. I almost wished Janine was there to watch it with me.

Then I heard a collective, ear-splitting moan from inside the theater, followed by what sounded like a gunshot, or a backfiring car, or an exploding zombie head, so I decided it was time to skedaddle.

I limped across the empty lobby, and about ten feet from the door, I heard a loud *pop*, then I fell flat on my face.

It was official. My ankle was done.

The zombie moaning was getting louder, and the rainbow clouds were getting smellier, and all I wanted to do was get the fuck out of there, so I crawled, like, I don't know, like a kid in some Vietnam movie who'd just gotten fragged by Charlie. The pain radiating from my ankle was out-fucking-rageous, and right when I got to the door, I realized I was moaning as loud as those damn dirty zombies.

My hands were so slick with sweat that I couldn't open the fucking door. The room was a big rainbow. I was getting dizzy; I still wasn't sure whether it was from the ankle or the smoke of the undead, but whatever it was, I was *sooooo* close to passing out.

I tried to center myself with a deep breath. And another. And another. And finally, I leaned against the door and got it somewhat open.

But before I could open it all the way, the Regal Arbor Cinema blew up, and I flew through the plate glass door. That last thing I remember thinking was, *The world smells like salami.*

EPILOGUE

1. IDENTIFYING INFORMATION

CLIENT NAME:

LAST: *Laughlin*   FIRST: *Alexander*   MIDDLE: *Erick*

DATE OF BIRTH: *9/21/1985*   SEX: *Male*

DATE OF ADMISSION: *9/2/2009*

TIME OF ADMISSION: *3:51 AM*

2. PRIMARY SYMPTOMS

Multiple facial lacerations. Multiple lacerations on the arms, legs, and torso. Second-degree burns on the scalp. Torn Achilles tendon.

3. INITIAL TREATMENT

Minor lacerations were flushed and bandaged. Major lacerations were stitched: fifteen stitches in the face, twelve stitches in the right arm, eight stitches in the left arm. Burns were treated with a cold compress. Emergency surgery was required to repair the Achilles tendon.

4. CURRENT PROGNOSIS

The stitches will be removed in twelve–fourteen days. The ankle will require six weeks of immobilization, then twelve weeks of physical therapy.

SIGNATURE: ATTENDING MD:

Dr. Sarah Bourne

THE AUSTIN CHRONICLE

INDEPENDENT MOVIE THEATER EXPLODES

ONE DEAD IN REGAL ARBOR CINEMA FIRE

SEPTEMBER 3, 2009

BY TROY KING

AUSTIN, TX—A two-alarm fire felled the Regal Arbor Cinema at 9828 Great Hills Trail yesterday morning.

Authorities initially believed that the theater, which had been closed since August 6, was empty, until body-sniffing dogs uncovered a single corpse.

The body was identified as Marcus Frost-McGee, 29, currently of Las Vegas.

The fire was extinguished almost immediately, but, despite the Austin Fire Department's best efforts, it continues to smolder.

Deputy Fire Commissioner Elvin Jones said, "We've dumped hundreds of gallons of water on the rubble, and it refuses to die. For some reason, the rubble remains exceptionally hot, so we won't go in there until it cools down to a workable temperature."

Authorities have asked for a voluntary evacuation in the immediate surrounding area.

TOBE HOOPER WITH ALAN GOLDSHER

Local resident Carlos Quintana of 9441 Great Hills Trail feels no need to leave.

Quintana said, "It doesn't smell all that great, but my gut tells me it's not hurting anybody."

Robert Charleston, the Regal Arbor Cinema manager, could not be reached for comment.

Welcome to the Truth About Zombies

September 12, 2009

We're back! And just in time. Because I have a story for you.

So I was in Chicago, and I was sitting out in Grant Park, on the Petrillo Bandshell (which is the main stage for Lollapalooza, for those of you who are keeping score), watching the nothingness, when this exceptionally red zombie skipped over.

Now, I know you're saying, "Skipped??? What do you mean 'skipped'??? Zombies sure as shit don't skip!!!" Well, chilluns, this one did. He was in such a happy hoppy mood that he skipped right up onto the bandstand and parked his zombie ass right down next to my human ass.

He stuck out his hand and introduced himself. (I don't remember his damn name, and even if I did, I wouldn't post it here, because would you want your name posted all over the web if you were a zombie? I didn't think so.) Being a polite fellow, I introduced myself right back, then said, "I hate to be rude, but you're undead, aren't you?"

He said, "Yeah. I am. But I'm getting better." He pointed at his arm and said, "Check this out. Yesterday, this was green. Now it's red. And a normal red. A normal healing red. It itches like mad, but I think that's normal. Things itch when they heal. Right?"

He was so eager for a positive answer, and he looked at me with such hope, that I kind of almost cried. I know that sounds pathetic, but imagine you're in a war, and one of your buddies gets shot, and he's gushing blood, and he grabs your hand and says, "I'm going to be all right, aren't I?" All you want to do is comfort him. That's what I wanted to do for this undead guy.

I said, "Right. Things itch when they heal."

Right then is where things got interesting.

The zombie stared out onto the park with a big smile plastered on his mug. He was scratching his arm, and scratching his arm, and scratching his arm. It seemed like he didn't even notice he was doing it. And I'm looking at the arm, and the red is going away. And I'm not talking like the red skin was peeling off or anything. The red was simply fading. His arm, once green, and once red, was turning skin colored. Holy shit, right???!!!

I gave the zombie a big AHEM to get his attention, then pointed at his arm. He looked at it for a while, and then, if it's possible, his smile got bigger. Then he looked at me and said, "I know this is going to sound weird, but could I hug you?"

So we hugged. I think he said something like, "Thank you for welcoming me back into humanity," but I couldn't totally make it out, because he was crying too hard. We stayed that way for a while, then I gave him my phone number and told him when he's feeling ready, we'll go catch some music or something. He said, "That would be great," then he jumped off the band shell and went about his merry way. I swear that with each step, he seemed stronger.

This is my last post here. I'm shutting down this website. I don't need it anymore. My search is over. I know the truth about zombies. And I ain't gonna tell you what it is, people. You have to figure that shit out for yourself.

COMMENTS

i don't know why u r making such a big deal out of this. that's normal in my hood. zombies r turning back to humans on every gottdam corner. it's not all that. chill. quit crying. don't b such a bitch.
miguel from compton represent, CA
September 8, 3:14 PM

My mother's okay, too. We had her locked in the basement for a month. We had to get somebody out to reinforce the door so she wouldn't break it down. Now she's okay. I didn't see the transformation happen, so I don't know if she came back to us quickly or gradually. All I know is that now she's okay. Thank God.
Donna from Cleveland, OH
September 10, 5:32 PM

TIME

September 21, 2009

SCIENCE NOTES

Easy Come, Easy Go

So-Called Blue Spew Downsizes

BY EDWARD LENNON

ATLANTA—The sexually transmitted disease known as the "Blue Spew" seems to have lost its momentum, and Dr. Daria Corbin of the Centers for Disease Control is baffled.

Dr. Corbin, who was in charge of researching the strain (*Puteulanus morbus*), claims that the petering out of the disease is unprecedented.

"Frankly, I've never seen anything like it," Dr. Corbin says. "Six of our patients here fully recovered at the exact same rate, at the exact same time. As much as we'd like to take credit for it, we simply can't.

"It's unexplainable," Dr. Corbin says, "and while we're all obviously thrilled that this has happened, and we're all crossing our fingers that the trend continues, it once again reminds us that nature is in charge, which makes all of us down here feel a tad insignificant."

twitter.com

 QuothTheRaven say yes to hugs. say no to drugs!
September 22 1:41 PM via web

 DonJuanTwoThree @QuothTheRaven Preach on, sister girl! Like Macca says, "It's getting better all the time."
September 22 1:46 PM via web

 DisposableHeroes @QuothTheRaven @DonJuanTwoThree Born-again freaks!!!
September 22 2:22 PM via web

 QuothTheRaven @DisposableHeroes @DonJuanTwoThree fuk you, dude. if your town burned to the ground, you'd UNDERSTAND!
September 22 2:52 PM via web

 QuothTheRaven @DisposableHeroes @DonJuanTwoThree if your bff blew up in a meth explosion, you'd UNDERSTAND!
September 22 3:03 PM via web

 QuothTheRaven @DisposableHeroes @DonJuanTwoThree if your house was vandalized by a bunch of fucking tweakers, you'd UNDERSTAND!
September 22 3:11 PM via web

 DonJuanTwoThree @QuothTheRaven @DisposableHeroes Yeah! What she said!
September 22 3:30 PM via web

JANINE DALTREY:

What a way to start a relationship. First, Erick has to wait on me hand and foot while I'm getting over my beat-down, then I have to wait on him hand and foot while he gets over his explosion. How very, very romantic.

In retrospect, it's a damn good thing we had each other, because we *understood*. We *got it*. When one of us woke up in the middle of the night screaming, the other one of us knew not to ask what was wrong. I'd hold him, or he'd hold me, or we'd hold each other. And we wouldn't say anything. What was there to say, really?

Is it our shared suffering that's kept us together? I don't know, some shrinks would probably say yes, but I'd like to think that we both have more substance than that. I'd like to think that we'd both recognize if we were getting married not because we love each other, but rather because we need a support system.

I think we're getting married for the right reason. No, I'm *sure* we are.

Erick wasn't a good boy about his physical therapy . . . that is, until I whipped him into shape. There were a lot of *loud* discussions about his laziness—I told him that I didn't care that the dreams were keeping him up at night and that he needed to get off his ass and get healthy—but I always came out on top of our little chats. Seriously, that boy can't argue his way out of a paper bag.

The Regal Arbor Cinema gave Erick a nice chunk of change so he wouldn't sue their asses—which he wouldn't have done anyhow, but he figured that he'd had a rough summer, so he didn't mention that to their lawyers—which meant that if we were smart with our money, we could get by without a salary from him for a year or two. So after we moved here to Cali, he decided to focus solely on writing his three screenplays. Yes, that's right, *three:* a romantic comedy, a silly action picture, and something he calls his Judd Apatow homage. Much to Theo Morrison's chagrin, Erick decided to quit music altogether.

Me, I'm doing personal assistant work for a big, fancy studio guy at Warner Bros. who wants to keep a low profile, so I am not at liberty to divulge his name. The big, fancy studio guy loves Erick and keeps trying to hire him to work for him, but Erick wants to write. Good for him.

I will tell you this: We love it here in Los Angeles. And no matter how much Theo begs us, we're never setting foot in Austin motherfucking Texas again.

TOBE HOOPER:

That rainbow smoke almost got me. It was the second-prettiest thing I ever saw, the first being the sixteen-year-old Claire Craft's eyes. She was a bitch, that one, but my Lord, those baby blues of hers could *slay* you. Anyhow, I'm not a believer in hypnosis—if you have a strong mind, it can't be bent—but that smoke, man, I damn near lost myself in it.

I wanted to get closer—no, I *had* to get closer—so I bailed out of the projection booth and walked, no, *jogged*, no, *sprinted* downstairs to the lobby.

And who's waiting for me at the bottom of the stairs, blocking my way out the door? That's right, the man, the myth, the motherfucker, Dude McGee.

I lowered my shoulder and tried to bull past him, but that boy was *heavy*. He was an immovable object, and I was *not* an irresistible force, so I bounced off him and fell ass-first onto the floor. He leaned down, offered me his hand, and said, "Let me help you up, William."

Now, that came out of nowhere. William is my given name, but I hadn't been called William since, I don't know, 1968 or something.

I ignored his hand and said, "I've got it," then, with great effort, hauled myself up.

He said, "Listen, this theater is going to explode in about two minutes. You need to get out of here."

I said, "Bullshit."

He said, "There is no bullshit being slung here, William. There will be an explosion, and you will survive the explosion, but you cannot be here when it happens. I've proven my point. The Game is over. I won. Now I'm hanging it up. I'm taking my ball and going home."

I said, "McGee, I don't know what the fuck you're talking about."

He said, "It doesn't matter." He looked at his watch. "Okay, you have about one minute to get out of here. If you're too close to the fire, there'll be problems."

I said, "But I thought you said I'm going to survive."

He said, "You will. But—"

I said, "No buts. I'm going to see the end of the movie, and I've got to get a better look at this smoke." And then I pulled the oldest trick in the book: I pointed over his left shoulder and yelled, "Holy Christ, a headless zombie!" When he turned to look, I bolted right past him.

He may have been an immovable object, but even though I'm an old man, I could outrun his fat ass.

I made it across the lobby, and right as I touched the theater door, *kaboom*, massive explosion.

And it was like the goddamn car wreck all over again.

I remember the doctors poking and prodding the shit out of me, and I remember it hurting like hell, the worst physical pain I've felt *ever*.

I remember a nurse telling me that I'd probably flown thirty yards in the air and landed face-first on the pavement, cracking my skull. Some of my brain fluid apparently leaked onto the street. There went *another* piece of my memory. The next time it rained, it got washed into the sewer.

After that, it was a bunch of nothing.

The next thing I remember, I'm in one of those SUV limo things, hooked up to an IV and a bunch of machines. There's a smoking-hot girl in doctor's scrubs diddling with a couple of the machines I was hooked up to. My mouth was dry as sand, and it took me a second before I could speak. I said to her, "Forgive me if I sound stupid, but what's happening here?"

The girl laughed and said, "Ah. Mr. Hooper. Hello there. Good to see you. And hear you."

I said, "Where the hell am I? And what day is today?"

She said, "We're in Los Angeles. You're on the 101. We're about half an hour away from your house. And today is September nineteenth. And we're glad to have you back with us. You've been out of commission for a while."

I said, "Who's 'us'? Better yet, who're you?"

She said, "I'm Cori. Dick Gregson from Warner Bros. sent me."

I said, "Whoa. Really?"

She laughed again—a beautiful laugh, I should note—then said, "He told me to—and this is a quote—'Treat Tobe right, and make sure you tuck him in nice and tight, because he's *my guy.*' Now, I've worked for Mr. Gregson for almost five years, and I've never heard him refer to anybody as 'my guy,' that's for sure."

I said, "Hunh. That's mighty nice to hear." I thought, *Holy shit, I bet I can make whatever goddamn movie I goddamn well please. How about that?* Then I told Cori, "Sister, if Gregson wants you to tuck me in, then you can goddamn well tuck me in."

And that's exactly what happened.

Cori stayed with me for a few weeks. When I was more or less strong enough to take care of my own self, I sent her on her merry way. I could've used the help, but she needed to split.

I haven't left my house since.

Everybody's cool about coming to me. But I won't see them. I *can't* see them. The only reason I'm seeing *you*, Alan, is that I had to tell *somebody* the goddamn story.

See, here's the thing.

The day before I sent Cori away, I'm peeing, and it starts to sting, and I look down, and there's this blue shit oozing out of my cock.

So yeah, she had to go. I've been alone ever since.

I don't really know what else to say. This is it. It's the end. All I can tell you is that I'm sorry, brother. I know none of this was my fault, but I'm still sorrier than the sorriest motherfucker you'll ever meet.

But on the plus side, I can guaran-fucking-tee you that it'll never happen again.

Which brings us to the moral of our story. And that is . . .

Tobe never finished that sentence. Instead, he stood up, gave me a companionable clap on the shoulder, turned around, grabbed a gun off his desk—it turned out to be that Colt he was always too damn lazy to take out of his safe—stuck the barrel in his mouth, and blew his brains out.

All over me. My face, my neck, my chest, covered with the gray matter of the man many consider to be the godfather of slasher flicks. His critics might call it poetic justice.

If you were to read something into that—and after you've worn someone's brains as a necklace, trust me, you read into everything—you'd think that maybe Tobe Hooper was trying to tell me that what's been done can be undone if you do it right. Or maybe he was saying that if you have the opportunity to make the ultimate sacrifice for the greater good, then you'd better goddamn well do it.

Or maybe he was saying, Walk a mile in my shoes, motherfucker. Here're some brains for breakfast. Enjoy your ride on the *Destiny Express*.

I suppose it's now worth mentioning that this morning, when I awoke, I noticed some blue slime oozing from the tip of my penis. And holy shit, I've never been so horny in my entire life.

—Alan Goldsher, April 2011

My deep thanks:

First and foremost to Alan Goldsher, for all the obvious reasons and then some, and for being a writing partner par excellence

To Jason Allen Ashlock who made Alan's good idea into a deal

To Julian Pavia who made that deal into a book

To Campbell Wharton, Heather Lazare, Tina Pohlman, and the entire Crown/Three Rivers team, from publicity to design and beyond, for making that book into a thing of creepy beauty

To Chris Ridenhour, my tireless manager

To Lee Keele, perhaps the classiest agent in the biz

To Howard Abramson, the attorney you always want in your corner

To Joel Behr

To Doreen Knigin

To Rebecca Hodges, the love of my life

To Louis Black and SXSW gang for making magic and letting me be a part

To dear friends Mark Rance, Mick Garris, John Landis, Guillermo Del Toro, and the Ale and Quail Club for their unwavering support

And most of all, to my fans, wherever you are across the world. I tell this story, like all the others, for you.

BONUS
MATERIAL

A Conversation
with Tobe Hooper

Tell us about your real *"lost" 1969 film,* Eggshells, *and describe its screening at the South by Southwest Festival forty years later.*

In the late sixties, there were a lot of movies coming out of Hollywood that were supposed to be about hippies—*Easy Rider,* which came out in 1969, is a good example—but even though some of them were quite good, the film hippies weren't anything like any real-life hippies I knew, so I wanted to make something that reflected my own experience. When it screened at SXSW, it was terrific to be seeing it with an audience after all those years, and the response was both positive and gratifying. And for the record, nobody contracted any virus from seeing the film. At least as far as I know.

Were you really in a car wreck when you were a teenager?

Yes, a serious one. To this day I can't even remember having gotten out of bed that morning. The pain was horrible, obviously, but one of the creepiest things about it was the memory loss. The whole incident was a big blank, and the concept of blankness is flat-out frightening—not knowing what did or didn't happen in any given situation is a mind-fuck—which is why we made that forgetfulness a theme throughout *Midnight Movie.*

In Midnight Movie, *you're portrayed as a loner. Is that the truth?*

Yes and no. Don't get me wrong. I like people. Working on a movie set with a good crew always gets me jazzed, and I love going to conventions and meeting my fans . . . but I do like my alone time. I'm not quite the hermit that I am in the book, but I sure dig staying in.

Is there really any Tobe Hooper memorabilia in a creepy film museum?

My house was robbed while I was out of town a couple years ago and a lot of my memorabilia was stolen . . . not all of it, but a good chunk. That event was the inspiration for putting the museum in the book. And if anybody does see any of my stuff in some weird museum, call the cops!

What is it about zombies that you find intriguing?

Part of it is that they're dead and alive at the same time, and the dichotomy gives you a lot to play with in terms of the story. Also, since zombie mythology isn't as templated as that of, say, vampires, you have more room to stretch. And it's always fun to write about a creature that's pure id, who has no motives other than a hunger for brains.

In the book, you're described as being obsessed with moviemaking when you were still in high school. How old were you when you decided you wanted to make movies?

I was barely out of the womb when I was bitten by the film bug. All I ever remember wanting to do was make movies, and director/writer is the only job I've ever had.

What was it about the medium that was so attractive to you?

I think the most interesting thing about film is that it's limitless. You can do anything you can imagine, and because of that, it always is a challenge, and it always will be a challenge, so I have a job for life.

Do you think your fans will follow you from the screen to the page?

I certainly hope so. These days, horror fans seem to be more open to more forms of literature than they were when *Chainsaw* hit—graphic novels, long-form books, etc.—and I feel confident that this book, which I think is quite cinematic, will be embraced.

Does this book reflect any frustrations you actually feel toward Hollywood?

Hollywood is a magical place where unicorns dance under rainbows, and everybody loves everybody, and everyone speaks the truth at all times. How could I ever get frustrated with that?

Why a book, and why now?

It's something I've wanted to do for a long time, and when my talented cowriter, Alan Goldsher, suggested we work together, I jumped. I'm as proud of this book as I am of any of my movies, and I could absolutely see doing it again. In fact, I have a fucked-up idea brewing as we speak.